THE CLUMSIEST LINE

JJY SMITH

CHAPTERS

BOX ELDER

The wise old ladies of West Didsbury gathered around her like pecking pigeons on a discarded chip bap. Renée Miller had gone down outside the Co-Op. She had not fallen over; worse, she'd had a fall. She looked up at the pitying pale faces and closed her eyes to shut out the world. They wouldn't fully open again.

For someone slowing down, it happened quickly. Under the sickly strip lights and to the lightweight radio station vomiting out middle-of-the-road pop music, dizziness took over. Renée zig-zagged across the sticky floor with her shopping basket, listing with the weight of a two-pint plastic milk bottle, a packet of ginger nuts and a box of Yorkshire Tea. Despite struggling, she managed to pay for the items, saving 10% with her membership card, with the student server ignorant of her distress.

After staggering through the exit, her knees buckled, and the world blurred. Her grasp on the handle of her Bag for Life weakened, and like a jaded boxer in the final rounds, Renée Miller collapsed into the arms of a box elder tree that stood guard by the store entrance. Eventually, she slid down it and could be at least grateful that her head stayed just outside the reach of the automatic doors that banged backwards and forwards, triggered by her presence.

Her friends, Janet and Sally, who were picking through the daily discounts close to the entrance, watched in a mix of shock and disbelief. Renée's fall was a spectacle that would later cause ripples across the Conservative Club when they heard the news, and the urgency of the situation didn't immediately grab them.

"Good grief, did you see that?" Janet said.

Sally, clutching her handbag like a lifeline, leaned in closer. "Is she?"

But before Sally could finish her sentence, Renée let out a low groan, her fingers clutching leaves from the box elder tree. The gossiping trio, Janet, Sally, and a third friend, Louise, who had splashed through two dirty potholes on her shuffle from the opposite side of the road, huddled around the fallen matriarch. Renée briefly opened her eyes, and the sight of the three women and the situation made her want to die.

"Get some water, dear," Louise instructed the callow shop assistant who had not witnessed the incident, only the furore that followed.

The boy scurried away through the Co-Op's automatic doors, which opened again to reveal a display of tumbled goods – boxes of pyramid tea bags and Jamaica Ginger Cake, both on discount deals. It seemed like the store's shelves had also toppled over to get a better glimpse of Renée's plight.

"Look at all that cake?" Janet murmured, eyeing the supermarket floor.

Sally shot her a disapproving look. "Janet, for heaven's sake, the woman's just collapsed."

Louise, ever the pragmatist, chimed in: "It's an awful mess. Perhaps we could get it for the foodbank as a gesture of goodwill for what's happened."

As the ladies chatted on, a small crowd gathered and the boy returned with an extra large mug of water. Renée, now sitting propped against the box elder, took a sip, her purple lips whispering a quiet "thank you." She would never dream of drinking water from a china cup, never mind a mug, and it added to her anxiety that she would do so in front of a gaggle of staring strangers.

"What happened to her?" one asked.

"I heard she just collapsed," replied another.

Louise, always in the know, added with a knowing nod, "She's been feeling poorly lately, poor soul. Probably just the strain; she does such a lot."

As the gossip spread, an ambulance arrived, its wailing siren and shocking blue flashes lighting up the gloom and drawing yet more rubberneckers. It was at that point that Renée's eyelids clamped shut, and the noise became distorted.

Paramedics approached her with a mix of urgency and professionalism. The ladies of West Didsbury stepped back, giving them room to work. They exchanged concerned glances as they assessed her condition. A few moments later, they gently lifted her onto a stretcher, her frail figure a stark contrast against the cold metal. The onlookers, now a growing congregation of curious faces, watched as Renée was wheeled towards the ambulance.

Janet, Sally, and Louise exchanged solemn glances. An important heartbeat of West Didsbury had been momentarily stilled. As the ambulance pulled away, its siren fading into the distance, the trio found themselves contemplating the fragility of life and another cliffhanger in their kitchen-sink, soap-operatic existence.

The day had begun much like any other for Nigel Miller, a man of routine and predictability. He rose promptly at seven, the same time as he had done for the past three decades. The early sun streaked through the thin curtains, casting a gentle glow over the room as it had on so many early spring mornings that he'd awoken there. With a practised hand, Nigel reached for his glasses on the bedside table, adjusted them to the contours of his face and brought the morning into focus.

Renée, his wife of 35 years, was still asleep beside him. Her shallow, rhythmical breathing was a lullaby to Nigel's ears, a comforting reminder of the constancy of their shared existence. He tiptoed out of the bedroom, leaving Renée to her dreams, and made his way to the kitchen.

The kettle boiled its familiar gurgle, followed by the aroma of brewing coffee. Nigel unfolded his newspaper - he still read them rather than going online - and with a crisp snap, he worked his way through the news, sport and finally, the arts section. The headlines were a collage of the failures and fantasies that existed outside their home. Floods in Florida, drownings in the Channel, $6bn dollar men arrested, an ancient sequoia lost to a storm. He skimmed through the articles before finally moving to the crossword, a daily ritual that brought a touch of mental exercise to prepare him for the day.

Renée soon joined him in the kitchen, her silver hair slightly tousled and her eyes still heavy with sleep. The routine continued as they exchanged pleasantries, their words a dance of familiarity that required no choreography. Nigel sipped his coffee, casting occasional glances at his wife over the top of his newspaper as she relayed a bad dream, a strange stalker and a set of high stairs with no balustrade.

As the clock ticked towards 10 o'clock, Renée cheerfully said: "I'll just be popping down to the Co-Op, Nigel. Need anything?"

Peering over his glasses, Nigel replied: "No, no. I'm good, love. Just get the usual, you know."

"The usual? Oh, I know, I know. A cheeky pack of biscuits for you, eh?"

"Well, who can't resist a good biscuit? Keeps me on my toes."

Renée chuckled and reached for her worn-out handbag on the kitchen counter. "We need tea and milk. And I mustn't forget a birthday card for Robin. Can't believe our eldest is turning 30."

"Time flies, Renée. Feels like just yesterday we were changing his nappies."

"You mean I was changing his nappies while you were supervising. Or working late to have your peace and quiet in the office."

Nigel smiled: "Someone had to make sure you didn't put them on backwards."

She returned his smile. "Now, don't you go solving the world's problems while I'm gone, Nigel."

Nigel winked and returned to his crossword, pen in hand. "Wouldn't dream of it, my dear. Off you go. I'll probably be in the studio when you get back."

"Another masterpiece," said Renée as she pecked him on the cheek, tied up her coat and headed out. Nigel looked back at his newspaper, not needing to acknowledge the warmth that transcended the years they had spent together.

He gave the crossword more thought but couldn't finish it and went to the garage, now a sort of converted studio, where he would generally spend his late mornings painting. He would enjoy listening to Blue Note jazz that he felt inspired his surprisingly erotic painting. His latest was almost finished: a mysterious mid-thirties woman lying naked on a sofa, arm behind her head and a sleazy smile.

Renée knew the content of his paintings but didn't say anything even though it left her bemused. It was what Nigel did. He'd always put great weight in the arts - theatre, cinema, music too - since they had first met, and she simply let him get on with it.

It was in the midst of his usual routine that Nigel's mobile phone rang; the ugly vibration cutting through the beauty of Wayne Shorter. The water jar was tumbled over in his rush to answer the call and he failed to hide his agitation when he finally put the phone to his ear.

"Mr Miller?" the voice on the other end was steady but tinged with an unspoken gravity.

"Yes, speaking," Nigel replied, the misshapen left eye of the woman in his painting glaring at him.

"I'm afraid I have some distressing news. It's about Mrs Miller."

Nigel felt a curious detachment as the voice continued, delivering the news with a clinical precision that seemed incongruent with the weight of its content. Renée, his anchor for most of his life, was gone. The words explaining her passing hung in the air, suspended in a surreal moment that refused to merge with the rhythm of Nigel's daily life.

"Mr. Miller, are you there?" The voice on the other end pierced through the fog that enveloped Nigel's consciousness.

"Yes, yes, I'm here," he replied mechanically.

The news settled in the pit of Nigel's stomach, a heavy stone sinking into the depths of his being. He clicked off the phone with an automated precision and heard the sound of an over-tuned car revving past outside at speed. Nigel remained motionless for some seconds, staring into the distance, before cleaning up the dampness where the paintbrush water was spilt.

Nigel moved back to the house like a ghost, his body on autopilot while his mind grappled with the immensity of the news. The familiar landmarks, the washing line with a black jumper, the grey azalea bought at the garden centre in the early spring, the faded crocs by the door, each step a struggle against the weight of the reality that now hung over him.

The kitchen door creaked open, revealing the silent house that echoed with the absence of Renée. The air felt thicker, the rooms emptier, as if the very essence of the home had already dissipated with her departure.

It was only much later at night, in the solitude of their bedroom, that the real emotion escaped. Nigel collapsed onto the bed, his shoulders shaking with sobs that seemed to have been trapped within him. The real grief, delayed by the numbness of routine, now banged with an unrelenting force. The reality of his loss hit him like a violent uppercut, smashing away the normality that he had initially clung to.

In that moment of vulnerability, Nigel realised he was now unmoored from the routine that had defined later life. The crossword puzzles, the coffee, the painting, the nods to neighbours – they all faded to black. Renée was gone, and with her went the light. The bedroom echoed with the rawness of Nigel's grief.

The final paragraph of the day was written in tears ending with an ellipsis to a life that would never be the same again.

After returning from the hospital, Nigel sat alone in the dimly lit living room. Radio 4 crackled on the 20-year-old DAB device unheard, barely audible over the persistent echo of memories that lingered in the air.

He absentmindedly traced the edge of the armchair, worn with years of shared laughter and quiet conversations. The room seemed to hold its breath as if acknowledging the absence of the one person who had given it life.

"Robin," Nigel whispered, his voice a gentle murmur, remembering that he'd forgotten to tell the children yet. His name alone carried a delicate, treasured memory—the day that Renée chose it when a tiny robin perched on the window sill and chirped a cheery tune.

"Wilfred, Lo," he continued to nobody. Renée had found inspiration for their twins' names in the pages of an Observer article about the World War I poets Wilfred Owen and Siegfried Sassoon; her motherly instinct wanting to care for lost and devastated souls that shone through the darkness of their works.

Nigel's mobile phone, short of charge, lay on the small table beside him, a connection to people who needed to hear words that could not be spoken easily. With a heavy heart, he went through three of the four names locked in the favourites directory, the conversations unfolding like a carefully composed elegy. "Your mother, she's left us," he uttered three times, the words lingering in the quiet spaces between them.

The following day, their three children arrived back at home and reclaimed their bedrooms. It was the first time they were all together for more than two years - except they weren't all together. Someone was missing. Still it was brighter to have noise and life in the house.

Robin Miller was a delicate first son. Nigel recalled Renée's concern for him, which began as a toddler tiptoeing around a swimming pool with giant water wings, refusing to jump in, and that anxiety never left her.

Now, he was a lanky, ruminative, bookish cricket journalist, but from his polished brogues to his tortoise-shell spectacles, he embodied the very essence of an enigmatic and stand-offish Englishman.

Aged six, Nigel recalled Robin briefly looking up from his Wisden Almanacs and self-marked scorecards to notice little Megan Posey - a girl with an infectious enthusiasm for insects. Fate took a whimsical turn when Asa Jones, Robin's best friend, won her affection with the simple yet profound gesture of gifting her a plastic ladybird badge.

Since that moment, Robin's romantic endeavours had seemingly become a series of unfulfilled dreams. Despite his eloquent way with the written word, he found it hard to articulate feelings and spent his time behind a laptop after a crushing end to his cricket playing days, despite huge promise as a youngster.

His aspirations as a cricketer suffered an early demise when, on his debut for Lancashire seconds, he fielded at backward point and was knocked unconscious by a wayward throw from third man. The incident left him with a perpetual fear of the ball and he lost his nerve in the field. Fortunately, he was able to channel his passion for the game as a writer and was now carving out a decent career.

His mother hoped he would find love, but she saw it as a rare butterfly fluttering out of his reach. The more he grabbed for it, the quicker it flapped away, and she sneered whenever she saw Megan, now a celebrity gardener, on the TV.

Wilfred, with his shaggy black hair and distressed wardrobe seemingly bought from a 1980s Los Angeles thrift store, existed in a world created by himself on a computer screen.

His closest friend was his slightly older twin sister, Lo although 'closest' could be exchanged for 'only'. South Manchester and their schools could be lively, even bohemian, but Wilf took a quieter path, an early life predominantly spent in solitude, save for the company of his twin.

The eccentricity of Wilf's character lay not only in his penchant for solitude but in the paradoxical fact that he was surprisingly attractive to the opposite sex. His stoic demeanour and unique style cast a magnetic charm that drew the gaze of many admirers. Yet Wilf lost in his world of thoughts and dreams, showed no interest in romance.

This contradiction, unknowingly to him, became the talk of the school when the prom arrived. The radiant Violet Hemp, the undisputed 'It Girl' of Year 11, extended an astonishing invitation to partner Wilf to the ball. However, true to his enigmatic nature, Wilf chose to attend the prom alone, a decision that drew a hum of whispers, shock and anticipation of how Violet would respond to the slight.

Affronted and annoyed, Violet did seek her own peculiar revenge. As Wilf stood near the punch bowl, clad in a velvet tuxedo, Violet approached and, without warning, upended Wilf's bottle of dandelion and burdock over his head. Undeterred, Wilf merely rubbed his hair and continued his evening as if nothing had happened. The incident only served to fuel his retreat into his own world of mysteries and inventions.

From a young age, Wilf had found solace in the glow of computer screens and the beeping symphonies of video games. His fascination with technology burgeoned into an innate talent, and he became an intuitive and intelligent software maker. Silicon Valley had already extended job offers, beckoning Wilf into a world that seemed both fascinating and alien, but he politely declined to the annoyance of his family, who so wanted him to fly.

Lo, the older twin by 12 minutes, was full of surprises from the moment she was born when the midwife's prediction of twin boys was proved wrong. Renée was elated by the surprise, but with her name, Siegfried, already chosen, she had to hastily alter plans and picked Sassoon's middle name Loraine.

Loraine hated the name from the moment she could talk, initially because it sounded like rain and later because of its connection with quiches. The family experimented with the name Laurie until she encountered a bin lorry. From the age of five, she stumbled across the nickname Lo and, from that moment, would only answer to that name, even to her most pompous and stubborn teachers.

On her 16th birthday, she officially changed her name by deed poll. At that age, a parent's permission is required, and Renée endorsed the move without question. She's always been a Lo, she said to Nigel, never a Loraine.

Lo navigated the hallowed halls of Oxford University with a pulp fiction novel perpetually spilling out of her jacket pocket and read more literary tomes in private. Her heart beat to the rhythm of the past as she daydreamed of a world where Clara Bow's silent film elegance mingles with the enigmatic charisma of Nancy Mitford characters, all to the soundtrack of the jazz age.

Despite studying English Literature, Lo was adrift in the sea of academia, uncertain of what the future held. Her dreams, shaped by the pages of novels from Jane Austen to Brett Easton Ellis, clashed with the stark reality of essays, exams, and the looming pressures of adulthood. Her professors often found themselves bemused by the outlandish references in her papers yet enchanted by the sheer creativity and confidence of her musings.

Lo's existential crisis was palpable to Renée and, therefore to Nigel. The weight of the future hung over her like the heavy curtains in a forgotten theatre. She refused to step onto the stage, grappling with the demands to act with conformity, dreading the day when her black-and-white dreams would be distorted by the colourisation of societal expectations.

In an attempt to escape the clutches of her own uncertainty, Lo sought solace in the dark corners of Oxford pubs, nursing Horse's Neck cocktails with, unlike her brothers, a wide network of friends.

And also, unlike her brothers, she confided to her mother about her trivial liaisons, much like the fleeting chapters of cheap chick-lit. She floated through romances with a detached elegance like the silent era flapper girls she so admired. Renée never worried about her in that regard.

But she fretted over all of them. And now Nigel would have to take that on by himself, and worst of all, he would add an extra burden to their blossoming lives. Their returns began with a warm hug that seemed to heighten the sadness. It was only the quarrels and steady return of laughter that brought any solace.

The practicalities of death demanded attention, and Nigel found himself navigating the cold waters of funeral arrangements. He spoke with the Co-op's undertakers, chose flowers that would bloom in solemn remembrance and pondered over the playlist that would accompany the final farewell.

In the kitchen, the kettle carried out its task once again, and Nigel mechanically prepared tea for the visitors who would soon arrive. Tea, a remedy for every sorrow, or so Renée had believed.

As he placed the tray on the table, Nigel marvelled at the juxtaposition of such simplicity in the face of life's complexity. Janet, Sally and Louise sat in the front room, and he composed himself, a façade of strength worn for the sake of those who would half-pretend to share in his sorrow but also peer behind the curtain of his reality.

The teacups were scooped up, and amid the quiet conversations that followed, Nigel forced himself through the mundanity; the clinking of teaspoons, the bitterness of the tea, and the dreary drag of making small talk. Once a sanctuary for Nigel and Renée, the walls were now breached by the gossipers and ghouls. But the happier ghosts of past years manifested through the more familiar sounds of creaking floorboards, the playful shouts of youths in the street and the occasional interruptions of the offspring asking about hot water for showers and the location of paracetamol.

Late afternoon sunlight shone uncomfortably through the window, blinding and warm, but Nigel didn't pull the curtain across as he had done a 100 times for his wife. Finally, it forced the visitors away, and he ushered them through the door in a flurry of 'thankyous' and 'that's very kinds' in response to the offers of help and statements of condolence.

Nigel sat in his favourite armchair, worn with years of use, staring at a wedding photo on the mantelpiece. His wife, Renée, smiled radiantly, frozen in a moment that felt both distant and painfully close. The room held memories like dust particles suspended in the air, settling over furniture and framed pictures.

After a simple funeral, life carried on. Days turned into weeks, but loneliness crept into Nigel's thoughts, transforming the air into a thick fog of guilt. His conscience tugged at him like a persistent child, demanding attention. The voices of Robin, Wilfred, and Lo, became distant echoes, and Nigel found himself on the edge of fear and self-loathing.

In the studio, he would flick through the paintings of women, forever lustful and unobtainable. None were of Renée. She was too precious to be captured in such elementary poses. Her images were photographs, family celebrations, sunny, happy holidays or simply the two of them.

Nigel quietly closed up the studio and prepared his breakfast, arranging his utensils with an obsessive precision. After brewing the coffee and neatly folding his newspaper, he filled in the crossword slowly and methodically, although made mistakes early on and neglected to correct them nor cross them out.

"The damn clues are wrong," he muttered on discovering one of his errors.

Saturday's paper was always too big, and when it arrived the following day, it was mangled through the letterbox. Nigel sat with identical precision for breakfast and the crossword, but the creases across the puzzle irritated him, and the pen would not stroke the paper smoothly. He calmly took out the ironing board and sorted out the issue. But the crossword would again be incomplete and riddled with errors.

"Note antique and very valuable stuff, four letters beginning with 'G'?" G I L T. Wrong!

Satisfied that he had given it a good stab, Nigel tended the garden and found himself slicing off the flowers from the purple hyacinths. He looked down at the collection with bafflement at what he had done. Picking them up, the wind blew many of the petals from his cupped hands. "Did you keep any secrets from me?" he said to the world.

Nights were difficult. Sometimes, he would spring up in bed, almost awoken by the emptiness. Eventually, he arranged the pillows to make the size and shape of another body. "I'm sorry," he whispered.

"Grief can manifest in mysterious ways, Nigel. Tell me what you're feeling," said Dr Barrelli-Minch. Her chunky wooden jewellery rattled as she adjusted her yellow glasses. Nigel had been seeing her for years, and although he thought of it as a middle-class affectation to see a therapist, he found it helpful. She hadn't known everything before, but now he was beginning to unravel.

"I hear her whispers in every room, but they're not comforting. They're accusing," he said.

Dr Barrelli-Minch was puzzled by his answer. "What do you mean?"

"She knew. She knew everything, but we never discussed it. We never settled it," he said.

"Settled what? Is there something you can tell me that you wanted to say to her."

"Not yet. I can't. I can't say the words yet."

As weeks passed, Nigel fell deeper into crisis. He rearranged the furniture, searching for hidden clues left behind by Renée. A framed photograph on the wall captured a moment of bliss, now tainted by uncertainty.

Wilf watched his father from the doorway. He sensed his anguish but remained silent, unsure how to comfort him. Robin and Lo were concerned and talked about his decline. They gave him space and care, but he instructed them to get on with their lives. They had time to hang around and believed their presence was helping to manage his demise.

Outside, the world was noticing and wondering too. Renée's death and funeral had dominated chatter for some time, but the shock was beginning to fade, and now the gossip was shifting to her husband left behind.

At the Co-op, Janet, Sally and Louise congregated by the box elder tree, not in homage but in ignorant coincidence.

"He's falling apart, poor soul," said Janet.

"She was his everything," added Sally.

"Is that so?" queried Louise.

Nigel simply sat among the artefacts, surrounded by the ghosts of his marriage, fearing for his sanity and wanting to share his reality while he remained lucid.

"I think I'm losing my mind," he told Dr Barrelli-Minch. "I'm being punished. There's germs in the house. They're eating away at me. Every night, I can feel them. Like a poison. I need to stop them. I shower and wash all the time, but I can't get myself clean. I'll never be clean."

"I'm very worried about you," said the therapist. "I'm going to refer you to a doctor. But remember, there's always someone there to talk to. Are you feeling suicidal?"

"No. I don't have the strength to commit suicide. It might hurt, and I might not be successful. That would be worse. I couldn't live like that." He lifted his head from hands and smiled genuinely. Then it slipped from his face. "I know what I have to do. The truth. Only the truth."

Subtle hints began with fumbled sentences and awkward pauses at home and in the therapy room as Nigel danced around the edges of an honesty he was terrified to utter. It was Robin who confronted his father, concern etched on his face like a map of worry lines and unknowingly speeded him to his destination.

"Dad," Robin said. "We're worried about you. Why don't you go away for a bit. You can afford it. Go and see Uncle James in Sydney and take a break."

Nigel refused and said it wouldn't be right, but they insisted he couldn't carry on as things were. Subconsciously, he agreed.

Nigel almost missed his afternoon appointment with Dr Barrelli-Minch. The road outside was being dug up, and the drilling vibrated around her office overlooking the workmen. Perhaps it was the discordant distraction that allowed him to try to sneak out his confession. The session started normally but it was in her minimalist office that the pipe burst.

After an initial 20-minute dance, Nigel was nudged and teased until he finally exploded in truth without warning.

"There were so many," he said out of the blue. Dr Barrelli-Minch held back, letting him fill the silence. "I loved her, I really did. I loved her so much. But…"

The therapist nodded and encouraged: "Take your time."

"They meant nothing. Nothing compared to her." The revelation gathered pace. "Women. A lot of women. Just lust and conquests.

"She was pregnant. With Robin. There was a woman at work. Heidi. We flirted. I knew she liked me and it was nice. I wasn't interested. I wasn't interested, but. Renée was having a tough time. Sickness. Fatigue. She lost interest. We got drunk. Me and Heidi. In the pub. She kissed me. I left and said no. But she was there. For weeks. Pushing me, pushing me. Then, one day. In the office. I was weak. It was terrible. I felt horrible. But Renée was happier. I took more care of her. Then, two weeks later, again. It was a bit easier. Then, right up until his birth. Then I said no more. I couldn't. I couldn't do it. Heidi was angry and threatened to reveal everything. She didn't. I don't know why, but she didn't. Then she left, and I was free of it."

Dr Barelli-Minch pushed her spectacles onto her bridge, making no notes, just listening.

"We were doing well. We really were. Then I had to go to France for a few days with work. Nathalie. She was playful. It just happened. One night. No strings. It was just a thing that only we knew about. I felt bad. But I was able to forget it. It was out of sight and out of mind.

"A few months later, in Zurich. Stephanie. I just met her in a bar. A stranger. It was easy. A night and then nothing. Then, more trips abroad. It was Italy I stopped. Giovanna. I didn't even like her. Then, nothing for four years. Until the twins were due. Then that hair. Like fire. Little Melanie. She was lonely. Friendly. Happy with the circumstances. For a long time. I cared. I loved Renée, but I cared. But it was six years I think. Off and on. Oh god, I'm so sorry. I was selfish. So selfish. But she was happy. The family."

Dr Barelli-Minch interrupted. "I'm afraid we're out of time. I have another person in 10 minutes, so we will have to leave it there. But before you go, I need to say a few things. Firstly, thank you for sharing. I know that wasn't easy. We can talk about your feelings in the next session, but you mustn't let this stop you from living your life. You've taken a step on a journey. A journey to forgiveness and unburdening a lifetime of guilt. We can talk about the reasons and the feelings at our next session, but I hope you realised the enormous step you've taken today. How are you feeling?"

"Like shit," he said. "Like a pig. There's moments. So many moments flashing in my mind. Her looking at my paintings. I was rubbing her nose in it. What a horrible, a horrible, nasty pig."

"Steady," she said. "We can talk about the reasons for the painting. I'm sure you weren't ridiculing Renée. I know you well enough to know that wasn't the case. Are you going to be okay? I'm worried about you."

"I'm okay," he said, wiping away tears he wanted to be there but hadn't actually arrived. "I'll be okay."

"You have family and friends. Take your time, and we'll work through it. Okay?"

"Okay," he said, rising to mirror Dr Barelli-Minch's decision to stand. He didn't know what he wanted to feel, but the only emotion was numbness.

The Shakepeare was badly named. It was an unusually grim pub for the area and couldn't be further away from the artful master it was named after. Nigel had only been there once in the whole time he'd lived in West Didsbury. He remembered the evening well. It was around 20 years ago, the first night the twins were entrusted to a babysitter. He and Renée went for dinner, got drunk, and stumbled into the pub for a nightcap in a stupor.

Despite its reputation, he seemed drawn there on this day following a long walk to clear his head. It was somewhere no one knew him and also he indulgently felt like the tragic hero of his own play.

The hours passed, and so did the drinks. Whisky after whisky until the karaoke started early in the evening. It was bad and rather than entice people in, surely it must drive them away, he thought. But it was too loud to think, and he stumbled outside with the world whizzing around his head.

A slow, long walk and the chill of the early evening gave him clarity. He couldn't tell Renée he thought, but he could tell the children; seek a surrogate forgiveness from those who knew her so well. Nearing home, his strides gathered pace, and he gained confidence, feeling strength for the first time since her demise.

He summoned Robin, Wilfried and Lo to the living room, and they squeezed onto the sofa like they had done as small children. Their faces looked worried, and he did little to assuage their fears. But Nigel decided that the only direction was to move forward.

"I'm afraid I've made a terrible mistake," Nigel confessed, his voice barely above a whisper. "I'm being tortured. I have to tell you before it's too late.

"I was unfaithful for a long time, and I can no longer bear the weight of this secret."

The room fell silent, the admission echoing like a shattered glass that couldn't be put back together. Nigel's gaze remained fixed on the floor as he unravelled the tangled web of his infidelities. Starting with Heidi and running all the way through to the most recent Carrie, each name adding another layer to the pain etched on his children's faces.

Robin, Wilf and Lo exchanged glances, grappling with the revelation that their father, the pillar of their family, had hidden such a profound betrayal. The air in the room became thick with a mixture of disbelief and heartache.

"Why?" asked Robin simply. "Why?" he repeated.

Nigel sat silent and they waited for him to say something. "I don't know. I don't know why. I don't know why my dad did it to my mother. Philandering is in the blood, I don't know."

"That's bullshit," cut across Wilf.

"I'm sorry," said Nigel. "You're right, that's ridiculous. I don't have an answer. I don't have an answer you want to hear."

"Give us the answer we don't want to hear," insisted Lo.

Nigel fell mute again and then eventually spoke out. "I don't know," he repeated. "Look, what do you want me to say? It was lust. Weakness. I'm not a great man. I don't have anything to say. I loved your mother. Always. Always I did. I betrayed her and I will have to live with that shame forever."

"Stop feeling sorry for yourself," said Robin. "Don't make excuses. It was you. It was all you."

"You're right," said Nigel. "It was all me. There are no excuses. I don't know what I can say."

"Enough," interjected Robin and he got up and left the room, followed by Wilf and then Lo. They regathered in the garage, surrounded by the semi-erotic paintings but didn't take in the strangeness of the backdrop and betrayed no signs of their inner turmoil. Robin looked at his siblings for inspiration.

"I think I'm going to go," said Lo simply.

"Me, too," added Wilf. Robin nodded.

A set of siblings that squabbled and argued through their shared youths needed barely a few seconds to reach a unanimous decision and one that would essentially break up the sanctity of family.

In an almost meticulous choreography of their movements, the children headed to their respective rooms. With efficiency, they packed their belongings — trinkets, books, and keepsakes collected over the years.

As they congregated in the hall, vintage suitcases, holdalls and backpacks in their hands, Nigel tried to speak, but the siblings left without a word. The front door swung open, revealing the pristine streets of West Didsbury bathed in the warm hues of a setting sun.

The trio walked away, their synchronised steps not too fast and not too slow. Nigel smiled as tears gathered in his eyes as he watched them march away. He finally claimed a small piece of peace amid the pain.

HEATONS 47

For Wilf, there were plenty of opportunities when he decided to leave. As a computer software prodigy, he had job offers from California, Texas, Wisconsin and New York in the United States, Japan and Hong Kong in the Far East and London and Amsterdam in Europe. University places had been offered unconditionally but were unnecessary.

Still, he found it the toughest of the three to depart despite the range of options and the fact that he was at his happiest in solitude. Even in infancy he had been mostly alone, with the warm and special love from his twin Lo and mother Renee his only external comfort.

Initially, Wilf accepted a job at a social media start-up in Northern California for a ridiculously high wage. The new company was seemingly incapable of failing due to the fact that it was being financed by a combination of faceless billionaire benefactors and managed by a hippy, tech-star pseudo-celebrity called Trent, who had made the breakthrough from geekery to the mainstream. The company's only problem was that they had little more than a vague idea for an actual product but Wilf didn't much care. He would be merely there to help build the user interface.

It was all agreed, and Trent arranged a five-bedroom eco-home in the small wealthy town of Sebastopol, Nevada County, which was a 20-minute bicycle ride from the Santa Rosa headquarters. Quite why his new 'eco-home' had to be so big Wilf couldn't quite understand. It had a large pool, which he wouldn't want anyone to swim in, large gardens he wouldn't use, a large kitchen, which he wouldn't want to cook in, and extra bedrooms that he thought no one would ever sleep in.

So two days after moving in, the house, rather than the job, influenced his decision to pull out of the agreement before he'd even done a day's work, much to the aggravation of the now-furious, hippy, tech-star pseudo-celebrity, and instead hastily take a job in New York.

Although it was also a spontaneous decision shortly after waking from a troubled night, the spacious and beautiful California was entirely the wrong place, swallowing him up like a plankton to a whale. The thought of moving to a big city had initially put him off choosing New York, but a walk around the Brooklyn Heights neighbourhood, where his airy and stylish loft apartment was located, quickly made him believe he would have all the isolation and solitude he desired.

The rain fell lightly as he skulked surreptitiously down Columbia Heights, along Pierrepont Street and across Monroe Street. The streets were wide and empty and full of shops. Most interesting to Wilf were the smart restaurants, particularly a classic Americana diner, a couple of unassuming bars, an upmarket liquor store and a beautiful bookstore on Smith Street.

Lively and bohemian, Brooklyn Heights was an exciting place to live, far cooler than he probably needed it to be. So, too was the gaming software company in Manhattan where he would be employed and just a short ride on the 3 train from Clarke Street to Penn Station followed by a six-block walk.

Bizarro Games created sophisticated, free-roaming game worlds heavily soaked in violence. And they refused to allow anything to be released until it was absolutely perfect. Often, years would go by between output and maybe even information on new releases. They avoided social and mainstream media, with updates seeping out through surreptitious back channels or opaque insiders. Fans didn't care. It only added to their mystique.

Success had brought an aura to Bizarro with rumours about their work gossiped about, as if they were rock stars. Some employees lived like they were. Drugs and alcohol were everywhere and caused work delays, but as long as each game that eventually came out set a new standard, which they always did, the money kept rolling in, and the hype continued to grow.

The work would suit Wilf. On his first day, he sat and programmed way past the 5pm standard finish, getting lost in the precision and technicality they couldn't help but bring. Around him, a table tennis tournament started amid the uncut cocaine lines and bottles of Westchester IPA that littered the table. Ziggy Stardust blasted out on the Bang and Olufsen speakers. He was startled when CEO Ciprian, a wealthy Oxford University alumni, pulled him away from his computer and forced a beer into his hand.

"It's not good to work too hard," Ciprian shouted into his ear. "We want you to be happy. When we're happy, then we do good stuff."

Wilf nodded. Ciprian had been excessively charming to get him to join them but it was one of those conversations where they had to shout into each others' ears to be heard, so there was no flow to the talking.

"I got to be honest, I'm happiest when I'm working," Wilf said.

"Huh?"

"I'm happiest when I'm working."

"That's okay, but you have to ensure you're happy too."

"That makes me happy. I get in the zone with work. I'm not happy until I've finished it."

"You can finish it tomorrow, Wilf. We want you to be happy."

"Yeah, okay."

"How's your first day? Everything okay?"

"I'm very happy. I like the work."

"And the company? What do you think of the office?"

"It seems okay, yeah."

"I think you'll be happy here, Wilf. We're like a family, we take care of each other, you understand?"

"I think so," Wilf nodded, looking down at the floor.

"But you have to have time to play."

"Huh?"

"You have to have time to play. A family that plays together stays together. You see?"

"Yeah, I see."

"We want you to be happy."

"I'm sure I'll be happy."

"It's a little different to Manchester here, huh?"

"It's not so different."

"Huh?"

"I said it's a bit different, but not too much."

"New York has got everything you could possibly want, Wilf. Whatever makes you happy, you'll find it in New York."

"It's been okay so far. I think I'm going to be okay here."

"You think you'll be happy here?"

"Yeah, I think so."

"You want some coke or is it not your thing?"

"No, it's not really my thing."

"You ever try it?"

"No, I'm okay. It's not my thing."

"You should try it. You might like it."

"That's okay."

"You ever try it?"

Wilf shook his head and took a big gulp of his Westchester IPA. It was nearly all gone now. Temporarily, he couldn't hear what Ciprian said next as he glanced around the room. The table tennis had stopped, and groups of people spread themselves across the room, talking animatedly as someone turned up David Bowie to another level. Ciprian said something about drinking liquor.

"I don't really drink," Wilf lied.

"You don't drink?"

"Not really. I'm okay, really. You don't need to worry about me."

"You've got to do what makes you happy. I'm making it my mission to make sure you're happy."

"I'll be happy, I promise."

"You swear?" Ciprian held out his arms, smiling and waiting for a reply. "You swear?" he repeated. Wilf nodded and smiled and Ciprian wrapped his arms around and laughed: "We'll make you happy, I swear." He patted him on the back. "Come on, let's get another beer."

Ciprian headed off to get another beer and Wilf slipped downstairs unnoticed and into the dark Manhattan evening. It was 8pm, and he put in his iPod earbuds, clicked on Belgian electronic rock and headed towards the Penn Station Subway.

Wilf had been into gaming from a young age. His first exposure came with an edition of NHL that was very popular in his class at school, and he would go on to become infatuated with it. He played it, or at least tried to play it, on his PlayStation 4 from the moment he arrived home from school until late into the night, depending on whether Renée was able to stop him. He got very good, playing online and against the computer.

That spring, he was invited to a birthday party with several boys from his school where an NHL tournament was to be the central focus. Wilf had never played his opponents but had boasted to them, in a factual way, about how good he was at the game. But when he played Stephen Frimmington, he met a type of opponent he had never come up against before, either online or through the AI. Frimmington kept the puck for large periods, making short passes and refusing to shoot. His players moved into strange areas and exploited the shortcomings of Wilf's lines. Eventually, he worked a scoring opportunity and took it ruthlessly. Then another, and another, winning 3-1 in the end.

Humiliate, tears involuntarily gathered in Wilf's eyes, and his cheeks turned red. The boys chuckled, Frimmington the loudest, and Wilf slowly put his controller on the floor. He remained through the laughter and managed to clear his eyes without a tear falling out. Stephen's mother arrived with a chocolate cake, and the boys began to sing 'Happy Birthday'. Wilf mimed along, but his mind was elsewhere.

From the moment he got home, he plotted revenge. Within the game, he created two ordinary players - a goalscorer called Sam Smith and a goaltender Jack James - and worked on their attributes incessantly over several weeks until they were as close to perfection as he could make them. Smith scored with every shot; James never conceded a goal.

A couple of weeks after that, Wilf invited the boys around for another tournament with the seemingly inconsequential Smith and Jones buried deep in his squad. Again, he faced Stephen Frimmington in the decisive game and again, the match was frustrating as he struggled to compete with the unorthodox attacking style, and he trailed 1-0 late in the game.

It was at this point that he turned to Smith and James, and within seconds, Smith blasted in a ridiculously fierce equaliser. James then made a remarkable save when it looked like the opponents were going to score, and from the resulting breakaway, Smith hit the winner.

Frimmington calmly put the controller down and chortled softly. "Well done," he said. "That was…" interrupting himself with a sneering laugh that the other boys began to join in with. He rose and added: "Congratulations on winning. That was truly remarkable."

Frimmington left the room followed by the other boys, chattering and laughing and patting each other on the shoulder. "What a save," he heard one joke to another just before the door slammed behind them. Wilf stood in the hallway, the controller still in his hand. It would be the last time he would see them away from school for more than a year.

For the next 12 months, Wilf taught himself programming. He locked himself in his room, reading programming guides, developing short games, working on graphics, and mastering the art of coding. By six months in, the books could teach him nothing. He was able to bypass their logic and shortcut his wait to better and more efficient games.

Next came the development of his own hockey game, which he thought could be even better than NHL. He stumbled across a section of the game engine on the dark web and developed the fundamental gameplay to make it a quicker and wilder experience, with even more vicious fighting, although the design and extras were more sparse.

AHL, or Alternative Hockey League, wasn't a particularly inspiring title, but Wilf thought it was the best he could do as he wanted to release it for free and avoid any copyright infringements.

Then, there was the difficult part of naming the teams, and Wilf randomly selected eight American cities and attributed original nicknames. The result was Spokane Punks, Rochester Animals, Sioux Falls Karambits, Chesapeake Characters, Oxnard Killer Bees, Grand Rapids Golden Oblongs, Port St Lucie Seamonsters and Topeka Lunatics. Player names were taken from the surnames of cricket players randomly picked from an old Wisden Almanack belonging to Robin and a forename generator, so Alex Laxman, Caleb de Villiers and Roger Tufnell were among the best players.

Bizarrely to Wilf, gamers were drawn to the strangeness of the names, and AHL soon grew in popularity, developing a small cult following. It was the gameplay that they stayed for. For hockey fans, it had a speed and craziness that no other game had been able to capture before, and, of course, the fights had an exaggerated violence and gory animation that made them unmissable. It didn't matter that the star teams and star names weren't in there or that the graphics were less refined or detailed; it soon became a cult classic, and daily players rose from hundreds to a few thousands in the space of a few weeks.

When Wilf heard Stephen Frimmington discussing an AHL match with his friends, he invited them all over for a tournament. Frimmington raised his eyebrows, but Wilf persuaded them that it was a good idea.

Renée was delighted to see Wilf have friends come around to the house and made a light tea of tuna, cheese and ham sandwiches and Stephen Frimmington and his friends were polite as they chatted about school and AHL in the kitchen while his mother flitted around fetching drinks.

Shortly after they went up to his bedroom, which is when Wilf revealed his big secret. The large server hidden in the wardrobe, the coding behind the game, network infrastructures, Wilf showed it all to them and they were astounded. Frimmington could barely speak except to mutter the odd "cool" or "incredible". To completely impress them, he added each of their names to the database of hockey players, and they all laughed when he gave Stephen Frimmington low statistics before bumping them up later.

The boys came back a couple of times over the next few weeks, but Wilf never truly made friends with them. As quickly as he had seen AHL's success rise, he had become bored with it. He discovered small faults in the game that annoyed him and found the team and player names preposterous. More than that, he realised that it was building the game that had given him the most satisfaction.

So, he set about building an even bigger game that would outstrip the popularity of AHL. To do that, he switched genres, focusing on a free-roaming world where players killed each other until there was only one left standing. Not the most original idea in the world so to make it stand out from the rest, he made his more believable. Guns and weapons were almost impossible to come across, so hand-to-hand combat was more common. Stealth was critical and kept players on edge. Killing an opponent by putting a plastic bag over their head or pushing them through an open window were deadly and revered skills.

Characters lived for longer, with games lasting for hours rather than minutes and hours, meaning that deaths or successful kills were more prized. If players wanted a break, they had to find a safe place to sleep for their character or risk them being smothered by a pillow while they rested. The world was small and clunky as Wilf tried to disguise the hard work and engine that he had stolen.

Still, Wormhole, as Wilf called it, took more than 18 months to build. When it went live, it was even bigger than AHL Hockey, which he had to remove to reuse the servers. Thousands were quickly hooked and it even garnered some mainstream attention.

That spotlight made Wilf feel very uncomfortable, not least the risk of being sued, but mostly for the occasional interest in who was behind it. He soon pulled the plug, destroying the game, writing a simple message: "The Wormhole is closed for good".

The reaction was mostly annoyance, and it increased the efforts to find its inventor. They wanted to know why he had sabotaged the game and whether he could bring it back.

Wilf knew that Stephen Frimmington guessed it was him. He had spoken about it to a friend when he noticed Wilf's double-take, a tic which had revealed his involvement. Their eyes would catch each other in class and at break times for the first time since they had briefly become acquaintances over AHL tournaments. But they never spoke.

A couple of days later, Wilf got a phone call from a gaming website asking if he had developed Wormhole. Wilf panicked and denied all knowledge, but it was unconvincing. Later that week, a small cult website published an article: "Revealed: The Master of the Wormhole," exposing Wilf as the inventor. It talked about how he had invented AHL and used a couple of pictures from a school trip to the Manchester Museum of Science and Industry. Wilf could barely read it but picked out words such as 'genius', 'loner' and 'weird' as he scrolled through the article.

Within days, a second expose appeared elsewhere, and Wilf stopped using his computers, running away from his virtual life and ignoring its existence. He went for long walks listening to music and would join Robin watching club cricket matches from the boundary edge. Once, he was approached by a website writer to tell his story but he physically ran away.

After a couple of days, the fuss had died down. Months after, Wilf turned on his computer and was met with a sizeable inbox of unread emails, but deleted the lot and set up a new account without immediately sharing the address. But shortly after, an email arrived to it. It was from a gaming company in Hong Kong offering him a job. Others followed. Meanwhile, his IT teacher was informing him of offers from leading universities across the world. California looked good, he thought.

A train arrived just as Wilf stepped onto the subway station platform. The carriage was mostly full. A young couple chatted and joked tenderly on the seat in front - bouncing shoulders off each other. The man glanced over his shoulders and caught eyes with Wilf, who decided not to look over at them again, although he could hear their distorted conversation faintly, along with the laughter underneath his music.

Across the way sat a smart middle-aged man in a navy suit with the shirt collar open and his tie pulled loose. Wilf glanced at his shoes. They were ghastly - cheap, plastic slip-ons that curled up at the toe. Wilf transported himself to the day they were bought. Imagining the man trying them on at the shoe shop. He strides up and down, catching glances in the angled, ankle-length mirrors. "What do you think?" he says to his wife, putting one foot on point. "I like them, yeah," she replies and the man nods in agreement. The assistant standing close by with a shoe box in hand ready to close a deal, too negligent and uninterested to be honest about how bad they are, even on sale. The man smiles at his wife; leans over to give her a peck on the cheek before he sits down to put on a pair of battered Reeboks and grins to himself contentedly. Wilf felt really irritated by the image, even though it wasn't real. But it was good to have these thoughts passing through his mind. He enjoyed his own thoughts more than anyone else's.

Then Chambers Street distracted him away from it. Wilf was worried about missing his stop and had to glare out of the window as they rushed into stations. His reflection stared back at him. He looked angry. And cool too, he thought. With the angry soundtrack in his ears, he felt like he could be in a movie. Wilf kept looking through the window, switching between his reflection and the stations. Park Place, Fulton Street, Wall Street. He stood up far too early for Clarke Street as the train passed under the East River. Wilf saw in the reflection that the man in the plastic shoes was watching him, standing at the door. The couple were kissing gently.

Wilf walked out into the street under the Hotel St George exit and briefly thought about going to a bar. But he had no ID with him and every bar he approached seemed cold and unwelcoming anyway, but he thought he would chance it an off-licence.

He stepped inside the first liquor store he came across and, searching down the beer aisle, was amazed to discover a case of Heatons 47 blonde beer hidden behind the door. The Heatons was a small brewery back home, based in either Heaton Mersey or Heaton Norris, Wilf couldn't remember which, and he'd been drinking it for a very long time. His father especially liked it and when he was younger, Wilf would steal one from the fridge before buying four-packs for himself when he got older. It was the fuel that powered the work behind AHL but particularly Wormhole. That and Starboard Jim's rum.

It looked out of place in a Brooklyn liquor store though; the simple design looked so very English. The wide-spaced Futura-esque words of 'Heatons' and 'blonde beer' above and below the heavily italicised script font '47'. It spoke only of home, but Wilf had to buy some.

He took a four-pack to the counter, and the girl serving, who looked barely 21, was writing in a moleskin notebook. "ID," she announced.

"Oh bloody hell," replied Wilf in his most English accent. "I completely forgot."

The girl peered upwards through her bleach blonde fringe. "Are you for real?"

"I'm very sorry. I'm new to America. I'm so sorry I didn't think."

"Are you for real?"

"I just moved here. Could you let it slip by, just this once?"

"Are you at the university?"

"Good god know. I just moved here. I got a job. I'm so sorry. It's different in England. There I've been buying beer since I was 13."

"When was that? Last week?"

"That's funny," Wilf smiled.

"Get the fuck out."

"I'm 22. I promise. I couldn't work in America if I wasn't 21."

"Oh come on."

"I promise. I swear," Wilf said, pushing forward the four cans. Could you let it slip by, just this once?"

"Fuck off, man." Wilf was shocked. "What even is that?" she added.

"Heatons 47."

"Never heard of it."

"It's from England. From Manchester, where I'm from."

"I don't know where you got it, cos we don't sell it here."

"I'll give you twenty dollars and the price of the beer?"

"I don't know what this is. We don't even sell it." She scanned the barcode, and an error message came up on the till. "See. We don't even sell it."

"There's a stack of them over there," Wilf pointed.

"I don't get it. We don't even sell it."

"Can't I just take these? I'll put them in my bag like you haven't sold them to me."

"But we don't even sell it."

Wilf waited. The girl huffed and put her arms on her hips. "Gimme twenty bucks and fuck off," she said finally. Wilf did exactly what she asked.

He walked the six blocks back to his apartment and thought about the first time he'd bought the same beers as a teenager back home. Then it had been a gruff Mancunian that he'd had to persuade to sell them, some story about buying them for his dad. It was as unconvincing as his latest lie yet somehow he walked away with them that time as well.

In his loft, Wilf poured the blonde beer into a handled tankard, the head spilling over onto the workbench, and he mopped it up. He stared at the beer and smiled as his mouth juiced up. He thought of Wormhole, and then when Wormhole had launched, which is when he had drank way too much of the Heatons 47. That wasn't a happy memory so then he thought about when AHL had first gone live. When the number of players started ticking up higher and higher. He grabbed the glass and quickly gulped down half of it. It was delicious and tasted so much of home. He burped, smiled and put on music.

Wilf woke with a familiar numb feeling and skipped breakfast to head straight into Manhattan. This time, he remembered to take his passport with him, feeling that he would probably want a beer later.

The subway was packed and still unfamiliar, or rather uncertain of the stops, Wilf had to peer between bodies as the train arrived at stations. Exiting Penn Station, the summer heat hit hard. The sun bounced off the skyscrapers and sidewalk, and the shaded sections were bustling.

New Yorkers were fraught and frazzled - men sweated in short-sleeve shirts with tattoos showing women in light cotton dresses. Wilf wore a sky blue polo t-shirt, dark rayon flared pants, and baseball sneakers but had forgotten his sunglasses. He looked skywards, shielding his eyes, but staring up at tall buildings always gave him vertigo, and he stumbled backwards with dizziness. A man skipped out of the way to avoid being trod on but carried on down the street without looking back.

Wilf called in at a coffee house to try to make himself feel better. The barista was brusque, and less than two minutes later, Wilf found himself back on a searingly hot 34th Street, holding a paper cup with what looked like the name 'Milf' untidily scrawled on it and the aroma of too-strong coffee dirtying the air.

Bizarro's office, in contrast, was like a refrigerator, and the cold air made him shiver happily. There was only a few people there when he arrived, but the desks steadily filled up as the morning went on. Punctuality seemed relaxed, which appealed to Wilf, who would rather work from lunchtime until late into the night, although he thought that would be difficult with the drugs and booze and music starting at what the Miller family would have called 'tea-time'.

His work was straightforward, building a seascape for a free-roaming game set in the Atlantic Ocean touching on the coasts of southern Florida and Cuba. Secrecy was what Bizarro took more seriously than anything, and all employees signed confidentiality agreements to not discuss it outside work.

'Untitled X' was focused around the world of drug smugglers and gun runners. Many of the staff had spent close to a month in Miami, followed by another month in Havana, mapping out the districts and building a flavour for the game. Drug lords, gangsters and petty crooks were interviewed and paid as consultants, and one programmer bought clothes from a smuggler and wore them to the office to help with his understanding.

As the project was already six months in, Wilf was tasked with building the ocean - a more generic mission. Others were building the important aspects such as cities, boats, cars, islands and characters. Still Ciprian had discussed sending him down to Florida for a fortnight to sample the light and the textures of the sea when he had offered him the job. He was to play a leading role in future projects but his ocean programmer role was seen as the perfect way to slowly acclimatise to the team.

Still Wilf wanted to push the creativity, studying the tides, the sealife and its population of the area and also wanted to add a realistic depth to the ocean. Characters in the game would be able to swim or deep sea dive, jettison cargo over the side or dump bodies into the ocean, and he wanted this to be as real as possible.

Around mid-morning, Ciprian wandered in, shouting hello to everyone there. Wilf forgot to head out for lunch, and just as he remembered he was hungry, Ciprian walked past his desk. "Crazy night last night, man," he said, tapping Wilf on the shoulder. He turned back and pointed: "What time did you stay until?"

"I'm not too sure," said Wilf.

"Yeah, I know. It went late. You have a good one?"

"Yeah, good. Feeling it today."

"You'll be okay. You'll be be happy here," Ciprian smiled and turned to talk to a colleague. Wilf forgot he was hungry again and carried on working.

It was still stifling when Wilf got back to Brooklyn. He had slipped out of the office late in the afternoon for a hot dog and thought it was probably fine not to go back. Instead, he wandered around Manhattan and took in the city until it was too hot to walk any more.

He made it to Central Park and went in for the first time. In one corner, young kids were playing baseball and the heat did nothing to sap their energy as they ran around chasing hits, both short and long, in eager groups. Watching on, a young man, of around Wilf's age had his arms stretched across the back of a park bench. The woman sitting next to him rested her hand on his chest and then buried her head into his armpit, but he never moved or showed any interest.

Checking the map on his phone, Wilf saw he was close to 72nd Street, so ducked into the Subway Station and took the IRT back to Clarke Street. The train was packed but he took a spot next to the door and spent much of the time looking at his reflection and listening to music as he checked the stops.

Wilf was thirsty from the heat and went into the first bar he found, although he missed the name of it, and ordered a Heineken. He took a seat at the bar and overtipped for his beer.

A baseball game was on the screens that filled every corner and around him, men in pairs and groups craned their necks and occasionally shouted their opinions at the TV or said them to someone close-by as if accusing them of being an ill-formed coach. The New York Mets were winning at the Los Angeles Angels, but you wouldn't guess it from the conversations. No one seemed particularly happy.

A guy, probably in his 60s, turned to Wilf and said something about the bullpen. He wasn't concentrating, so missed the first half of his sentence. "I don't know anything about baseball," he said. The man turned back to the screen. Wilf finished his beer and headed back into the street, where the low sun blinded him.

He made his way back to the liquor store where he'd been the previous night. The Heatons 47 was in the same corner and he picked up another four-pack and took them to the counter. It was the same girl serving, and again, she was writing in a notebook.

"Just a second," she said, noting his presence but not looking up from her writing. Wilf watched her pen move and glide sideways. A fan was barely two feet away from her and she brushed her blonde fringe away from her forehead, exposing her black roots, and she sighed deeply in the dry air. She was wearing a tight Sonic Youth t-shirt with a drawing of a woman smoking and a man with his arm around her. Both were wearing sunglasses. Wilf read the cartoon-style text on it:

I stole my sister's boyfriend. It was all whirlwind, heat, and flash. Within a week we killed my parents and hit the road.

"What the fuck?" she sighed.

"Hi. Can I take these again?"

"I left a message for the manager to take those away."

"Oh sorry. But they're right over there." Wilf pointed to the stack of Heatons 47s in the corner.

"But like I told you last night, we don't sell them."

"Can I give you twenty dollars again?"

"Man, what is this?"

"Yeah I know. But this is my favourite beer. Can I just give you twenty dollars again?"

"I knew that was a mistake. We don't even sell it." Wilf stood silently. His hands were resting on the counter with a 20 dollar bill poking out from underneath his left.

"We don't even sell it. And I bet you don't even have ID again do you?" she added. Wilf took out his passport, and she looked at the page with the picture and date of birth on it. "What the fuck is wrong with you? Go and get some other beers," she motioned.

"I know. But," Wilf started replying, but before he could finish, she ripped the bill from between his fingers.

"Fucking jerk," she said as she slumped back onto the stool and picked up her notebook. Wilf smiled back, although she didn't notice, and he turned to the door.

The Heatons 47 tasted even better than the previous night; deliciously refreshing in the oppressive heat. Wilf put on some music and thought about home. He would normally have been programming at this time but it felt good to have worked hard in the daytime and have a clear night.

Opening the second can, Wilf put on Sonic Youth. He hadn't heard them before. They were raw and rowdy, and he liked them.

The following day was a Saturday, but Wilf felt like heading into the office to do some work. He got dressed and took the subway into Manhattan, but as he entered the block of Bizarro's building he changed his mind. Ciprian would give him a hard time for working on the weekend; talk about him needing to be happy, and maybe he was right anyway.

But New York was just too hot in summer. He had to get off the street and ended up back in the coffee house with the brusque barista and stayed inside to take in the air conditioning. The coffee was bad; too strong. Wilf thought about a can of Heatons 47, but it was too early for that.

Instead, he Googled Manhattan for ideas for his day off. Central Park was discounted because of the sun and everything else, like going to the Museum of Modern Art, seemed too touristy, even though he hadn't done the tourist things yet and wanted to.

An arthouse cinema was showing a double bill of Stanley Kubrick films. Wilf enjoyed the first, A Clockwork Orange - a famous movie from the 1970s. that he hadn't seen before. It was very violent, with a twisted morality, and Wilf couldn't help looking at it through the eyes of a game-maker. In some ways, it was similar to what he had wanted for Wormhole and the loss of Alex, the main character's, free will was reminiscent of the way he had lost control of the world he created.

The second movie was an erotic thriller called Eyes Wide Shut and Wilf felt uncomfortable watching it in the cinema on his own. He was gripped by the paranoia and claustrophobia, but the eroticism took him out of the film and back into the auditorium, which was largely empty except for a smattering of couples. He heard one couple laugh, and the man looked over in his direction and it made him embarrassed.

It was still mid-afternoon, but he decided to head back to Brooklyn and his first thought was about getting a pack of Heatons 47. Riding the train, he was starting to get more comfortable with the stops and barely had to check he hadn't passed Clarke Street.

He headed straight to the liquor store where a young lad with a conservative haircut was reading a maths textbook. Wilf took two steps inside before deciding it was too early for a drink. Instead, he headed to the bookstore he liked the look of and wandered inside.

They served coffee, and the small cafe area was a mixture of sofas, armchairs and small table-sets. Most of them were filled with single people engrossed in books and with the air-conditioning set to sensible, Wilf thought it would be a good place to stay for the rest of the afternoon.

He spent too long picking a book, searching the shelves for something he really wanted before eventually picking out Money by Martin Amis. Returning to the cafe area, he bought a latte and took it to an armchair. A couple of people looked up from their books to see who the new arrival was. A man with rimless glasses and a floppy parted fringe peered over his book in a school-masterly way. A chubby girl with a book resting on her middle briefly looked up.

Money was pacy, grim and brilliantly entertaining. Wilf occasionally thought about going to buy a pack of Heatons 47 and reading it in the huge window of his apartment but stayed in the bookstore and ordered another latte. The cafe slowly emptied and when the chubby girl put her book on top of her hemp bag overspilling with vegetables, Wilf was the last person left and decided to depart.

Instead of heading straight to the off-licence, he stopped for noodles, taking a seat at a bench looking out into the street. The restaurant sold Starboard Jim's and he ordered a double with coke along with pork-belly udon. He carried on reading Money but was distracted by the people passing by on the street, and after quickly drinking a second double Starboard Jim's and coke he started to feel dizzy.

Montague Street seemed to attract a slightly wealthier and hipper crowd than that close to Wilf's apartment or the area near the subway station. The men were either too muscly or too thin, but hardly ever overweight. Their clothes were tight or tailored, and sunglasses were almost requisite, even as the sun was beginning to dip. The women were almost all slender and tanned. Every pristine haircut seemed to bounce enthusiastically, and from large handbags, cellphones, water bottles or toy dogs were forever being pulled. Everyone looked very healthy and very American.

The liquor store girl appeared across the road and looked like she wasn't a good fit with the rest of the passers-by. She wore no sunglasses, and her shaggy bob haircut had been tied scruffily into two short and uneven pigtails. Her hoodie was zipped halfway and pulled to the left and below a pair of ripped jean shorts, her legs were dotted with bruises and scrapes.

Crossing the road, she stopped midway to dig deep into her backpack. It was clearly full of all-sorts of stuff, and she finally picked out a pack of cigarettes and stuck one in the mouth. Then she dug back into the bag to find a lighter, eventually lighting the cigarette, inhaling the first puff deeply and exhaling high into the air like a firebreather before continuing across the road. Wilf watched her until she disappeared out of view, striding away with little interest in anything on Montague Street.

He finished his noodles, ordered another drink and tried to carry on reading his book. But concentration was hard, and he finished the drink and paid for the meal, which was surprisingly expensive - even more so with a large tip.

From Montague Street, Wilf headed straight to the liquor store, carrying the book as he had no bag or pocket to put it in. The girl was now sitting behind the counter, writing in her notepad, and he headed straight over to the Heatons 47s and picked up a four-pack. The crate was the same size, missing only the two packs he had bought before - now three.

Putting them on the counter, he cleared his throat and said: "Hey". The girl looked up and stared back at Wilf with an expressionless face. "You know me, I love my Heatons 47," he smiled.

She accidentally smiled and turned her gaze away, muttering: "Oh my God."

"No one else is going to buy it. The only person buying it is me."

"We don't sell it, you fucking weirdo. No one is buying it because we don't sell it."

"I appreciate it, I really do," said Wilf, placing a twenty dollar bill on the counter, which she snapped up. "It reminds me of home. It's very special."

"Take the lot. If it's that special, take the lot. There was some sort of mix-up on the order, and they might take it away so if it's special, take the lot."

Wilf stood silently for a few seconds. Then he ripped a can from the pack and passed it over. "Take one," he said. "Take one, it's great."

"I'm not allowed. I'd get fired."

"Take it with you tonight. Get home tonight, light a cigarette and have a Heatons 47. Please, for me."

"What? And think of England?"

"Yeah. Make a toast to the King."

"And will I start eating fish and chips?" saying the last bit in a spoof English accent.

Wilf half-laughed. "If you don't like it, then I'll buy the lot. How about that? Deal?"

"I don't care. It's all the same to me."

"Try it? Let me know what you think when I come to buy a four-pack tomorrow."

"I'm not working tomorrow Martin Amis, so you'll have to wait for your little review."

"It's good, You know it?" he said, acknowledging the book and then being embarrassed that he had nowhere to put it. "So when are you back in?"

"What is this?"

"I'm interested in what you think?"

"Why? Who cares what I think?"

"You in on Monday night?"

"Look, I'll try it okay, and maybe you'll find out what I think at some point."

Wilf smiled and picked up the three remaining cans. "You won't be disappointed." He added a goodbye, but she didn't respond as she buried the Heatons 47 in her bulging bag.

Sunday morning began late and only because his mobile phone was pinging with WhatsApp messages. There were six one-line messages from Ciprian that landed one after another but it was only the fifth that had any pertinent information. He was having a rooftop party on his building in midtown and said Wilf should swing by. He left the messages unticked for some time.

He considered taking the N train from Borough Hall to Coney Island to check out the ocean as much as anything. But the temperature had dropped, the sky was cloudy, and he thought he would save it for another day.

Instead he found himself once again wandering the streets of Brooklyn and ended back on Montague Street, this time heading into the diner. It was busy with families sharing huge plates of pancakes, bacon, eggs and waffles and healthy couples eating smashed avocados and drinking smoothies. He was about to back out of the door when the waitress spotted him and took him to the table closest to the restrooms.

After ordering corned beef hash and eggs, the waitress returned with a large mug and poured coffee into it. It was good and jerked him into life and a refill even moreso. The breakfast was just as delicious, and Wilf cleared a massive plate of food.

Midway through he picked up his phone and messaged Ciprian that he would see him at the party later. He grimaced when the phone pinged back after a couple of minutes. It pinged another four times with none of the messages worth reading other than the details of the address.

He instantly regretted saying he'd go, but then again, if he played it right, he could avoid any more gatherings for maybe a few weeks or longer. The afternoon was spent playing video games, but as the apartment descended into gloom, it was time to head out to the party.

One good thing about the Bizarro crowd was that there was no need to make an effort to dress. Everything was cool - either ironically, unironically or any way they decided to explain their keenness. Wilf wondered what they would make if he were to wear those cheap plastic slip-ons that the guy on the subway train had been wearing. That might see him blackballed from the clique and it was worth considering for the future. But instead he put on his cotton hooded smock and $200 sneakers that drew coos of praise.

Ciprian's apartment was entirely as he had imagined. Minimalist white walls covered in expensive, unimpressive graffiti paintings with banal slogans like "Fuck the rules" and "Dream but don't sleep". Technology everywhere and incredibly new, with deep throbbing house somehow both loud and quiet at the same time.

Wilf grabbed a bottle of weak Australian lager from the table piled with beer and ice. Its mediocrity was familiar and refreshing. A group of maybe 20 people from the office hung together, and Henk, Arthur and

Bebe made room for him to fit in and feel comfortable, although he felt anything but.

He had to field a few questions about what he'd been doing: "This and that," he unsuccessfully replied before saying, "I'm still on UK time," to follow-up questions. He was relieved when Ryder arrived, and they moved on to grilling him about his Sunday. Wilf took a half-step back from the circle where he wouldn't be noticed.

Glancing around the group and then the room, he noticed that Ciprian was missing. He tapped Bebe on the arm: "Hey, where's Ciprian?"

"He's had to fly down to Miami this afternoon," she said. "There's alway something going on down there. But he usually brings back some good shit. You want a line?"

"Not my thing," Wilf replied, lifting up and rattling his bottle that was already empty.

Bebe nonchalantly answered: "Sure thing," before motioning the sign language for snorting a line of cocaine towards Ryder as they headed off to an anteroom. Wilf cursed his look that Ciprian wasn't there, and now he was. What a waste of a night out. Maybe he could let him know he was there and get the best of both worlds as he headed over to the cocktail bar to make a cuba libre before moving to the balcony.

From the 20th floor, he had a good perspective of Manhattan. All those straight lines, the rows of lights and windows, the parked cars, the double parked cars, the cars driving, the taxis and the people. A group stopped, turned around, then, after a couple of yards turned back again and carried on walking. A man chased a woman walking at pace, grabbed her arm, she shrugged him off, leaving him standing. He watched her walk away.

"How you finding it?"

"Hey. Oh hey Amber," Wilf said. Amber was also English, from somewhere in the home counties, he guessed, and worked at Bizarro.

They'd had a brief awkward chat about being English at the office but nothing further. Wilf thought her rather plain, particularly compared to their co-workers.

"You settling in?"

"Oh sure," said Wilf, staring across the avenue. "It's a big city."

Amber smiled. "It is. Have you got an apartment?"

"I'm in Brooklyn."

"Me too."

"You been here long?"

"Six months," Amber replied. "I love it here. You can be whoever you want to be and do what you want to do. You know what I mean?"

He didn't, but said yes anyway.

"What you drinking? I'm going to get myself another."

"Rum and coke. Cheers."

Wilf stared across watching a couple on the opposite balcony. They were in silhouette, backlit from the low light behind them, drinking from champagne flutes. He moved in for a kiss, and she responded by throwing her arms around him. He put his hand on her backside, and she took the glass out of his hand and led him back inside.

"Lucky them," said Amber, offering the rum and coke to Wilf.

"Cheers," said Wilf. "Good luck to them," offering his glass to the other side of the street.

"Do you have many friends in New York, Wilf?

"No. I moved out my own. I'm happy alone you know. It suits me. I came for the work.

"Yes, I know. I came here alone too, but you have to get out there.

"I know," he nodded.

"This is the greatest city in the world. Restaurants, bars, glamour, people, everything. There's everything."

"Okay," he said, sipping his drink. Amber looked at him, refusing to break the silence that hung. "I mean, I don't need everything, but I'll get round to, you know, finding something."

"What do you want?" she shot back.

"You know… well… I don't know." Amber again allowed the silence to hold. Wilf downed the rest of his drink, shaking the ice over his tongue. "Well, cheers. I'd better get going," he smiled. "See you at the office tomorrow," before a short wave to the Bizarro group, who did not respond.

Wilf had drunk four drinks, and he figured that was enough to be able to leave if any of his colleagues had been counting. He couldn't be bothered to go back to the Subway, instead hailing a passing taxi, giving his address.

The driver, Hernando Villalobos, according to his pass, was talking to him, but Wilf couldn't really hear him or understand him. After a couple of "Sorries" and "I don't understands", Hernando gave up, waved his arms, said something in Spanish and turned up the Latin music on the stereo.

Upbeat and sunny, it felt like it should be incongruous to driving through nighttime New York, but somehow it provided the perfect soundtrack. Passing through quickly through the bright lights and neon sides gave a languid strobing effect and Wilf saw the city as a set of slow-motion moving Polaroids. Wild faces, big smiles, angry rows, romance, skaters, religion - all revealed in the space of a few blocks. He felt drunker than he had leaving the party. He thought of Amber. "There's everything," she'd said.

Crossing Brooklyn Bridge sobered up Wilf. It wasn't a big deal, he just didn't like looking down at the East River. He looked at his $200 sneakers. They were cool. How could you wear those plastic slip-ons? He looked up just as they were passing the local liquor store.

Wilf rose late on Monday morning. The heat was overwhelming when he hit the street, and he considered turning back. It wasn't much cooler on the subway and he didn't open the cold soda can he bought from the store, instead rubbing it on his neck and forehead.

There was only one other passenger in the carriage - an elderly Chinese lady who was wearing a cardigan and writing on the back of an envelope in elegant easy shapes. They both got off at Penn Station, the lady carrying a large washing bag.

Heading straight to the office, the air conditioning gave him a shiver when he arrived. Amber was sorting through the pigeonholes, and Wilf sidled past her without being spotted. He took a hot desk seat two down from Ryder.

"Hey," Ryder said. "Good night?"

"Yeah, it was good."

"Got a bit wild, right?

"Yeah. Hey, is Ciprian in today?

"No, I think he's still in Miami. He might be a couple of days.

"That's cool," said Wilf, putting his headphones over his ears. Ryder got up and made the sign of a drink towards his colleague. Wilf shook his head, although he would have loved a coffee. Instead, he opened his soda and flicked open his laptop. He didn't move for another eight hours. Progress was being made on the seascape but it was slow, laborious and thoroughly enjoyable to Wilf.

Hunger finally wrestled him free of his work; he hadn't eaten all day. Closing the laptop, he realised that Ryder and Amber had gone. In fact, there was only one person at the other end of the office who he didn't know. No parties tonight. Straight down to the street and straight into the sushi chain two blocks down. He ate two plates of avocado and salmon maki off the conveyor belt before his rum and coke had even been delivered. A second with his chicken ramen gave Wilf a buzz, and he felt content.

Now would be a good time to explore Manhattan at night. The evening was warm, it was busy but still a Monday so maybe head down to Greenwich Village.

Wilf started walking downtown but ducked into the Subway on 28th Street and jumped on the 2 Train. Eyes closed, sinking into his seat, he soon altered his plans to go back to Brooklyn. He decided against earphones and instead listened into a conversation between two millennial women. He couldn't quite make out the full chat, but the crux of it was that Brad was a jerk and that Simon was also a jerk but not as big a jerk as Brad or maybe the other way around, but one of them was a "total fucking loser". He was about to discover the full role and deception of a third person called Chloe when he jolted to his feet, arriving at Clarke Street.

His internal sat-nav sent him in the direction of the liquor store, and he was outside five minutes later. He stood by the doorway watching the girl behind the counter, sitting uncomfortably on a stool, reading a book and stopping the pages turning over from the fan that stood next to her. She looked up and gasped, seeing Wilf standing.

"Jesus Christ," she said, flipping the book on the counter. "You scared me you dick."

"Sorry, sorry," stammered Wilf, catching the step with his toes as he stepped into the store.

"Fucking Heatons. It's still here," she said.

Wilf grabbed a four-pack and, walked over to the counter and pulled a twenty-dollar bill out of his back pocket.

"So what did you think?"

"What? Of you standing there? Fucking creepy."

"No. Of the Heatons?"

"What?"

"Of the can of Heatons?"

"Right. I didn't…" she grabbed for her bag. "You want it, it's in here somewhere." She rooted through. Cigarette foils and sweet wrappers fell out before she produced the can and held it out towards him.

Wilf noticed she had goosebumps on her left arm from the fan and noticed an arrow tattoo on the inside of her right arm. She had brown eyes too.

"No, you keep it," he said.

"It's fucking heavy, and I keep forgetting to take it out of my bag until I'm halfway down the street."

"Think of it as an emergency can. One day, you might need to pull it, and it could save you from the gloom."

"Gloom? Listen, I don't need saving. I've been gloomy my whole life, and that's how I like it."

"How can you be so gloomy when you look so good?" The girl looked shocked and then sniggered before pulling her shaggy hair out of her eyes. "I mean, would you like to go for a drink with me? Maybe. One night. If you're free."

"Come on man," she said, angling her head to the right, still holding out the can. Wilf still didn't take it, just smiled.

"Is that a no?"

"That's a no."

"Okay. You don't like me? I mean, all I've done has been a pain in the arse with this beer. You might like me otherwise?"

"I didn't say that I didn't like you."

"Right?"

"I'm just not interested. I don't need it right now."

"Okay, okay," said Wilf. "I can work with that. You're not interested right now, but you don't not like me. I can work with that, right?"

"Oh you can?" she half-smiled. "I don't think so."

"I think so."

"Take your beer and get out of here."

"How about this?" he suggested. "If you don't say yes between now and when that stack of Heatons are gone, I'll never bother you again?"

"I can save you the bother right now. Buy all the Heatons now, take them away, because the answer is going to be no."

"You're not interested right now."

"Take you beer," she said, thrusting the can into his chest.

"No, you keep it. You might like that too one day," he said and turned towards the exit. She rolled her eyes, shook her head, put the can in her bag and picked up her book.

The following night, she wasn't working.

Wilf had spent the day at the office programming in solitude for about 10 hours. He nodded at Ryder arriving but didn't speak again, putting on his headphones and barely shifting his gaze from the screen. He was making good progress, everything was beginning to take shape. The office was emptied fairly early again and he wolfed down a Katsu curry from the close-by independent, small sushi bar. It was called Okina-Yummy. It was cheap and wonderful. The food was amazing and whichever of the three generations of the same family that served him were smiley and non-intrusive.

He caught the train and listened to Belgian electronic rock very loudly, getting off at Clarke Street instinctively and went to the liquor store. Wilf looked over at the stack of Heatons and worked out there were 36 left. Buying a four-pack every visit gave him nine nights. So instead of beer, he asked for a bottle of Starboard Jim's. But he had forgotten his ID, and the monosyllabic 'dude' working that night refused to sell it to him.

A similar schedule on Wednesday. Work, no party, no real atmosphere. Maybe it was building up for the weekend. Dinner at Okina-Yummy, then the subway and a short walk to the liquor store.

She was there. Sitting behind the counter, messaging on her phone, when he walked in. He picked up a pack of Heatons 47 and put them on the counter.

"Hey," she said first.

"Hey. You okay?"

"Oh yep. I'm over-easy."

"You look amazing," he said.

"Not tonight, man."

Wilf half-smiled and left, leaving two ten-dollar bills on the counter. He pulled one of the cans out of the plastic carrier in the street, clicked it open and poured the beer into his mouth. It was finished before he got back to the apartment.

Thursday, he took off. Ciprian hadn't been into the office all week and he'd done so much work he figured he could get away with it. He'd looked on the database, and he was blitzing his colleagues and they would probably appreciate it if he didn't rush ahead and embarrass them.

Also it was heating up quickly. A thunderstorm had broken late at night with forks of lightning smashing into the city. It was spectacular and refreshing. The rain reminded him of Manchester.

He thought about the time when he was six or seven, standing at a bus stop with his mother. Robin had taken Lo to a cricket match, and Wilf and his mum were joking about what a waste of a day they must have had. A car speeded past through the puddle in front of them and they were soaked by rain water. "You stupid bastard!" she shouted after it. It was the first time he heard her swore and he started giggling. She turned around and started laughing too. "Don't tell your father," she said. They had ring doughnuts stuffed with chocolate when they got home.

What with the storm and everything, he hadn't slept much, so he just stayed in bed and read his book, eventually getting up for some breakfast - but it was too late, and he had to order a lunch. So he had a bacon and fried egg sandwich and two cups of coffee which was like a breakfast anyway.

Then he went back to his apartment and waited for the sun to go down. Reading, dozing and playing video games.

At 8pm, he went to the liquor store. She was there again, standing with her palms resting on the counter, looking downwards. The arms of her threadbare jumper were pulled over her hands, stretching it all out of shape. He stood in the doorway, and she saw him. She looked straight at Wilf and shook her head.

He walked in and held the four cans of Heatons 47 in his fingers. She looked up. Her eyes were watery.

"Twenty bucks," she said.

Wilf put the cans on the counter and reached into his back pocket.

"Listen…" he said as he stumbled for the money.

"Twenty bucks," she interrupted, looking away.

Wilf placed it in her hand. She looked up at him again. He smiled. She put the money in the cash register. He left.

Bizarro was rammed. Wilf had got there fairly early - 9.30am - after his day off but he couldn't find a hot desk to work at. Laptops and bags took up every single space while the workers stood or sat on the arms of sofas or the floor. Some herbal trance music was playing and the talking was so loud you could hardly hear it. Wilf figured there was going to be a big party tonight and made a mental note to disappear mid-afternoon before he got stuck.

"Hey man," Ryder touched him on the shoulder.

"Busy today."

"Everyone's in. Never seen it like this."

"Right. How come?"

"You not heard?"

"I don't think so."

"It's Ciprian. He got arrested in Miami, apparently. With some coke."

"Oh shit. What does that mean?"

"I don't know."

"Does it affect, you know, the company?"

"No man. We're all good. Too much money in this."

"Okay. But what about Ciprian? Is he coming back?"

"Well, no one knows. Bebe reckons he was with some real bad guys when he was picked up. Real bad guys. And the cops or FBI or DEA or whatever are going to give him a real hard time."

"Oh shit."

"He'll probably be able to pay bail. But I don't know. We got mixed up with some real bad guys when we started making this game man."

"Oh shit."

"They're not going to be happy with some rich English dude running around knowing their secrets. Well, so Bebe says anyway."

"What does that mean?"

"I don't know to be honest. Could be bullshit. Could be serious. Until Ciprian gets in touch or one of the bosses, we don't know."

"Bullshit that he's been arrested?"

"I don't think so. But it came from Bebe."

"Is that good or bad that it came from Bebe?"

"I don't know," shrugged Ryder. "The game could be wiped, though. Who knows? We're just speculating. Hey Henk!" he shouted, grabbing Henk as he walked past.

Wilf stood by himself, watching the groups laughing and joking or looking serious. A champagne bottle popped on the far side of the office and the music was turned up with the rhythm a little faster. Wilf left.

It was a beautiful morning with the warmth coming from the sun, even in Manhattan, rather than the humidity of the past weeks. He jumped on the Q train all the way to Coney Island and ate a hot dog before arriving at Brighton Beach. It was already busy, but Wilf found a spot and lay on the sand.

He didn't really have the right stuff for the beach but he was in shorts and sunglasses, had water, music and a book. No towel but that was okay, he did have sun cream in his backpack. He took off his sneakers, socks and t-shirt, lay back in the burning sun and closed his eyes. It felt good.

It felt good to rest his eyes. It felt good to be on the beach and not be constantly bothered to be asked to play cricket like on family holidays by the sea. He thought about Lo and his mum and the girl at the liquor store and his dad and Ciprian and then he fell asleep.

In the afternoon, it was getting too hot. He walked two blocks back from the beach and found the Rikitar Tiki Bar. It was interesting, Honolulu meets New York. He took a seat at the bar, ordered a cold beer and popcorn shrimp and took out his book.

"You're from England?" said the bar girl as she poured his drink. She was young, wearing an Hawaiian shirt and had bright white buck teeth and wavy blonde hair. She didn't sound like a New Yorker; maybe Texas.

"Yes," said Wilf. "Yes, Manchester."

"I love England," she said. "I'm hoping to go soon. To Oxford."

"Oh wow, to study."

"No. God no. I have a friend there. She said I can come and see her and she'll take me to London."

"London's great," nodded Wilf. "My sister's at Oxford, but I don't know it. But London's great.

"I love your accent," she said, putting the beer on the bar. "So cute."

"Thank you," he said. "I've been working on it all my life."

She laughed revealing dimples in her cheeks. She held out her hand, her arms were thin and perfectly tanned with coloured cotton straps wrapped around her wrist. "I'm Michelle."

"Hi Michelle. Wilf." They briefly, limply shook hands.

"Wilf, cool."

He took a big slug of the ice-cold beer and flicked open his book.

"What you reading?" she said.

"Martin Amis," he said, holding up the cover to Michelle.

"Cool," she said and then served a customer that arrived.

Michelle came back after, wiped the bar and buzzed around. Wilf was engrossed in his book. He took a slug of his beer.

"How you like New York?" she said.

"Yeah cool," he replied.

"You move here?"

"Yeah, couple of weeks ago. It's cool."

"You like it?"

"Yeah I think so. I'm in Brooklyn which seems pretty cool."

"Yeah Brooklyn," she said. "Me too. You want another beer?"

Wilf finished his drink, put the glass on the bar and nodded. She poured a beer, and a hippy-type man with a bandana and apron laid the plate of popcorn shrimp down next to him without speaking. He dipped one into the light pink sauce and ate it; unspectacular but he was hungry. Michelle came back with the beer.

"So do you know your way around?" she said, putting her elbow on the bar and resting her chin on her hand.

"Not really," he said.

"No?"

"I know some places. But you know, just exploring."

"You heard of Tiger on the Roof?"

"What's that a film?" She smiled.

"A bar."

"A bar. No, never heard of it."

"It's a rooftop bar in Williamsburg."

"Okay."

"Amazing views of Manhattan. Great DJ."

"Okay, cool."

"I'm going to be there tonight with some of my friends if you want to come down."

"Right."

"Or if you don't want to, you know. It's all good."

"Yeah sure," said Wilf, wiping his mouth after eating the last shrimp.

"Well we'll be there from 10 anyway."

"Sure," said Wilf as he finished his beer. "Sounds like a cool place. Can I pay up?"

Michelle came back with the bill. She pointed to the bottom of it where she'd written down some numbers and a smiley face with a tongue dangling out of its mouth. "That's my number," she said.

The bill was for $27.45. He left three ten dollar bills and picked up the piece of paper, smiled at Michelle and said: "See you later," before heading towards the subway station.

Sun, beer and sleeping had taken away all Wilf's energy. He drew a bath, the first time he'd done so in his life without being told to by his mother. He had no bubble bath, so had to use shower gel, which didn't last long before the water turned a flat and an ugly colour. Still it was pleasant to lie there in the hot water, reading his book with the steam rising and going into his lungs.

He smelt and felt better when he got out. His skin was soothed, his body warmer and less achy, and his head felt clearer. Wilf wandered around the apartment with the towel wrapped around him, took the Vitra Eames armchair in front of the large window, which he slid open, and watched the sun come down over the city. The cool air brought down his body temperature, and he stayed until the goosebumps appeared on his arm.

Clean t-shirt, clean underwear and clean trousers, he headed out into the Brooklyn air. It was gentle and warm, and he slowly wandered over to the liquor store. She was inside, sitting at the counter, reading a large book.

Wilf grabbed a four-pack of Heaton's 47. There were 28 left or seven four-packs. He put it down on the counter and softly said: "Hey."

"Here he is? Mr English beer boy."

"How are you?" he asked.

"Tickety boo," she said in a mock English accent.

"Good, good." Wilf took out twenty dollars and handed it over.

The girl took it and looked at him. "Okay then." She had big brown eyes and maybe six or seven earrings in each ear, which Wilf had not noticed before. Her hair was frizzier today, and she was wearing a deep red lipstick and mascara. "Thanks," she said as Wilf stood, holding the beers in his left hand.

"I love your look," he said. The girl didn't smile or, get angry or show any kind of emotion. They looked at each other. "I'm Wilf," he said. She sat on her stool and picked up her book. Wilf turned and left.

When he got home, Wilf put the beer in the fridge and got into bed. He was tired but didn't sleep. He got up in the night and sat by the window. When the sun started to rise, he saw a black and white cat was in the street watching a pigeon pecking at a hot dog roll. It crawled towards the pigeon but didn't even get in striking range before the bird flew away. Wilf was happy for the bird. It didn't know how close it had come to being snaffled.

A strange loud noise buzzed. Wilf was momentarily confused. The third time it sounded, he jolted out of bed, and looked at his bedside clock. It was 10.17. The buzz again, it must be the intercom; he hadn't heard it before.

He pressed a button next to the front door of the apartment and said hello.

"Hey Wilf, it's Ciprian."

"Oh hey."

"Let me in, man."

Wilf pressed the second button on the wall and heard the click of the building's front door being released. It came back to him what people had been discussing at the office and his arrest. He let the door off the latch and started making coffee in the kitchen.

"Hey man, how's it going?"

"Yeah good. You want a coffee?"

"Yes, thanks, Wilf."

"How's it going?"

"You enjoying the work?"

"Yeah sure."

"It going good?"

"I think."

"You happy you're here?"

"Sure. Well, I think so."

"You heard then?"

"No. Well I heard something. Just rumours."

"Drug rumours?"

"Something like that."

"Oh man. It's bullshit."

Wilf said nothing. He pressed the top of the cafetiere and poured the coffee into two cups. He lifted the milk, and Ciprian put his hand over the top of one of the cups. Wilf poured milk into the other one. They both took sips simultaneously, it was a little too hot, and they both returned them to the counter.

Ciprian was sitting on a stool. He looked tired. They both looked tired but in different ways. Wilf was just short of sleep.

"Something about being arrested?"

"Yeah, I was arrested."

"Okay."

"Drugs though, that's bullshit. It's my bullshit, but it's bullshit."

Wilf nodded and took a sip of the hot coffee.

"I told Bebe that. But it's not true."

"Okay. Worse?"

"That's the thing, it's not even worse."

"Right."

"Look Wilf. I don't know, I thought of you. I need advice but it's kind of embarrassing."

"I'm not good at advice."

"Can I tell you?"

Wilf went to the bread bin, put two slices in the toaster. "You want some?" Ciprian shook his head.

"I'm going to tell you. Maybe you'll help me, maybe you won't."

Wilf took out the margarine and marmalade from the fridge. Ciprian began to tell his story anyway. The toaster sprang up and noisily he spread margarine and orange shredded marmalade. He didn't interrupt.

It began about 18 months ago when they first started doing reconnaissance for the game. Executive producer, Dominic, who Wilf had never met, had the idea, and they went to Miami to scout locations, meet some of the locals and generally get the lie of the land.

From the start, everything was going well. Some local gang members took to them, turns out the boss Redacted was a big fan of Bizarro and loved the idea of being involved. They wanted to be the stars of it but we advised against it, although Bizarro agreed they could do some voiceover work and also get paid pretty nicely as advisers.

Everything was going well, they'd do coke, visit hangouts and nightclubs, the ports and harbours. One night in a backalley, Redacted jabbed a knife into his neck as a warning that if anything went wrong he would be in serious trouble, but other than that, he was becoming one of the gang.

Dominic flew to Tokyo to talk to the company's big bosses and to get moving on making the game a reality by selling the dream, and they organised for two guys called Sam and Logan to go out to Cuba and start making things happen from that end. Everything was going really well.

Ciprian stayed in Miami for a few months to ingratiate himself with the gang. Another night Redacted took them to this bar just off Ocean Drive, which turns out to be a lot seedier than the tourist bars. It was small, dark and loud. There's not many men in there, maybe a dozen in small groups or by themselves and maybe twice as many women in cheap dresses. It's pretty clear that they're prostitutes.

There was this one woman who caught Ciprian's attention. A small Colombian with big brown eyes. He couldn't help but keep catching her gaze, and five minutes later, she came over. Redacted puts her arms around her, and they begin to make fun of Ciprian's shyness. But after a while the boss started goading him, saying have some fun. Another woman came over and flirted with Redacted . He was less shy, grabbing and touching before disappearing with a wink.

After an awkward conversation, Ciprian discovered his girl was called Beatriz and eventually they went to the condo he was renting. Sex and coke and more sex and more coke until finally, they collapsed into the bed. When they woke up, Ciprian said she was even more beautiful. More sex and then a healthy breakfast, he gave Beatriz her money, plus a healthy tip and told her to come back in the evening.

She did, and the evening after that. Pretty soon, if he wasn't with the gang he was with Beatriz. Eventually, Ciprian set her up in her own apartment and he would spend almost all his spare time there. Even after he had to come back to New York he kept paying for Beatriz, nearly $10,000 a month, and would go to Miami at every opportunity.

Sometimes, they'd go to the beach or restaurants and even once to the theatre. They were in love and he didn't know what to do. At the end of the day, she had a lot of rough edges, and he couldn't bring her into his life. He just couldn't.

After a few weeks in New York and a week on holiday in Bali, Ciprian decided to end it. He went down to Miami, started a row and used it as a pretext to get out. He told her to move out of the apartment. She left immediately in tears. He kept his burner phone and waited for Beatriz to ask for a pay-off or to blackmail him. He had taken a $100,000 hush money in cash to the apartment, but she fled before he had time to offer it.

Ciprian thought about her every day, but the phone never rang. Last week, he spoke to Redacted and he'd located Beatriz; she was in a neighbourhood called Overtown; a rough area, really dangerous. Ciprian was devastated. That's why he went down in a hurry. He saw her standing on a street corner and begged for forgiveness. She told him to get the fuck away and never come back. They rowed, and she walked off down the street. He followed in the car, pulled up ahead of her and got out. He took out a huge wad of cash and told her that he'd paid for her time. She kept walking. He grabbed her. She shrugged him off and he grabbed again. That's when he heard the police siren.

Both of them were arrested and taken to the station. The cops thought it was funny, it's not a major felony, but Ciprian's work status is under threat. The British consulate were informed, and he could face deportation, although, of course, that won't happen. On top of that, Beatriz sent a message saying simply: Stay away.

"Another coffee?" Ciprian asked.

"Sure, I'll make it."

"So what do you think?"

Wilf puffed out his cheeks. "I don't know."

"I can't tell people the truth. I can't tell people I'm in love with a cheap… well a hooker."

"I don't know. Why not?"

"Come on. It's not a… it's just not a thing I can do."

"So why the drugs thing?"

"What drugs thing?"

"The drugs story?"

"I panicked. I was arrested and I needed bail money. And I didn't want to say I'd been arrested for soliciting in a rundown neighbourhood of Miami full of Colombian and Mexican crack whores."

"Right."

"Redacted knows. He knows everything. I feel like I should just go back to Britain, you know?"

The coffee was made. Ciprian put his hand over the top of the cup when Wilf went to put in the milk.

"Just say. People will forget soon enough."

"Drugs in one thing. Drugs are cool. Colombian hookers are not cool."

"Tell them the truth. The way you told me."

"Wilf, I can't. I just…"

"People think the game is in trouble. People think that you're in danger and that the game might get cancelled."

"Shit," he drank the coffee. "Shit. What the fuck, what's my way out of this?"

"I don't know. Say it like it is."

"Can I stay here? Just for a couple of days. I need to figure it out. I need a plan. Is that okay?"

"Sure. But what about work?"

"I'll have a plan. Don't go in. Don't tell anyone you've seen me."

"Okay."

Ciprian was shattered and took the spare bed. There was no spare quilt so he had to make do with a blanket and a single pillow borrowed from Wilf's bed.

The spare room was essentially a dumping ground, and its door had only been opened on a couple of occasions since Wilf had moved in, and that was only to chuck more stuff in. With no window and little attention, there was a fusty, musty smell, but Ciprian didn't care too much and collapsed into sleep.

His arrival was an annoyance. A friend you can get rid of, but a boss is more difficult to lose. And Ciprian was unpredictable - potentially the sort to hang around for days and days or on the other hand, he could disappear once he'd woken up.

Asleep, he was fine. Wilf pottered around the apartment; thought he'd better tidy up a bit. Work hadn't been in touch, which was a relief. Not that he would tell them the secret, just that it was easier not to communicate with them and taking two successive days away without anyone noticing was what he expected, but still good to know.

Around mid-afternoon, Ciprian appeared. He looked even more drained than before he'd gone to bed. He asked for coffee, which Wilf made for him, but they barely said a word to each other. Certainly, the revelations and Beatriz remained taboo, and there was no request for any advice.

"I need to get my shit together," Ciprian would say like a tic every five minutes.

When he went for a shower, Wilf decided it was a good time to escape. He shouted through to the bathroom that he was just going out and didn't wait for a reply, not knowing whether he had been heard.

It was getting on for tea time, and Ciprian wanted to be out until late so he could quickly go to bed. Killing some time, he took the Subway to

Manhattan to go to Okina-Yummy. Listening to a band that had been recommended to him by Spotify - Boss Hog (he wasn't sure about them yet) - he looked forward to more noodles but then worried it was too close to the office, and he didn't want to bump into anyone.

So he remained seated at Penn Station and contemplated a plan. That resulted in riding the 2 Train all the way to the terminal in Wakefield.

Checking Google it was certainly different to Manhattan and Brooklyn. Certainly around the station, where he didn't want to stray too far from. Fried chicken, fast food chains or Mexican food seemed to be the choice so Wilf ended up at a sort of Irish pub a few blocks down called Kennedy's Bar.

Under elevated train tracks, it somehow managed a magic combination of both welcoming and unappealing. He took a seat at the bar; ordered a Starboard Jim's and Coke, and put a $10 bill on the bar. Scanning the room it was lively, a couple of small booths with people, a group playing pool, a long bar with a few stools taken. Country/pop music played over the randomly placed TVs showing two different baseball games.

"Limey?" said the fat, balding man sitting a couple seats down.

"Little bit of lime, sure."

The man laughed. "No you doofus. Limey? You English?"

"Oh right. Yeah, Limey." He looked straight ahead.

"I was in Liverpool for like two months. Had a great time. Great city."

"Don't know it too well."

"Met a pretty girl there. Wow, she was pretty. Penny. You know, like the song Penny Lane? The Beatles and Liverpool. I used to sing that to her."

"Right. That's sweet."

"Had to come back to New York. She wouldn't come with me. Said she was too young. Her parents and things."

"That's tough."

"You want another?" He said as Wilf shook the last bits of ice to get the last bit of liquid.

"I got to go," he said, standing up and leaving.

"Get yourself to Liverpool, Limey," the fat, balding man shouted after him.

Wakefield wasn't a place he wanted to hang around so he jumped back on the subway and went to Okina-Yummy for some Ramen noodles. He took a table at the back of the restaurant so he couldn't be seen from the street. Bebe and Henk walked past but they wouldn't have seen him even if they had looked in. They stopped outside, framed in the window, lit by the bright orange neon signs. He thought they might come in. But they kissed gently, like it was their first time. They walked on.

The noodles were so good, thought Wilf, why would he eat anywhere else. He stayed longer than usual, ordering a second and third Starboard Jim's and Coke. The youngest of the family buzzed around him, asking if everything was okay. It was mostly an in-and-out sort of place, especially for Wilf, so his long stay was unusual.

Still he felt the need to leave before ordering a fourth, which he wanted, and it was only around 9.30pm. Greenwich Village was again a possibility for a late drink, and the booze was giving a nice buzz, but he ended up riding back to Clark Street, listening to Belgian dance music loudly.

He went to the liquor store; she was there, wearing the Sonic Youth t-shirt and listening to music, the first time he'd heard it in the store. Rock music, but no one he knew. She nodded her head in time to the rhythm and didn't see Wilf walk in or approach with his four-pack of Heatons 47.

"Hey," she said. He handed over a $20 bill and looked over at the stack of Heatons 47s. Six left.

"Not many left," he said.

"Nope," she said. He smiled. "You smoke?" She added.

"Me? No."

"Dope?"

"No."

"That's a shame," she said, presenting a spliff. "Was going to have this."

"I don't smoke. I can join you."

"Sure," she replied and locked the front door; turning the sign to Closed. "We're done in like 10, and no one's coming by now except strange Englishmen." They passed behind the counter, through a scruffy stockroom and into a dank, dirty yard.

Sitting on a wooden crate, she sparked up the spliff and inhaled it deep into her lungs. Wilf was another crate, slightly lower and felt intoxicated by the smell and the strangeness of why he was there. "So why you in New York?" she said on the exhale. "Not pretty England?"

"England's not so pretty. I think I like it here so far."

"I like it, but I'm from New Jersey, and anywhere's better than New Jersey."

"Well, you know, Manchester's not exactly paradise."

She inhaled, offered the spliff and said, "You sure?" holding her breath before forcing out the smoke.

Wilf shook his head and looked down at his feet. "What's your name?"

"I might tell you, Wilf. But then I'd have to kill you."

Wilf cracked open a Heatons 47 and took a swig. "You want one?"

She laughed. The weed was hitting nicely. "Sure," and they clanked tins. "So what do you do Wilf?"

"Software engineer. In Manhattan."

"You gave a geeky vibe."

"Yep. 100% nerd."

"I'm just fucking around."

"I know."

"So how long you been here?"

"Met you on the first night. So when was that, like two weeks ago or something?"

"I don't know," she said, scratching out the lit end of the spliff and leaning back to look up to the sky. "So how you like it?"

He started to tell her a little about the job, modestly about his prodigious history and how he earned it. She dotted in questions had heard of Bizarro but wasn't really into gaming. Then he told her about Ciprian, the full story, and she interspersed with "Jesuses" and "Fucks" as she relit the second half of the spliff.

At the end of the story she offered the same advice that Wilf had offered Ciprian. The conversation seemed to end abruptly. Wilf looked up at her.

"Woah. That was good shit. I think I'd better call it a night."

"Yeah. I don't really want to go talk to Ciprian though."

"It's like 11.30 now. You won't need to stay up too long, right?"

"Shit. Really?"

"Look. I've swapped shifts tomorrow night, long story. But you can come over for a spliff and a beer at the same time if you need to get out."

"Is that a date?"

"No, my English friend. It most certainly is not."

They smiled as they rose to their feet.

"Strawberries, mango, bananas and spinach."

Ciprian was refreshed, up early for a four-mile jog and back with a brown paper bag full of fruit. The kruzz of the blender woke Wilf. He put the kettle on and made fresh coffee, the condensation on the side of the smoothie sliding onto the counter undisturbed.

"I think you're right. I should tell everyone the truth."

"Cool," said Wilf, sipping the hot coffee.

"But there's something I didn't tell you. There's Portia."

"Portia?"

"Portia De Lange."

"Okay."

"My fiancée. We've been together a long time. We're not in love or anything but we're getting married."

"Right."

"She's a fuck-up. Drugs, alcohol, crazy. We sort of get on, and it works."

"Okay."

"And she's the daughter of Alexander De Lange. A major Bizarro investor."

"Shit."

"So I can't tell the truth. It's impossible."

"Right. But is the drugs line any better?"

"No. But I can spin it. Undercover with the gangs, misstep etc."

"So you going to stick to that story?"

"I'm going to stick to the story."

"Right."

"Portia's been messaging me. I need to speak to her today. She's worried."

"Sure."

"Listen Wilf. There's only you at Bizarro that knows the other story."

"The real story?"

"Right. I'm trusting you man."

"No worries."

"You can't tell anyone. Anyone."

"Sure, no worries."

"If this comes out and I'm dead."

"Okay."

"Finished. You know. Fucking done."

"Don't worry."

"Please Wilf."

"Don't worry."

"I'll never forget what you've done for me."

"I didn't do anything."

"I'll never forget it. What you've done."

"Okay. But I didn't do anything."

"You need anything. Just ask, man. All you have to do is ask."

"Okay."

"I don't know why but I just knew you were the right person to come to." He downed the rest of his smoothie and rinsed it under the sink. "Don't go in today okay. I'll go into tomorrow and give everyone a debrief and get the game moving."

"Okay."

"I need to speak to Portia. And her dad. It'll be fine. I know just what to say to them."

"Sure."

"Yeah. Things will be sweet."

"Cool."

"Thanks man. Thanks for everything. I won't forget it. Anything. Anything at all."

With that he left. Wilf thought he'd better let the office know he would not be in again as it would be three days since his last day there. He emailed Amber and told her he was working on some designs and went back to bed.

The day was a waste. He lay awake in bed, read the news websites for a bit, thought about the liquor store girl, ate toast and marmalade, played video games, made noodles, watched a film, had a shower, thought a bit about Ciprian, read by the big window.

Eventually the clock ticked around to 9.45 pm, and he went to the liquor store. Music was playing, too loud for customers really, and she didn't see him stroll in and grab the Heatons 47. He stood at the counter watching her writing in a moleskin book and nodding along to the music. Each finger had a silver ring, some had two, and her index finger had a small tattoo of a delicate Picasso-like dove. Her nails were clear and either neat or bitten. Her t-shirt was an anime girl, holding a sword, in front of Japanese writing. Her...

"Here he is."

"Here I am," he said, holding out a $20 bill.

"The till's always wrong. The boss can't understand why it's always over. He's completely forgotten to send them back. So you might as well take them for free."

"Have you not been taking the money for yourself?"

"Fuck no. I need this job."

"Why? What for?"

"Come on, let's go in the yard," she said, locking the liquor store door.

They took exactly the same positions as the previous night, Wilf just by her feet. She lit a spliff that had already been started and took a can from Wilf who drank half a tin with his first gulp. He looked up at her. It was a dark night for Brooklyn, and he could even see a couple of stars in the sky behind her. He went to speak but she spoke first. "So come on. What's going on with Ciprian then? I've been dying to know."

Wilf cracked open his second can and gave an update on everything that Ciprian had said, the fiancée, the father, the knowing what to say and how he was so grateful.

"I don't know what I did. But he kept saying anything you need, anything."

"Ooh and he's rich."

Wilf had now finished his third can, and the girl was rolling another spliff and still had half of hers left. The Heatons 47 had never tasted better, like when he was a teenager.

"Go get yourself some more beer," she said.

"Well, I can't drink Heatons 47. That will cost me a night. You know the deal."

"Okay. You'd better go then."

"Why?"

"That's a rule I just made up."

"You got Starboard Jim's haven't you. I'll buy a bottle and some coke."

"Register's closed."

"You can put it through though, right?"

"Nope," she lit the spliff. "It's Heatons 47 or time to go home."

"I'll get one and take three next time."

"We only sell them in four-packs."

"You don't fucking sell them."

"You want a beer or not? It's four or none."

"Should I?"

"Up to you Wilf."

"I'll take the beers but you have to tell me something about you. You know plenty about me, and I know nothing about you."

She stayed quiet and smiled. He went into the store. There were just five four-packs left, four after he took one away.

"So you're from New Jersey, that's as much as I know."

"Yep I'm from New Jersey."

"Where in New Jersey?"

"What the fuck does it matter to you? You know Jersey? I'm from a shitty little town in Jersey, like all the shitty towns in Jersey. It wouldn't mean anything to you."

He nodded and drank another beer. "Okay. Well, tell me something? What's your dream?"

"Now that's a good question."

"Oh good."

"Hmm. I don't know."

"That's not a good answer."

"Well what's your dream?"

"Come on, I asked first. You've got to give me something."

"I don't know, I'd just like to be happy, I guess. I mean I dream of being a singer or a writer or something. But ultimately, I don't know. Just. I would like to be happy."

"You happy now?"

"What right now? Or right now?"

"Right now."

She sucked on her spliff and stared off into the distance. "Right now, you have to answer my question. What's your dream?"

Wilf talked a little bit about his gaming ambitions. He didn't really know what they were, but something like he wanted to make the greatest game ever. She asked questions, and he told her about what had happened with Wormhole and how he'd pulled the plug on it.

Somewhere around the sixth or seventh can, he talked about his parents. About what had happened just before he left for New York. She put her hand on his shoulder and rubbed it caringly. At the end of it, they sat peacefully and listened to the siren of a fire tuck, a dog barking and a shout in the street: "What the fuck you looking at? Yeah, I got body parts in this bag. Deal with it, motherfucker."

They both burst out laughing hysterically. Eventually, it petered out but the liquor girl couldn't help sniggering.

Wilf looked up at her: "You have a great laugh."

"Come on, we'd better get going."

They stood up.

"You working tomorrow?"

"No I'm not back in until… shit I can't even think when."

"You got plans on your night(s) off?"

"Yes Wilf. I got plans on my nights off."

"Well, when will I see you?"

"I think I'm in maybe Monday if you haven't bought all your beer before then. Come on, I gotta go."

Wilf could see she had goosebumps on her arms as she frizzed the back of her hair and then stretched them both out. He touched her gently between her shoulder blades. She stood briefly, then opened the stockroom door.

Other than an email sent just before 11pm, there was no sign of Ciprian at the apartment and no suggestion that he was intending to return.

Subject: Meeting

Hi guys,

I understand there's been a lot of speculation in recent days so I wanted to get everyone together for a brief chat and to put some minds at rest.

It would be great to see you around 12 for a quick update but don't worry if you have other plans, it's nothing urgent.

It won't be on Zoom I'm afraid, so come along if you can.

Cheers, Ciprian

Elsewhere in his inbox, there was no automatic receipt that his message had been read by Amber.

The following day was very hot. The subway was breathless and uncomfortable. Emerging in Manhattan, Wilf ducked into the coffee house to take advantage of the air conditioning, ordering a fruit juice and cooling off in the corner as he read his phone.

It was getting on for 11.30 when he made it into the office. Once again, it was packed, and all the hot desks were claimed, although no one was sitting in the chairs. Wilf leaned against the wall, put his bag at his feet and read some more on his phone. Ryder and Henk both said hellos but didn't stick around to chat.

Around an hour later, Ciprian appeared. He stood for a while, and it took some time for the office to go silent, like a slow-motion wave that finally made it to the far end of the room.

"Hi guys, and thanks for coming in. Look, you know I hate doing stuff like this, and you hate listening to stuff like this." Slight titter. "I know there's been lots of talk in recent days so I just want to very quickly clear everything up. Firstly, Project X. Simply, nothing's changed. It's game on. Carry on. You've all put in an awful lot of hard work, and it's coming along great. We're so excited about how everything's going, so thank you to everyone and let's make it the best ever.

"Secondly, I understand there's been a lot of rumours about me. It's a little embarrassing, but yes, I was arrested. You know I have an opinion about drugs. It's not the same as the United States of America, so we go with it. In terms of what it means for me. Thank you for your concern. It means a lot. It really does. I don't want you to worry. I've spoken to the board, they understand and we continue as we were. Nothing's changed.

"So there we are. It's business as usual. If anyone wants to talk about anything, come and see me anytime. You know you can all talk to me, and I'd hate for anyone to be anxious. Other than that, let's keep on as we were." The office started to clap with even the odd whoop. "Thanks guys. Thanks so much. Bizarro forever!"

The end of the speech was like a fire alarm, with the office emptying quickly. Most people went for lunch, but the odd hotdesk came available. Wilf hadn't done any work for a while and wanted to get back into it over the next couple of days. As people came and went, picking up their bags, some staying to work, he made good progress.

It was nearly seven when he realised there was only a couple of people left, and this is when Cipiran wandered over.

"Hey man, how's it going? Everything okay?"

"Good, yeah, good. What about you?"

"Beautiful, absolutely beautiful. Everything is beautiful."

"Great."

"I won't forget you know."

"Sure."

"Listen. I was thinking. You've not been to Miami yet have you? How would you like to go to Miami?"

"Miami?"

"For the game? To do some research for the game. What do you think?"

"Sure. I mean, if you think it would help."

"Well, it certainly wouldn't do any harm."

"Okay, sure. On my own or?"

"There's someone you want to take? Of course. Yeah, take someone. I'll get you a suite. It's beautiful, you'll love it."

"No I mean, anyone from here? I don't think I have anyone to take."

"If you want to take someone, sure. Who you want to go with?"

"No, I mean for work."

"Take whoever you want. How about Bebe huh? You want me to send Bebe with you?"

"Oh no. That's fine. I can go by myself."

"Listen, whatever makes you happy, okay. Go when you want, stay as long as you want, and take whoever you want. Make it a holiday. Just you know, take some pictures or something so we can, you know, write it off."

"Right, okay. I'll have a think."

"Great. You've earned it, Wilf. Don't think too long, get yourself down there. It'll be very hot, hotter than here. But get yourself down there and have a good time."

"Okay."

"You've earned it," he tapped Wilf on the shoulder. "I'll never forget what you did."

Wilf nodded, and Ciprian went back to his office. It was a good time to call it a day and he packed up his stuff and headed to Okina-Yummy for noodles. They were pleased to see him. But he didn't eat too much, other than four or five maki, and drank four Starboard Jim's and coke in quick succession, which went straight to his head. The matriarch of the family asked him if he was okay. He said yes but felt dizzy and flustered as he followed her to the till.

"The heat, the heat," he said.

"Yes, very hot," she nodded and smiled.

It was still hot in the street, and he drank a litre of water before he made it back to the apartment and had to run the final two blocks to make it to the toilet in time.

He immediately stripped out of his clothes and jumped into a lukewarm shower, staying there for maybe half an hour, feeling the water fall over his stiff neck and running down his cheeks and neck, watching the bubbles dancing by the drain.

The next two days took a similar pattern. The heat was intense, and Wilf travelled to the office for around 11; there were plenty of hotseats available now. He didn't see Ciprian either day but had brief chats with Amber and Ryder, separately.

In the evenings, he left the office around eight but decided not to go back to Okina-Yummy, instead walking down West 34th Street, in the opposite direction to the Empire State Building and the pedestrians going in that direction.

Giuseppe's Pizza was okay, not as good as Guiseppe thought it was, but after his quick sales pitch, he left Wilf alone except to bring over a pepperoni and salami stromboli and a couple of Westchester IPAs.

The next day was the hottest of all and the neighbourhood was melting. There was no one on the streets, and Wilf stayed in the apartment too. He was now reading London Fields by Martin Amis and spent the afternoon with it in a lukewarm bath before going back to bed to snooze.

Waking up around six, he made salad, played video games and had a hot bath. Around half past nine, he headed towards the liquor store. She was there, and Wilf grabbed a pack of Heatons 47, the third last, and went to the counter.

"Oh hey," she said.

"How've you been?"

"Yeah, good."

"Good, good."

"Listen, I don't know if you can come back tonight. I got a lot of schoolwork to do."

"Oh. Okay."

"I'm sorry, it's just, you know."

"No, no that's fine."

"Yeah, I'm sorry."

"Look, I'm running out of chances. So before I go I might as well ask," She shook her head. "Well, I'll ask two more times and then you won't be bothered by me any more." He smiled and left.

"Wilf," she called. "I really need a spliff. Come on, let's go in the back."

"You sure?"

"Yeah, close the door."

They took their familiar positions on the crates and started on their vices. Wilf asked what she'd been up to. She was vague. She asked about Ciprian, he filled her in on the meeting.

"He wants me to go to Miami for a break."

"At this time of year? Jeez."

"He says I can take someone." Wilf looked up.

"No, no, no. I'm not going to Miami."

"It would be an amazing hotel. And a suite."

"No, Wilf."

They smiled and then sat for a bit. Eventually, the silence was broken.

"I know I don't tell you much. It's not easy. I have my life Wilf and it's complicated."

"Sure, I know. But if you ever wanted to say something. You know?"

"Thanks. It's nothing bad. It's just me."

"You don't need to explain."

"Okay, thanks."

"But can't you tell me your name?"

"Come on. I've got to work."

Wilf had two cans left which he took with him. She followed him to the door. "Jackie," she said. "Jackie Sixty." He smiled, she closed the door.

Wilf went into the office around lunchtime. Five minutes after arriving, Ciprian came over.

"Hey Wilf, how's it going? Everything good?"

"Hey. Yeah sure."

"Good, good. You thought any more about Miami?"

"Oh yeah. Not yet."

"Why don't you go next week? I'll get it booked."

"Right. Next week. That's soon."

"No time like the present. You've been working hard. Go have a good time. I'll fix you up with the good shit, women, whatever you want."

"Next week is a bit soon."

"No way. Get yourself to Miami. Have fun."

"How about in two weeks?"

"Wilf. I'll be honest with you. I can't ask anyone else. I need you to find Beatriz. Please, you've got to help me."

"I don't know. What can I do?"

"Don't worry. It's nothing dangerous. I just need you to talk to her. Tell her to come up to New York."

"Can't you go?"

"I can't, no. There's no one else. There's only you that knows."

Ciprian looked up and saw a stylish man in sunglasses walk in. "I got to go. Can we talk?"

Wilf nodded and watched him greet the arrival with a handshake and an arm round the shoulder. He asked Logan who it was and he said Dominic, the executive producer of the game.

As they closed the door to Ciprian's office, Wilf packed up his computer and dashed out. He walked all the way to Greenwich Village despite the heat and the humidity. When he stumbled into a dark dive bar below street level called Cellar E. It was cool, refreshing and pretty empty.

The fridges were rammed with a thousand different types of beer bottles and cans. On the bar was a menu divided by countries of the world. He ran his finger down to the United Kingdom and saw Heatons 47.

He took his can and glass to a small table. Cellar E was a ramshackle dump with random drawings etched on the peeling white walls. He sat below a huge y and b, of large writing which read said: Why bother? Above the toilets a sign read: Don't think your shit don't stink, and behind the bar it said: You shall live by the sword and serve your brother, but when you rebel, you will tear his yoke from your neck.

Wilf sat there all afternoon, reading his book and watching the people come in and out. There was no pattern, two men in fitted shirts and chinos, a hippy with denim flares, sandals and no shirt, a middle-aged woman with heavy make-up, two construction workers, and an old man with a long straggly hair and beard.

After four or five cans, Wilf said farewell to the barman. They'd said nothing to each other all afternoon other than "Another beer?" and "Yeah" and he happily overtipped.

Opening the door, the sky was a violent colour - black, purple and grey like a bruise. The rain smashed down, and thunder vibrated through the air. Wilf stood under the awning of a bakery, not knowing where the nearest subway station was. He wanted to hail a cab but none were free.

Checking his phone, he saw the nearest station was West Fourth Street–Washington Square station. He sprinted the first couple of blocks but was instantly drenched, his shirt and trousers sticking to him. He looked up to the sky, laughing as the lightning flashed and thunder rumbled, eventually squelching to the entrance with a few other drowned rats and riding back to Clarke Street.

The rain had eased by the time he got to Brooklyn, and the thunder was echoing in the distance. He ate, bathed and fell asleep, waking at 10 with a headache. After two paracetamol, he went down to the liquor store.

The door was locked. Wilf could see Jackie through a gap in the window, she was cashing up and the music was loud. He watched her for a while and then banged on the door, getting louder the second time.

Jackie looked up and came over to the door. "I thought you'd given up on me."

"Not yet." There were two fourpacks left. "But almost." She didn't hear the second part.

The rain had stopped but the crates were wet and Jackie brought some plastic sacks to sit on. Drips fell at various locations around the yard, but everything was still, even the two people were silent for the first few minutes while Jackie rolled her spliff.

They talked a little about the weather; Wilf spoke about the weather in Manchester. Jackie shared a memory of a downpour from her youth when her and her best friend Molly had got soaked at the skate park when they were kids. Wilf thought about asking if she was still friends with Molly but didn't.

He didn't talk much. Jackie asked if there was any news on Ciprian and he filled her in on the latest episode and how he didn't want to go to Miami and definitely didn't want to get involved in tracking down and speaking to Beatriz.

Just then, it started to rain. Jackie pulled out an umbrella from the side of her and sprang it out, patting the space next to her. Wilf sat under the umbrella, with their bare arms touching. Almost as soon as it started raining it stopped again.

"Well, that was a waste of time," said Jackie as she closed the umbrella. Wilf didn't move. He didn't feel like it. They sat for a while in silence, maybe five minutes, maybe 10, looking up at the sky and the surrounding buildings.

"There's only one four-pack left," Wilf said eventually. Jackie didn't reply. They sat quietly a little longer, both part-relaxed, part-tense.

A few minutes past, and Jackie tapped his leg and said softly: "We've got to go." Wilf took her hand and looked into Jackie's eyes. She looked back: "We've got to go." She rose. He rose. She picked up the plastic bag, coughed and went inside. He followed. She gently said: "Goodnight." Wilf looked at her, smiled and left, carrying the three cans he hadn't drunk.

Around mid-afternoon, Wilf rode the subway into Manhattan but wasn't going to the office. He got off at Washington Square, bought a cheap hot dog from a street vendor and then went straight to Cellar E.

He ordered a Heatons 47, took the same seat under the y and b, and took out a new copy of The Goldfinch by Donna Tartt.

Six hours, eight cans and 120 pages later, he was still there. He went to the bar and thought about ordering a ninth but found himself saying: "Cheers, mate," grabbing his jacket and leaving. The barman nodded.

Wilf climbed the stairs out of Cellar E, and his senses were overwhelmed. Bright lights blurred both fast and in slow motion. A police siren and someone shouting split the loud noise of people talking and music coming out of windows. The warm air brought beads of sweat to his forehead, which he wiped away as he paused at street level.

A couple walked past and then a group and Wilf felt he had to move on. He moved towards Washington Square slowly and then quickly, sneaking into a tourist's bar to use the toilet but was challenged as he left.

"Hey man, you ordering a drink?"

"Er. I'm terribly sorry, but no."

"You can't just come in and use the john."

"Look. I'm very sorry. It was a mistake."

"Fucking asshole. How about I come to yours to piss?"

"Yeah sure," said Wilf, walking out of the door.

"Fucking asshole," the waiter shouted down the street. "Hey you. Cheap English asshole. You fucking dick, man."

Eventually he had the relief of seeing the Subway station and gave $10 to a homeless man outside before descending off the street.

It took around 15 minutes for the train to arrive. Wilf was worried about missing Clarke Street and stared at the window, his reflection looking back at him. He kept looking, gazing at his own eyes, sometimes imagining it was a stranger, sometimes seeing himself or Lo or his dad.

When the train arrived at Clarke Street, Wilf was slow to react and then stumbled through the door. Autopilot took him to the liquor store. It was just before 10 pm, and Jackie was working. She was listening to music loudly. It sounded old, maybe from the 1960s, singing along and moving her head as she wrote in her book.

Wilf stood outside the door watching her, but she didn't look up. He stayed for a few minutes and then left.

Wilf woke around lunchtime with a terrific headache. The apartment was a mess. Three empty cans of Heatons 47 were crushed on the counter next to a half-eaten kung-Po chicken and rice.

He took alka-seltzer, a pint of water and coffee and went to sit by the big window. It was a sunny, cloudless day, and he felt the heat coming directly from the sun. He put on sunglasses and sat in the warmth, slowly coming to life like a microwave meal, better but still not good.

After a warm bath, he walked into Brooklyn, his head still a little sore but starting to ease. He stumbled across the noodle bar where he'd seen Jackie in the street and took the same seat at the window, ordering a bao bun and a coke. The coke was good and he had another, which wasn't quite as refreshing. He didn't see Jackie. He read his book but only a couple of pages; he couldn't really concentrate.

Leaving the noodle bar, he wandered down to the river, looking across to the imposing Manhattan skyline. He traced the skyscrapers from left to right, wondering what was going on inside, some lights on, some lights off. He thought of Cellar E, a dingy bar under these giants, like a rabbit hole at the foot of an old, gnarled tree.

Cold air was making goosebumps, and Wilf left the view behind and went back to the apartment. At the front door, he turned and went in the direction of the liquor store. He waited a few minutes in a side alley before restarting his journey. As he reached the door, he realised he kept walking on. Not looking in, just a brief swivel of the head, but not seeing anything.

His feet kept on walking, and he was back at the river looking over at Manhattan. He could hear noise from a nearby roofbar and a car revved past. This time he stayed through the goosebumps for another half hour, hypnotised by the view.

Eventually he left and went back to the apartment. Turning the key in the door, he was startled when someone spoke. Jackie said: "Don't you want these?" holding a four-pack of Heatons 47.

She was wearing a leather jacket with the Sonic Youth t-shirt. Wilf didn't answer. She pushed the door open, and they both went inside.

"I have to go," said Jackie, putting on a boot.

Wilf was awake but not really alert. "Okay," he stuttered. Jackie sat on the bed and clipped her necklace shut, but it took two or three attempts.

"You want coffee before you go?"

"I don't have time."

Wilf got out of bed and started to make coffee. It was made by the time Jackie emerged, and he poured her a cup. She picked it up and drank it.

"You want some breakfast?"

"No, I can't."

"It will take two minutes to make toast. Just give me a sec."

Jackie walked towards Wilf, kissed him softly on the cheek, burying her head in his chest. She let go and he put bread in the toaster and went to the bathroom. When he came out she'd gone.

Wilf searched for her, but then realised that she'd left. He smiled to himself about Jackie, about everything. "Man," he said out loud.

The toaster popped and he spread on the marmalade and took it to the big window with his coffee, making a second trip for his laptop. He checked his emails and saw a message from Dominic.

Subject: Update

Hi everyone,

I would like to thank everyone for their hard work on Project X. The game is progressing wonderfully and while we're a little behind the ideal schedule, I'm sure we can get close to the target.

To that end, there have been a number of changes within the business that I would like to update you about.

"Shit," Wilf spoke aloud to himself for the second time that morning. He thought it was probably something to do with Ciprian. It was already around 9am, so he had a quick shower, put on something semi-smart and headed into the Bizarro offices.

His instinct was right. There was a different atmosphere in the building, the hotdesk seats were being used properly, rather than for bag storage, and there wasn't the usual groups and gangs of people. Ryder looked at him and nodded a yes, with his head in a straight line. Wilf scrunched up his face like he was in pain.

Almost exactly at 11am, Dominic arrived and addressed the room. He thanked everyone again for their hard work and said how well Project X was going and that Bizarro thought this game could potentially take them to another level.

He said he was happy with everyone, and then he got to the crux. Unfortunately, Ciprian was leaving. No details. Just that the company was hugely grateful for all his hard work but they would now be looking for a replacement to take charge of the New York operation. Dominic would be in temporary charge and oversee Project X to its publication.

Only one question, asked by Amber. "Can you give any more details on why Ciprian's leaving?" Dominic said he was leaving for personal reasons and that the company had accepted his resignation with great sadness.

The meeting broke up and the groups got together. Wilf joined one with Ryder, Henk and Dylan. The consensus was that it must be something to do with the drug arrest. That he was likely going to prison, and Bizarro wanted to cut ties. Henk said he'd call his cell phone that morning, but there was no connection. Bebe wandered over and said she couldn't get hold of Ciprian this morning either.

Gradually, everyone returned to their desks and got to work. Dominic came out and spoke to a few people as he wandered the floor. Wilf was listening to Belgian house music on his headphones when Dominic touched him on the shoulder, making him jump. He looked much older close up, Wilf thought. His eyes were sunken and his hair had holes in it when you looked closely.

"Sorry, didn't mean to make you jump."

"Oh, no worries."

"We haven't properly met, I'm Dominic," said Dominic, holding out his hand, which Wilf shook.

"Wilf, hi."

"I know. Listen. I just wanted to say fantastic work. I've seen what you've done and it looks terrific."

"Oh, thank you. That's great."

"How are you settling in?"

"Yeah, good. Yeah, I'm enjoying it."

"Good. We're really excited about you. We've got big plans. I think this is going to be a great place for you."

"Okay. Good."

"We'll have a proper catch-up. Let me know if there's anything I can do for you."

With that, Dominic was gone, and Wilf put his headphones back on.

Around 7pm, he went to Okina-Yummy for ramen and coke. He chatted to the matriarch for a little bit. She was having problems with an app on her cell phone, and he was able to sort it out. She brought him a caramel custard that he hadn't ordered. He didn't really like it but ate it anyway and then gave a bigger-than-normal tip.

On the Subway back to Brooklyn he listened to some Sonic Youth. He was still listening to it when he got to the liquor store. He took off the headphones, but Jackie wasn't working, and there were no Heatons 47. He bought a Coke Zero from the fridge and left.

Returning to the apartment, his headphones were balanced around his neck in case Jackie jumped out again, but she didn't.

For the next two days, Wilf followed a familiar routine, arriving at the office around mid-morning, working through until early evening, dinner at Okina-Yummy, then back into Brooklyn. Jackie wasn't working either night, just a guy with long red hair and beard, and he entered and left with an ice-cold Coke Zero both times.

The following day, Dominic was near the entrance of Bizarro when he arrived and asked him if he wanted to grab some lunch. Wilf agreed, and around 1pm Dominic came over, put his arm on his shoulder and said "Let's go."

Outside, he hailed a yellow cab and told the driver to go to Opisthodomos. They made small talk in the back; Dominic pointed out a few buildings: "Great sushi there", "Best John Dory I ever tasted", "Try the Old Fashioned, incredible". They talked a little bit about how Wilf was settling in, but his answers were short and unrevealing.

Opisthodomos was an ordinary door, a long corridor that then revealed a huge dining room. It looked like an English stately home, with wood panelling, 17th-century portraits, solid silver cutlery, pale pink table cloths and parquet flooring.

Dominic ordered celery soup, guinea fowl and a glass of white wine, Wilf chose celery soup, Beef Wellington and a still water. The food was incredible, light and full of flavour.

"You're doing an incredible job," Dominic said.

"Thanks. I'm enjoying it."

"It's a great place to work. I know people thought a lot of Ciprian and it's a shame he had to go. The atmosphere was relaxed and that produced good work. But slowly. It was maybe a bit too relaxed, you know?"

"Sure."

"I don't want that to change too much. Just a little. We just need to step up the professionalism a bit more. I've looked at what you've done. You've produced way more than others. Way more. And it's all so good, so clean, no bugs, no issues."

"Thanks."

"I know you don't come in every day, and that's absolutely fine. You're what we want. With Ciprian going, we need to find the right person to take charge of the New York office. Now, I don't think you're ready for that, but certainly, it's something to aim for in a few years."

"Okay."

"But I want you to head up a team. Report directly to me but you know, get them to step it up a bit. We want to go faster and bigger. And you're perfect for that. Look, don't answer now, have a think."

"Right."

"But we'll double your wages. And rent out a duplex in Manhattan for you. Make everything as you want it. Okay?"

"Okay."

"Have a think."

"Sure."

Dominic moved the conversation on. He told stories about his holiday in Bali with his boyfriend, meeting Taylor Swift in Los Angeles and playing golf in Scotland.

After coffee and Amarettos, it was time to leave. Dominic told him to take off the rest of the day, have a think and insisted there was no rush.

Wilf watched him leave in a yellow cab. He had no idea where he was.

Google Maps instructed him that he was four blocks from the nearest Subway station, but he was tired and hailed down a cab.

They didn't speak once the destination was given. The driver was focusing on the baseball on the radio, and it reminded Wilf of his brother listening to the cricket on hot summer days in the back garden while he played on his handheld.

Back at the apartment, no one jumped out when he got out of the taxi. In the kitchen, he found a tin of PG Tips that had been missing since he first arrived, lost behind a vase he put in a cupboard.

He drank three cups of tea by the window, reading The Goldfinch as the sun went down and that took him back home, too.

After a shower, he headed to the liquor store, but Jackie wasn't working again. It was the red-haired guy with the beard.

Wilf grabbed a Coke Zero from the fridge and went to the counter to pay for it.

"Hey. Do you know when Jackie is working again?" he said.

"Jackie?" he replied.

"Yeah Jackie. The blonde-haired girl who works here."

"I don't know a Jackie."

"You been here long?"

"No, I only started last week. But I'm pretty sure there ain't no Jackie."

"She works most nights. Jackie Sixty? Blonde hair, cool style."

"Oh, you mean Jenny Fifty?" he started to laugh. "Jackie Sixty! You mean Jenny Fifty."

"Blonde hair, this tall?"

"Yeah, that's Jenny Fifty. She quit last week. I took her shifts."

"She quit?"

"Yeah. Needed the shifts I got to be honest."

"She say where she was going?"

"Not to me."

Wilf stood there a while. "You got her number? Address or anything?"

"No, man."

"What about anyone else here? They must have her address."

"I think she was leaving you know? I think she was getting out, going somewhere."

"You know where?"

"I wanna help you. But I don't think we know anything, man. I'm sorry."

"Right, right. Listen can you ask your boss or something? Anything? Number? Last address, anything?"

The man got him to write his contact details down and said he'd ask his boss to call. Wilf said it was urgent and the man believed him.

Wilf found himself walking the streets. Eventually, he ducked into a small bar that was playing country and western music in a semi-ironic way. It was packed. He took a seat at the bar and ordered a double Starboard Jim and coke and then another.

He finished a third inside 10 minutes and then went to the gents and hurt his hand, punching the wall. He came back and had a fourth and fifth inside the next 20 minutes. Finally, it caught with him in a big wave as he rocked backwards off his stool, his foot stopping him from falling flat on his back but he knocked a girl and apologised.

She didn't look entirely happy and then her friend jumped in. "I know you," she said.

"I don't think so," he said.

"Yeah, it's Wilf right? You're the English guy?"

"That's right. You know me from where?"

"Michelle. I work at the Tiki Bar near the beach."

"Right," he said, but he couldn't be sure. "I'm awfully sorry about bumping into your friend. Would she like a drink as an apology?"

Michelle broke off to ask her. "Vodka Lime Spritz. I'm on Tequila and Cider."

"Jesus Christ. Tequila and Cider? I got to try this."

He ordered the Vodka Lime Spritz and two Tequilas and Cider. The girl accepted the drink and his apology and returned to their group of three other girls and two boys. Michelle stayed and watched him try his drink. It was strong. His eyes widened, and she laughed.

They made small talk for a while and he ordered two more Tequilas and Cider when Michelle briefly returned to her friends. She asked him about books and he made some grandiose comment about literature, which he didn't believe but just vomited out on autopilot.

"You've got beautiful eyes," he blurted out mid-conversation.

"Jeez, thank you," she smiled.

Wilf ran the outside of his hand down her bare arm and loosely grabbed her fingers. She stopped smiling and looked at him. He pulled her towards him, and they started to kiss. Gently but enthusiastically. Eventually, they broke and smiled, embarrassed.

They didn't speak for an uncomfortably long time, although it was maybe only 30 seconds. Wilf laughed to himself and was about to say something when the girl he'd stood on earlier came over and said she needed Michelle to accompany her to the ladies.

Wilf thought it was a good idea to go too, but standing up, he instantly fell back onto his stool. He closed one eye to concentrate his focus, and looking up, he saw Jackie or Jenny leaving. His balance came back and he followed her out of the door into the street.

"Jackie," he shouted after her. She was with a friend. "Jenny," he shouted. Both girls looked back, uneasy. It wasn't Jackie or Jenny. "Shit," he muttered to himself. He looked into the bar and saw Michelle had returned to his stool. He suddenly threw up, with the sick bouncing up off the pavement onto his boots and the bottom of his trousers.

Wilf didn't really know how he got home. He had a few Polaroid snaps in his brain, strange roads, uneasy conversations with strangers. He'd definitely gone to the liquor store and been told to "Shut the fuck up" after banging on the metal shutters. Remembering the incident with Michelle, he ran to the bathroom to be sick again.

After Alka Seltzer, a shower and a coffee, he sat by the big window. He'd made a phone call in the early hours but didn't know the number, and the conversation lasted 13 seconds. Then it came back to him. He had a strange idea that he could guess Jackie or Jenny's number. Miraculously, it connected. It wasn't her number.

Around mid-afternoon, he went for lunch. He found a food hall and ordered a feta cheese salad and power smoothie. It made his stomach wobble but was just about staying down.

He had a mouthful of lettuce when his phone vibrated. Unknown number. He picked it up and nervously said: "Hello."

"Hey, is that Wilf?"

"Yeah."

"Hey listen, it's Joe I own the liquor store on…"

"Right," he interrupted.

"I was told you wanted to get hold of Jenny Fifty."

"Yeah."

"Look I'm sorry she just took off. Gave me like 48 hours' notice. No details, no numbers, nothing. To be honest, I don't even know where she was living when she worked for me, okay. You don't need to know those details. But anyway. Noel said he thought you looked kind of desperate, so I thought I'd just let you know, that I can't help. Sorry man."

Wilf tried to press him for any information but he didn't seem to know anything about her. Friends, family, addresses. She just came in and did a good job. He asked if he knew about the order of Heatons 47, but he said that Jenny had mentioned something about returning it and he figured it had been picked up.

Finally, he hung up and chucked his late lunch in the bin. He felt drunker than he had the night before. Dizzy, lost, confused, desperate and in physical pain. He needed to get drunk for real.

Within an hour, he found himself inside Cellar E and ordering a Heatons 47. Wilf stared at it for a good while in the glass, almost lost in its allure. The orangey glow, lit by a neon sign making it look almost celestial. Finally, he took a large swig and let out a refreshing sigh at the end of it.

He stood up, left a fifty dollar tip and headed back into the street and hailed a cab. He told the driver to take him to his apartment in Brooklyn and he enjoyed listening to the baseball game, hearing three or four innings.

The taxi waited as Wilf went to his apartment and gathered up a bag of things. When he came down, the radio was playing Latino music.

"Who won?" he asked.

"Not the fucking Dodgers," he said, pulling into the road.

They didn't speak again as they put the city behind them, although he didn't look around to watch New York disappear. Finally arriving at LaGuardia around 30 minutes later, Wilf was again overly generous with his tip in a rush to get out of the country and home.

At the British Airways desk, they said there were no seats on the next flight back to London, but he could get on the one the next morning. He organised a follow-on flight to Manchester.

The night was spent in the airport hall, playing pinball on his phone as the floor cleaners rotated noisily, followed by the bleachers. At 6am, the coffee stall opened and half an hour later the cafe for breakfast and another coffee.

An hour after that, he checked in and went straight to the gate. There was only one other person there, and Wilf could tell instantly from his profile that he knew him. It was Ciprian. He was bent over with his head in one hand, next to him a small leather holdall.

Wilf kept walking. When the flight was called, he hung back and watched the passengers board. When Ciprian was gone, he put on his headphones, Sonic Youth, which he skipped for Belgian house music and boarded the jet.

He made slow progress up the aisle, with passengers squeezing and forcing their bags into the overhead lockers. Wilf could sense he was being watched but he focused on looking to the back of the plane where he was seated. He never looked around to notice.

SELSEY BILL AND
THE HOUNDS

St Olave's Hotel was a place of intrigue and mystery for Lo from the moment she happened to spend a night there the previous summer. Situated in a forgotten, hidden street in the centre of Manchester, it was a glorious four-storey Georgian building in a square of law firms and private properties where the few people that walked around it emitted easy style and sophistication. Lo certainly looked the part in her cloche hat and tailored overcoat and carrying a vintage suitcase.

The hall was elegantly silent as Lo took in the hunting pictures and antique furniture. Every inch was thoroughly thought-through, from the chessboard mosaic tiles to the mini chandelier. A curling butler's bell tinkled gently to summon a mousy receptionist. There was only one of the 12 rooms available which Lo took at the cost of £250, just over half of the money she had left in her bank account.

She took the creaking antique lift to the second floor and used the mortice key in the lock. For some, the room would have been too garish, plum patterned walls, chintzy four poster bed, art deco dressing table and lights, thick rug and booming wardrobe. There was too much for such a small room but Lo cooed enthusiastically.

The bathroom looked like it was transported from a 1920s country house and Lo immediately turned on the taps to the roll top bath using the distinctly modern Medea of Mayfair coconut and lime bubble bath.

She soaked for a long time, seduced by one of her favourite books, Party Going by Henry Green. The troubles of five miles south, forgotten in the luxury getaway.

Finally getting out before becoming a total prune, she dried herself on the fluffy towels and then went over to the steamed up freestanding mirror and stroked the letters 'L', 'O' and a smiley face, pausing for a few seconds to look back at her dark brown eyes. She stayed in front of the mirror as she rubbed in Medea of Mayfair coconut and lime body moisturiser all over, occasionally seeing the blurred outline of her body and her warm skin where the symbols pierced the condensation and gave a sharp, true reflection.

After putting on her own cherry blossom silk kimono, she lay on the bed and read more of her book. Eventually snapping it close, she jumped out of bed and put on a simple but elegant summer dress and went downstairs to the bar.

It was a beautiful room with a stylish oak bar in front of shelves of coloured and misshaped bottles; at least a dozen gins, whiskeys, vodkas, brandies, rums, and every other spirit she could think of.

To the left was an open door to a small library with a fire, two walls filled with leather books, tables with accountant's green lamps and a small mezzanine balcony where an older gentleman was relaxed into a high winged armchair with a book. On the right was a more modern minimalist white room with floor to ceiling windows the full width of the building, and showing off the low-lit walled garden filled with exotic plants and a small table shared by two lovers.

Lo took a stool at the bar and ordered a Horse's Neck. It arrived with the lemon rind bowing smartly over the side of the glass and tasted heavenly. She smiled at the barman and he smiled back.

But she was there for a reason; deciding what to do next. University was over and she had no real ideas on starting a career. She was short of money. A holiday would be great - staying at St Olave's would be better - but even paying for a flat in Manchester was not an option. She'd stayed at a shared house in Oxford but now everyone had gone and it was waiting for a new flock to move in. Lo was not going home so she would have to stay with friends. But who?

School friends in Manchester had long been discarded and forgotten. She briefly thought about joining Wilf in California, before his move to

New York, but she was excited for him, taking a chance on freedom, so wanted to let him give it a try by himself.

Relatives were out. Too much private sympathy over her mum and too much public sympathy for her dad. She needed a break from it.

So that left only university friends and there wasn't a single obvious candidate. She had friends, but not many good friends and certainly not a best one.

Lo wasn't the type to have a best friend. She'd had one at high school, Emily. But Emily would get frustrated that she would see other friends, have friends that were boys and didn't seem to get caught up in the drama of her life, offering half-thought advice and unperturbed when it was ignored.

Then there was the time Emily went on an exchange trip to Chemnitz. Lo accidentally had a drunken kiss with her boyfriend Colin, only because she was interested in what it would be like, not because she wanted to steal him or hurt Emily. Of course it got back to Emily within an hour of her flight touching down from Leipzig and after saying sorry, and not having her apology accepted, she realised that she actually wasn't too bothered.

It wasn't obvious who to pick from Oxford. In the final year she'd been in a house with two boys and three other girls but felt like an outsider. Those five were close but Lo spent much of her time in her room, reading books and was rarely around for communal meal nights.

Starting at the top, she went through her most recent WhatsApp messages and groups to get some ideas of possibilities.

On her course, there were a couple of options. Charlotte would be delighted to have her stay but Lo knew that she couldn't bear to be isolated with her for more than a couple of days with her constant moaning about anything and everything. Saskia was a big drinker; too dangerous. Victoria was obsessed with relationships; boring. Olly would be great but he had twice asked out Lo and been turned down so that was a no. Olivia was also out for a similar reason. Ignacio had gone back to Vigo and his family seemed odd when he talked about them. Paul, no single reason but definitely not a possibility. She kept scrolling through her phone without finding an obvious name.

"That must be a serious message the way you're focusing on that." She looked up to see a tall, youngish man in a suit standing next to her. "To a boyfriend or something?"

"No, nothing like that," she smiled.

"In that case, can I buy you a drink?"

"Sure."

He pointed to Lo's half-empty glass and signalled two to the barman. Lo put down her phone and locked it.

"Henry. Nice to meet you."

"Lo."

"What's that short for?"

"Nothing."

"Lo? Okay. That's unusual." Lo said nothing. "So you work around here Lo?"

"No," she said. "I'm guessing you do."

"Yes, I'm a lawyer. Commercial law. So busy at the moment. Got this case about a joint stock company. Been going on for months."

"Interesting."

The barman returned with the two drinks.

"Are you interested in the law?"

"Not particularly."

"What are we drinking?"

"It's called a Horse's Neck. Brandy, ginger ale and bitters. Cheers." They clinked glasses.

"Cheers. You like horses?"

"No."

"You don't like law and you don't like horses. Okay so what do you like?"

"I like books."

"Okay books. Are you a writer?"

"No."

"Okay, just reading."

"Just reading."

"I don't read much myself. Unless you count magazines. I get Men's Health every month. I like to work out, keep fit. I run 10ks twice a month. And I like to eat well."

"Right."

"Do you like to eat well?"

"Everyone likes to eat well."

"There's this terrific Spanish tapas place not from here. Would you care to join me?"

"Rafa's?"

"Yeah, you know it?"

"Yeah, it's good. Great sardines."

"Shall we go?"

"No, I don't think so."

"Oh okay. What would you like to try?"

Lo shrugged and said: "I'm good," with the first word elongated and the second almost inaudible.

"You just want to stay here?"

"Yeah I think I'm going to stay here. But you should go to Rafa's. Have the sardines."

"So you're just going to get a free drink and then bin me off? Is that how it works?"

"I didn't realise I was signing up for something when I accepted a drink. Let me pay you back."

"No, of course not. I just thought…"

"You came over. I thought you might be interesting. We talked. Now I think you're a dud."

"A dud?"

"A dud."

"A dud. I'm 26 and I get paid £110,000 a year. Does that sound like a dud? If you saw my six-pack you'd know I wasn't a dud."

"That's what a dud would say."

"Fuck you. Fuck you, is that what a dud would say? Fuck you. Put that in your fucking book."

"I'm not a writer."

"Ah, fuck off," he said slamming down his drink and leaving the bar.

Lo picked up her phone and restarted her search.

Then she saw the name. Chloe Newbury. Chloe was a friend of Olly's and they'd met up a couple of times. She was quiet and straight at first but then had a marvellous sense of humour once she unravelled. She was plain looking and mostly unadventurous but was solid and good company. Never asking too much or too little and occasionally surprising with bouts of spontaneity.

They'd had quite a laugh at Olly's expense in the World's End pub and met a couple of times afterwards, and Chloe developed a mutual liking for a Horse's Neck.

Lo remembered a drunken conversation where they said it was sad that they'd met so late. It was midway through Hilary Term of both their third years, and the last few weeks Chloe threw herself into revision for her 'finals'. Lo did too, but still found time to go to The Dolphin most evenings.

They bumped into each other briefly shortly after Chloe's last exam and lazily promised to stay in touch. One of those promises that neither expected to keep.

Chloe had said that she didn't know what she was going to do in the summer and was hopeful of going back to Oxford to study for a master's degree in marine palaeontology. Lo remembered that because she responded with something insulting about her choice of subject, having never thought to ask what she was studying previously. She couldn't remember exactly what she'd said but knew it was instinctive and true and that she'd desperately backtracked and apologised, then burst out laughing which Chloe kindly responded to.

Nor could Lo remember her hometown. Somewhere on the south coast, somewhere that sounded small but not very pretty. Not one of the major towns. A third Horse's Neck didn't oil her memory any.

She thought about what she was going to say and then decided it was a bad idea to plan. Chloe would be guided into inviting her to stay, it was better if she thought it was her idea.

"Chloe. I'm on my third Horse's Neck, and I was thinking about you. How are you?" she said when the phone connected after the fifth ring.

"Hey Lo. I wouldn't have thought you'd be doing anything else. You're such a poet."

"Yes, but I know you Queen's College girls aren't as reserved as you'd have us believe. I'm sure you've got some wild boy down there, attending to your every whim."

"Down where? Nobody's been in those parts since the clocks went forward!"

"Chloe. How disappointing. I was calling for a gossip. You're not going to let me down, are you?"

"I'd love to have something interesting to tell you. But I now have the dreariest existence. I've got this job at a tea room, and I've only been out once since I got home and that was only to the local pub."

Lo was tempted to jump in there and then and say she was on her way to fix her problems and to bring some excitement to her village, wherever it was. But instead they caught up for a little while.

Chloe talked about missing Oxford and her friends and wanting to go back. And that her mum was hardly around now that the summer season had started, working six nights at a restaurant in Eastbourne.

"How far away is the restaurant?" Lo asked.

"From Bexhill? Oh, not far. But she's not back until after 11 most nights. Later on Fridays and Saturdays. If I don't see her at breakfast, I don't see her all day."

Bexhill pinged in Lo's brain. They talked some more, about her brother Benjamin on a gap year in Thailand and Australia and the rude people that came into the tea room.

Then Lo told her about her mother dying. Chloe apologised for going on, and Lo told her that she wanted to hear her stories to take her away from a dreadful time. She signalled for another Horse's Neck and then told her about her father's confessions.

"I had to leave," she said. "I had to get out. I'm staying at this wonderful boutique hotel for now, but I don't know what I'm going to do next."

"Oh Lo, you poor thing. I'm so sorry. It sounds like you've been through the wringer. If only there was something I could do."

"No, I'm sorry Chloe. I didn't mean to bring you down. That wasn't my reason for calling. I wanted to speak to you because we didn't see much of each other in the final weeks. It's been tough, but I wanted to hear happiness, and you always struck me as someone wise and content."

"I feel dreadful, moaning about my life after everything you've been through. Listen to me going on about being lonely and working too hard. I'm sorry Lo. I shall have a Horse's Neck tomorrow night for you, I promise."

"And I will too. Cheers my dears!"

"Listen. You don't have to if you don't want to. But you know you can always come down to stay for a bit?"

"What, to Bexhill?"

"Yes. It's not the liveliest. Not like Oxford or Manchester. But you can get away for a bit, and I'd love to have you."

"What about your mum?"

"She would be happy. She feels bad that I'm left alone. She still thinks I'm 10. It would be great. It's only a small cottage, but you could sleep in Benjamin's bed, he won't mind."

"That's very kind of you, Chloe. Truly. But I couldn't."

"Oh Lo it would be a break for you. Get down to the beach and clear your head for a bit. I'll take care of you and I won't bother you."

"Chloe, you really are the best."

"Is that a yes?"

"Maybe I've had too many Horse's Necks. But okay yes."

Chloe yelped with delight, and they made some earnest plans. Lo's new host even booked and paid for her train tickets from Piccadilly to

Bexhill for the following day. More than five hours, two changes and an open return.

It was a tiring journey, particularly having to get from Euston to Victoria on the Tube. It was a sticky London day, and the commuters and tourists all seemed particularly sweaty, and Lo was determined to avoid being dripped on.

Even in her light summer dress, the one she'd worn the previous night at St Olave's Hotel, she was feeling the heat and intensity. She loved London most in autumn and then spring and tried to avoid it the rest of the year.

This could not have been any different to the previous night, she thought to herself in a crowded carriage. Apart from the brief interlude with the young nuisance, the stay had been divine.

After her call to Chloe, she moved into the library with her book. The man on the mezzanine came down the spiral staircase and introduced himself as Robert something or other. He was a terrible flirt and obviously wealthy and asked Lo for a game of backgammon.

She accepted and he insisted on buying her drinks and ordered some snacks of olives, cheese and biscuits and French crudites. Lo was quite drunk but still beat Robert in four of the five games and was happy to spend time in his company.

After the final game, he said he was going to bed and invited Lo to join him. She laughed a no, and he said something along the lines of "You can't blame a guy for trying," and they kissed on the cheek.

Lo slept wonderfully and then had eggs benedict and coffee for breakfast in the white room and felt better than she had in a long time. Thinking that made her mind turn to her mother and father and she banged the table in frustration at bringing herself back down, alarming the other three tables eating. She giggled an apology and finished her coffee in the walled garden.

Finally, the Tube train pulled into Victoria, and she waited only 10 minutes for the train to Bexhill. It was slow but gave her an opportunity to finish her book, although a boy listening to grime music without headphones was a distraction. He caught her glaring and smirked to himself.

He got off at Eastbourne and the rest of the journey was magical as the train line followed close to the coast, giving charming views in the light of the late afternoon sun. Stops at Pevensey Bay, Normans Bay, Coodens Beach and Collington somehow seemed enticing.

Bexhill railway station was ordinary. But the 10-minute walk up the hill gave hope it was going to be an interesting town and finally spotting Chloe's house which she thought instinctively was marvellous. It was small and looked like it had been added as an afterthought to the street, squished in between two much larger homes. But Lo thought it was exquisite.

Waiting for Chloe, she thought about going back down the hill to the George and Dragon pub that she passed but decided to sit outside on her suitcase and enjoy the last of the sun.

Just as she sat down, she could see Chloe running up the hill, still, presumably, in her work outfit of black culotte trousers, white shirt and black tie with a small apron around her waist. A pencil fell out, and she grabbed it before it rolled down the hill, then yanked off the apron and held it in her hand.

"Chloe," Lo hugged her tight. "Oh, Chloe."

"I'm sorry. I tried to get off early to meet you, but we had a minibus of Americans arrive."

"I'm so glad to see you. Thank you, Chloe. Thank you so much."

"No, I'm so glad to see you." She pulled in Lo for another hug. "Was the journey okay?"

"It was long and hot, but I read my book. And it was worth it. This place looks wonderful."

"Oh, it's small. But hopefully, you can find some peace here."

"God, I hope not."

"Well, I hope you can have a great summer."

"I'm sure I will."

Chloe opened the door and told Lo to mind her head. Lo gasped at the quaintness of the tiny cottage. "It's perfection!"

Chloe and Lo sat in the small garden at the back of the house as the sun went down with a bottle of white wine and then another. The air turned chilly and Lo borrowed a hoodie and pulled it over her head while Chloe was already in a styleless but comfortable thick tracksuit and puffer jacket.

They talked incessantly and laughed a lot. About everything and nothing. Places to go in Bexhill, friends at Oxford, the people at the tea room, the two men at St Olave's Hotel, their siblings, their parents. Lo brought up her rude comment on palaeontology and apologised again earnestly this time. Chloe burst out laughing, and then Lo joined in.

Just after midnight, Chloe's mum walked in with the girls laughing over a story about one of Lo's old housemates but she never got close to telling the punchline and couldn't remember if there even was one.

"Mum. This is Lo," giggled Chloe.

"How do you do? Thank you so much for letting me stay."

"It's a pleasure. If you have this effect on Chloe, you can stay as long as you want."

"Have a glass with us?" asked Lo.

"Yes, why not? Are you staying outside?"

"It's summertime. Of course," said Chloe, thrusting her glass into the air.

"Cheers," said Chloe's mum and they clinked glasses. "Now you must make yourself at home. Help yourself to anything in the kitchen and let me know if you need anything. There's towels in the cupboard in the bathroom and Benjamin won't be back for…"

"Mum," interrupted Chloe. "We've done the tour, don't worry. Lo will be fine," she added looking over to her guest.

"Yes, sorry. I just want you to feel at home. Chloe's told me a little about what's happened to you recently. I'm sorry to hear of… I want you to relax and make yourself comfortable."

"Thank you, that's very kind. It's so beautiful, I am sure I'm going to remember this place forever. There is just one thing. I just realised I only know you as Chloe's mum."

She smiled. "Veronica. Call me Ronnie, everyone does." Lo nodded.

Ronnie finished her drink and tidied up the plates and food they'd had as snacks - hummus and vegetable sticks, then crisps and finally, a portion of cheesecake brought back from the restaurant and split in half.

"I know you're all excited and I'm not going to boss you about. But you've got the tea room in the morning so don't be too late."

Chloe rose and gave her mum a hug. Ronnie then placed a hand on Lo's shoulder. "Night girls. Have fun."

Tiredness descended quickly, and they stayed for only another 10 minutes to finish off the last of the wine. They whispered and laughed in the bathroom as they cleaned their teeth and moisturised.

Outside Benjamin's room, Chloe stopped and held Lo's hands. "I'm so glad you came."

"So am I," said Lo before they hugged and said their goodnights.

It was well after 10 when Lo awoke. Disorientated at first, she finally gathered her senses. She felt devilishly comfortable in the bed with its crisp sheets and thick pillows while wearing a pair of Chloe's tartan pyjamas.

On the pillow next to her was a key on top of a small square note:

You looked so cute sleeping I didn't want to disturb you. Make yourself at home, come and go as you please. I'll be at the tea room until five unless I get off early. Chloe xx

She smiled and stayed in bed for another hour reading Nancy Mitford's Don't Tell Alfred before going downstairs for coffee. A selection of sliced fruits - mangos, pineapples, strawberries, kiwi, melons and watermelons, was prepared in a bowl on the kitchen table, and she made a cafetiere of strong coffee and took them out in the garden in her bare feet.

Midday was hot and she treated herself to a long bath after hearing Ronnie leave. She could only find a small towel and it barely covered her as she wrapped it around herself and returned to the bedroom to moisturise.

Lo felt comfortable although she had the feeling that there were a lot of people in the room with her. There was a curious selection of pictures on the wall, not ones that could give much of an indication to the normal inhabitant.

Either side of the door were vintage Vogue covers from the 30s, 60s, 80s and 90s, distinct in their transition from demure to glamorous.

On the main wall were two original garish paintings by, presumably, the same artist whose work was unknown to Lo. The first was a curious picture of a fancy dress scene in an Edwardian bedroom. A vampire sat on an iron bed in a majestic room with a woman wearing a fox's head and orange skintight catsuit kneeling in front of him with a second woman, naked but for a mouse's head, in the corner of the room, facing away.

The second was three astronauts standing on the moon in bright blue lycra suits and large silver helmets. The centre person, who is clearly a man, has his arms around the two other astronauts, who are clearly women, with one of them reaching towards his middle.

Above the bed was a huge print of presumably Jesus Christ, arms out with a woman at her feet. It wasn't a particularly nice painting, dark and unappealing, but somehow hypnotic. Around it were dotted various flyers and tickets to events.

Lo, like the Vogue pictures, they were effortlessly stylish, and while she was always naturally drawn to the 1930s covers, they all appealed to her. The rest of the pictures in the room were odd and slightly unsettling once she studied their contents.

She wandered around the rest of the house still in her towel, and everything was charming and tasteful. Ronnie clearly had exquisite taste, carefully straddling a liking for art deco, modernist and oceanesque in an uncluttered and clear fashion.

Lastly, Lo wandered into Chloe's room and it was delightfully homely. Plum walls made it dark and cosy with a large double bed covered in cushions and blankets and a gypsy throw over a chair, standing on a thick rug. Fairy lights dangled around a busy desk, which was both neat and full. Unapologetic Polaroid snaps of Chloe and friends, Chloe and Ronnie, Chloe and presumably her dad, Chloe and presumably her brother were dotted around. The posters on the wall were all something to do with physics, obscure but at least done in Helvetica. A very small en-suite with just a sink and toilet smelt of wild flowers.

She heard the door open and heard Chloe shouting her name.

"Up here," she replied from Chloe's bedroom.

Chloe entered and was slightly surprised to see Lo looking out to the garden from the window in her tiny towel.

"It's just so beautiful. I hope you don't mind. I had a bath and then felt quite at home."

"No, of course not," said Chloe, collapsing onto the bed. "Mi casa es su casa."

Lo climbed onto the bed, and the extra weight meant she rolled quite close to Chloe. "What shall we do tonight?"

"I don't know. What did you have in mind?"

"Let's get drunk and do something stupid."

"I've got the tea room tomorrow. Why don't we save that for Friday and relax tonight."

"Quite right Chloe. Very sensible."

"Don't be mean."

"I'm sorry. I was being silly. Why don't I make you a nice dinner and we could watch a movie."

"No, you don't have to do that. I can make us something."

"Let me. You've been working all day. I can be your little woman. Make you dinner and wash and clean. Would you like a cup of tea?"

"Do you know Chloe? I really would."

After a brief stroll to the supermarket, while Chloe had a bath, Lo started dinner. It was only a simple peppery seafood linguine with rustic homemade garlic bread, but Chloe thought it was sensational.

Best of all, Lo had bought a bottle of brandy, ginger ale and lemons and emerged with two long and strong Horse's Necks. Dressed in their comfies, they settled on the sofa and eventually settled on watching the first of The Hunger Games.

Darkness descended on the room unnoticed until the film ended. "Let's watch the next one," said Lo and Chloe agreed, saying that her mum had left two portions of tiramisu in the fridge. They were rather big so Chloe decided to split one portion in half and turned down a second Horse's Neck when Lo offered. She made one for herself.

Midway through, Chloe confessed she was beginning to feel tired. Lo clicked the remote control to see how long was left. "There's only another half an hour."

"I'm not daft Lo. I can see it says 43 minutes."

"Yeah, but that includes the credits and everything."

"What 13 minutes of credits?"

"They go on and on and on and…"

"How about this? I wash the pots, and we watch the rest in bed."

"No, I'll wash up. You got to bed."

"No it's okay. You made tea. You relax, I'm good."

Lo was back in her tartan pyjamas, and scrolling on her phone was Chloe's bed when she arrived 10 minutes later. Chloe cleaned her teeth, scrubbed her face and faced the wall as she stripped and got into her own pyjamas before lying next to Lo.

She was on the right side of the bed but generally slept on the left. She perched the iPad between them after it had fallen over several times. She then clicked off the light, knocking over the iPad again and they both chuckled.

Eventually, the film restarted and within minutes, Chloe had fallen asleep. Lo didn't immediately notice but then moved the iPad to the bedside table and rolled onto her side, away from Chloe, to watch the rest of it.

When it finished, she put the cover back on and rolled back to face Chloe, who was demurely still unconscious. Lo closed her eyes and quickly fell asleep too.

In the night, both separately noticed the other was there and were initially confused and then returned back to sleep.

Chloe was getting dressed in the corner of the room when Lo slowly awoke. She watched in between passages of closing her eyes before croakily whispering: "Morning. You want a coffee?"

Turning around, Chloe whispered: "Morning. No, I've had one. I can get you one, or just go back to sleep."

"I'd love one."

Chloe smiled and went to the bathroom to clean her teeth. She went downstairs and returned 10 minutes later with a coffee but Lo was dozing but exhaled a weak "Thank you."

"Mum's still in bed. She's working again later, so probably won't see her again today. But do what you want to do," Chloe said, swiping the fringe from Lo's eyes.

"I thought I might explore the wonders of Bexhill later," she said, smiling and closing her eyes. "But I'm so comfortable right now."

"You stay in bed for a bit. You've had it tough recently."

Lo opened her eyes. "Thanks, Chloe. Thank you so much."

"I've got to go," she said, rising quickly. "I'll see you tonight."

Chloe gave a weary wave and rolled over to the other side of the bed.

It was a couple of hours later when she woke up properly, disturbed by the sound of Ronnie vacuuming downstairs. Glancing at the clock she thought about hiding out in Chloe's room but decided to go downstairs in her pyjamas and messy hair.

Ronnie jumped when she spotted the guest and switched off the vacuum cleaner. "I'm sorry did I wake you? I had to have a quick clean up and I'm leaving for work in an hour."

"Oh no, that's okay," said Chloe. "I'm not normally this lazy. I'm just catching up."

"Don't worry, sweetheart. Why don't you go to bed or into the garden while I have a tidy. And I'll bring you a coffee. I've got some nice bread left over from the restaurant and some lovely local honey. Would you like that?"

"Oh Ronnie, I really would. Can I go out into the garden? I promise tomorrow I'll be up to speed."

"Of course, sweetheart. Don't you worry. Let us look after you."

Lo felt the need to hug Ronnie and bury her face in her shoulder. Ronnie rubbed her back then they went in different directions. Lo went to get her book and sit in the garden, Ronnie appearing shortly after with a cafetiere, warm bread and a small jar of Sussex Sea Bees Finest. An hour after that, she came to check Lo was okay and left her in the sun, still in her pyjamas, and departed for the restaurant.

Bexhill beach was a shingle beach, which Lo didn't realise until she saw it. She had planned to have a lazy afternoon in the sun and finish her book but there was no chance of anywhere to lie without something comfortable.

However, the promenade was delightful to walk along with the plodding pensioners, dogwalkers and their energetic dogs and the floating ice creams, dripping from the very small and wolfed by the very tall.

It was pleasant and pleasing until she spotted the modernist building jutting out. The De La Warr Pavilion - a spectacular building from the 1930s stylishly renovated. Instantly captivated, Lo spent far too long admiring it from the outside, from different angles near and far, and then venturing to see the wonders inside.

She was moved and wanted to remember her first feelings about it forever. It made her happy to write it down in her notebook from the cafe's veranda overlooking the beach with a tea from an art deco style pot and cup and saucer. It was the first time she'd written anything in months; the words spilt out rather than crafting them too carefully.

June - the De La Warr Pavilion may be just about the most perfect thing I have ever seen. It's strange to think that I had no idea that it even existed until I actually arrived in Bexhill. Had I seen even the smallest picture, I would have come here in a shot. But I feel lucky to have stumbled across it and fallen in love with it at first sight.

It stirs emotions in me that take me to a place where I'd like to be. A forgotten era of glamour and adventure that I long for. It's brutal and romantic, powerful and sexy, clean and soft, both handsome and pretty.

The exterior is strong and purposeful, with its iron and glass with a bulging centre-piece the most appealing of its characteristics. It flaunts itself like the proud bow of a sleek liner waiting to be launched into the sea in search of exotic places on a mystery ride.

Inside is even more alluring; all hard edges softened by the gentle lines and holes and curves enticing further intrigue to explore. The staircase seduces a desire to go upwards and stare through the windows, giving glorious sight of a heavenly vista.

On this summer's day, the salty smell of the sea and the warmth of the sun are an invitation to stay on the balcony, peering over the edge to enjoy its proud white sharpness in the muted colours of its surroundings. No doubt, the dark storms of winter that surround it would not take away its attractiveness.

A place I didn't know I was looking for and somewhere I'll find difficult to leave.

She lay back and smiled, looking out to sea, her literary instincts considering storylines and dramas and romances that would benefit from having the pavilion as an extra character. Her eyes were watery, hidden behind her dark, oversized sunglasses.

The George and Dragon was an exceptionally plain pub. The contrast to the De La Warr Pavilion could hardly be greater. It was all cluttered garbage, horse brasses, hunting images and bad imitation Hogarth prints, hulking, glowing fruit machines, a threadbare, dirty patterned carpet, and discarded peanuts in so many locations, like a postmodern take on the Hansel and Gretel fairytale.

Unidentifiable pop music was piped in seemingly for the enjoyment of no one, certainly neither the two elderly gentlemen on separate tables nursing pints of Guinness nor the two women on stools at a high bar chatting over crisps and cider, nor the rotund middle-aged man sitting at the bar with his newspaper, phone, stubby pen and frothing beer.

Lo ordered a brandy and ginger ale with a slice of lime. It was weak, lacked any heat, and the fruit was semi-shrivelled. She took a booth in the corner near to the women. The music and their chatting made it hard to continue her writing ideas, so she listened in to their conversations. It was about men and was coarse and unappealing.

She went back to the bar and interrupted a lively conversation between the barman and man on the stool to order another drink.

"You on holiday, love?" he said. She glanced up from looking at the faded tattoos and gold jewellery on his podgy fingers and arms.

"Kind of. Although I might be here for a bit. I've not decided."

"Very cryptic," he said.

"Oh no, nothing mysterious. I'm staying with a friend. I just don't know how long."

"A boyfriend? Three-sixty please love."

"No, just a friend. But I don't know how long. I don't have much money and don't want to take advantage."

"You looking for a job?"

"I don't know really."

"You ever pulled a pint?"

"No."

"It's easy. Want to do a few shifts here? I always need extra help in the summer."

"I don't know."

"It's fifteen quid an hour, plus any tips. We can see how it goes if you want?"

"Yeah, I guess."

"Lovely. Nick Guest, nice to meet you, love." They shook hands. "Come round here. You can't start now."

"Lo Miller," she said. "What about forms and stuff?"

"Don't worry about all that shit, we'll sort it out later. I'll show you the till, where everything is and we'll get you started. And I'll just be over there if you need anything. Alright sweetheart?"

"Yeah, okay," she said.

Lo went to the other side of the bar. Nick pointed out the spirits. There weren't many and were served by the gill with a simple press under the upturned bottle. The draughts were served by simply pressing a button and the bottles and mixers in the fridge were straightforward. The till was a little more complicated and Lo logged on as someone called Leeanne and was given a crash course in how it worked.

Nick then left her to it and sat around the other side of the bar and ordered a lager which she poured and put through the till. He let out an exhalation of satisfaction. "Very nice," he said, handing over a £5 note. "Keep the change, your first tip." He winked and she smiled.

Over the next three hours Lo had the odd moment that required the intervention of Nick. He came around the bar to help, putting his hand on her back or shoulder or arm and saying "Don't worry, love."

But she was quickly up to speed and didn't need his help. He stayed at the bar with his mate and was joined by two more men as the pub began to fill up.

After a couple of hours, three others arrived behind the bar: Joe and Melody, who were around the same age as Lo, plus Leanne, who was older. They said a quick hello before getting on to work.

Nick came around the other side of the bar and served himself two whiskies which he sat in front of his group. "Well done, love. Same time tomorrow?" he said, handing her a £50 note.

"Joe can't work tomorrow night either," Leanne interrupted.

"Fancy it?" Nick said. "Five until midnight? It gets pretty busy but just over a ton."

"Yeah, sure," she said, taking the money.

"Sweet."

"Do you know the Smokey Oak Pizza Rooms?"

"Hey Lo, I wondered what you were up to."

"There's a Horse's Neck here with your name on it, so get a wriggle on."

"You'll have to give me some time to get ready. Are you there now?"

"It's not exactly the Ritz darling. Come quick. There's some Bexhillian boys or whatever they are, that I'm worried might come over if I'm here on my own any longer."

With that she clicked off, leaving Chloe without any alternative. She threw on a pastel blue skater dress and white tennis shoes but still looked demure after the 10 minutes she spent putting on soft make-up and brushing her hair.

But she'd taken too long. Three Bexhill boys were sitting with Lo by the time she got there. Lo threw her arms around her. "Oh, thank goodness you're here. Rescue me from these Bexhill barbarians."

Chloe looked confused while the boys smiled. "Can I get you a drink, love?" One of them said in a gruff Southern accent.

"She'll have a Horse's Neck and could I possibly get another one, Harry?"

"That's the spirit, Lo, love it. Same again lads?" The other two nodded and he went to the small bar on the opposite side to the kitchen and its large, glowing pizza oven. Chloe hadn't been to the restaurant before and looked a little overwhelmed as her head revolved around the well-lit dining room and the long benches, which meant strangers were sat next to strangers.

Lo grabbed her by the arm and pulled her down alongside her. "Don't look so worried," she said. "They're lovely boys. This is Dennis and Kane." They nodded. "And that's Harry at the bar. They're all builders. Bexhill builders."

Harry returned with three pints of lager and two Horse's Necks and introduced himself to Chloe, shaking hands. They were a curious trio. Thick and muscly, two were covered in Maori tattoos on their arms. Kane had only the name Rebecca in small typewriter font across his wrists. They smelt rather good and their clothes were football hooligan chic and expensive.

The five of them laughed a lot, although Chloe was always the last. She looked like an outsider both metaphorically and, at times, physically.

Two large pizzas arrived, and the drinks kept coming. Dennis tried to flirt with Chloe but was very bad at it. His innuendos were naff and tawdry. Harry tried to flirt with Lo and was very good at it. He hit the right notes between suggestive and innocent. She was actually a little charmed by him, and he was handsome and ruggish. Kane didn't try to flirt and was bad at conversation. He looked lost and was more comfortable having banter with his two mates.

But they were there for over an hour, getting more and more drunk, particularly Lo, who ended up squashed between Harry and Chloe. Harry was funny and his teasing was making her giggle loudly. Dennis and Kane, meanwhile, were in conversation, leaving Chloe on her own.

"We're thinking of heading to The Dome if you fancy it?" said Kane across the table. Lo felt a squeeze on her elbow coming from Chloe. She turned to look at her. "I've got to," Chloe said. "But, you know, you go if you. But I've got to."

Lo turned to the lads. "Chloe's got work tomorrow and I've got to be up early, so I don't think we can."

"That's a shame," said Harry. "Maybe I could take your number and when you're free?"

"Sure," said Lo and gave it to him. Neither of the other two asked for Chloe's, and they stood up from the bench to leave and hovered uncomfortably.

Harry rose too, pecked Lo in the cheek, and said to Chloe: "Nice to meet you." He turned to Lo: "And I'll message you in the week."

"Okay," said Lo and then watched Harry and his mates disappear. She turned to Chloe and smiled.

"What are you going to do if he messages you?" said Chloe.

"I don't know. Message back."

"So you're going to go on a date with him?"

"I don't know. Maybe. He's sort of funny and good-looking. I don't know."

"A builder?!"

"Oh, you snob," said Lo, pinching her playfully on the shoulder. "You only go in for the geek-types?" Chloe blushed. "I'm only joking. So what do you want to do now?"

"I don't know."

"Well. To be honest, I'm shattered and fairly drunk. So bed is very appealing right now."

"Yeah, that really sounds good."

The drinks were all bought by the boys at the bar and Lo took care of the pizzas and then remembered about her job to Chloe. They laughed that it had only just come up.

Then Chloe told her about her experiences at the George and Dragon. Going in and trying to get served as a 16-year-old. Again, as a 17-year-old. And then being refused when she was 18 by "the pig behind the bar" when she had legitimate ID. Last summer was the only time she'd had a drink in there with Benjamin who was there with his mates playing pool. They laughed all the way home at what a dump it was.

Lo put on her pyjamas and got into Chloe's bed without thinking. She was still a little drunk, but in a nice way. She wasn't going to be sick or anything, and she was fighting the tiredness. Chloe scrubbed her face in the little bathroom, and only the fairy lights were on as she got undressed in the corner.

"So you didn't like Kane or Dennis then?" Lo said quietly.

"Jesus. I don't know which one was worse."

"Is there anyone you're interested in?"

"In Bexhill? No." She got into bed. "There was this person at Oxford that I liked. But it's complicated. And I don't even know if they like me back."

"Of course, they would. They'd be crazy not to."

"I don't know. I can't think about it."

"You can always talk to me, Chloe. If there's anything you want to say."

"Maybe."

"You're a shy girl."

"It's not so easy."

"Okay. Whatever suits you. Do you want to fall asleep to the TV or something?"

"Let's listen to the Shipping Forecast. That makes me happy."

She found the BBC Sounds app on the iPad and clicked on Radio 4. The news was still on.

"Sandettie Light Vessel Automatic is so romantic," said Lo.

"You listen to the Shipping Forecast too? I don't believe it."

"Of course. Did you know Sandettie Light Vessel is unmanned? It doesn't even have an engine. It just floats off the northern coast of France, powered by solar panels. My dream is to live on that boat. All you would hear is the sound of the waves, and never have to speak to anyone. Lie on the deck naked in the summer and stay in the galley with hot chocolate and books in the winter. Just a handsome, strong sailor coming out once a week to deliver provisions and a quick shag before sailing off again."

Chloe burst out laughing. "You'd go crazy out there on your own with no one to talk to."

Lo started laughing too. "No I wouldn't."

"You'd be talking to the dolphins and whales."

"It's a 40-foot-long, beautiful red boat. It would be paradise. I'd be so happy. I really would."

"Have you any idea what the sea is like in winter? The waves can be like 15 metres high. You'd be smashed all over the place. And in the summer, you'd have seagulls shitting on you from a great height during your naked sunbathing."

They both laughed again. "Okay, I wouldn't. But it's a nice fantasy. It's okay to pretend."

The news was coming to an end as their laughter stopped.

"Selsey Bill," said Chloe.

"Oh yeah."

"That's where I would go. Selsey is such a beautiful name. So soft and inviting. Not the Bill part, but they go well together. But Selsey is really gentle. It's not. It's dangerous. Because of the rocks off the coast, but it's so pretty, especially at dawn or sunset. I haven't been for a few months. There's an area called Selsey Bill and the Hounds, which is a marine conservation zone."

"Sounds more like a punk band."

"Yeah I know. But it's extraordinary. There's fascinating geological features, with small trenches and steep underwater cliffs. And there's amazing sea life. Sponges and anemones. Sea squirts and the short-snouted seahorse. It's where I want to study if I got the chance. I went to Bracklesham Bay when I was young and collected shells on the beach. That's where it all began. My love for the sea and fossils."

Lo squeezed Chloe on the arm gently. "I think you'd be better at Selsey Bill than I would on Sandettie." She smiled back lazily as the music for the Shipping Forecast started. They closed their eyes.

"Sandettie Light Vessel Automatic. Southwest by South. Seven. Rain. Two miles. 1,001. Rising."

"It's wet and wild," whispered Chloe.

"North Foreland to Selsey Bill. Southerly or southwesterly. Two or three. Fair. Good. Selsey Bill to Lyme Regis. Southwest. Three or four. Mainly fair. Good."

Veronica thought it was hilarious that Lo had got a job at the George and Dragon. She was off for the day and the three of them were enjoying a lunch of olives, cheese and salad in the garden, although it was slightly cloudy overhead.

She'd grown up in Bexhill and said the pub had barely changed in the last 20 years. In fact, she couldn't remember the last time she had been in. It was that long ago. It had a reputation as being a bit lively and Veronica warned Lo to be careful, especially at the weekend.

It was a shame that she was working that evening because Veronica was off and wanted to get a takeaway and have a lazy night with a bottle of wine and a catch-up. Lo said it would be better for the two of them to have a mother and daughter night. But Chloe and her mum both agreed that they wanted her to be there too.

Lo left just before 5pm to start the shift. The pub was already busy and she immediately started serving. Leanne asked her to be in charge of collecting glasses and putting them in the dishwasher, saying it would get very busy. It was an order rather than a request, but she was happy to wander the floor and capture the atmosphere every now and again.

However, two hours into the shift, the place was absolutely rammed and collecting the empties was difficult. She had to squeeze through groups of people chatting loudly and the tables were quickly filling up with glasses faster than she could collect them. Leanne told her to get a move on abruptly which she didn't enjoy.

A glass slipped out of her hand on the next way round and a huge cheer went up around the pub after the smash. She came back with a dustpan and brush and while she bent over, she felt a hand touch her on the backside.

"While you down there, love," a voice boomed, followed by laughter. She turned around and saw it was Kane from the night before. Next to him was Harry, Dennis and a fourth man, and they were all guffawing.

"Oh hello Kane. I was just looking for your personality," she said with gusto, but was shaken by his groping. The other men made a noise like they were taken aback. Kane obviously tried to think of a retort but nothing came quickly and he took a slug of his lager.

"Don't ever fucking touch me again," she said, and the trio laughed and jeered.

Behind the bar, she told Leanne what happened. She said it sounded like she had handled it well and to expect a bit of flirting, but that was way over the mark and next time to bar him. There were two very large bouncers in bomber jackets on the main door who were always up for a ruck. But she told Lo to stay behind the bar for the rest of the night and Joe would take over on glasses.

It was more comfortable on that side, although there was the odd lascivious leer, including from Nick, who always told her to keep the change no matter whether it was a pound or as much as ten.

"Well, this is a nice surprise." Harry had come to the bar. "Can I have four pints of lager and a Horse's Neck for the most beautiful barmaid in Bexhill?"

"Is one for your dickhead mate?"

"Come on Lo. He was only having a bit of fun."

"It wasn't fun Harry, you prick. And you could have said something."

"Woah. Don't have a go at me. I didn't do anything."

"Exactly. You didn't do anything."

"I bet you would have been happy if it was me who'd done that."

"No Of. course, I wouldn't."

"Okay, okay. Touchy, but no touchy. So when are we going to go for a night out then?"

"You've got to be kidding."

"Oh, come on. We had a good time the other night."

"We did. But now I've seen what you lot are like."

"You need to lighten up. It's only a bit of banter."

"£17 please."

"Where's your cocktail?"

"I'm not thirsty."

"Jesus. Here take that."

He thrust a £20 note into her hand and walked off without turning back. She didn't see them for the rest of the night and the remainder of the shift passed off without incident, although she was still a little wired.

An hour after closing after cleaning up, they stayed and had a quick drink. Leanne told her she'd done well after they'd split the tips of £30 each, and Nick gave her £150 in cash and put her down for another four shifts that week. Leanne asked where she was staying and told her to get in the taxi with her, dropping her off on the way.

Lo was shattered when she walked through the door and a little upset about the evening. Chloe and Ronnie were still up, and she told them what had happened with Kane. Chloe gave her a cuddle and then reheated some Chinese food as they watched episodes of Friends.

Before going to bed, Ronnie said she'd done well and that it was probably a one-off, but if it didn't feel right working there, to quit. Lo thanked her and said she'd give it another try.

Fatigue suddenly hit Lo, and she rested her head on Chloe's shoulder. She cuddled her with the soft blanket she had wrapped around her and then suggested bed too. Moments later, Lo collapsed into bed, her body aching as she closed her eyes and listened to the opening music to the Shipping Forecast.

The next few weeks settled into a pattern. Lo would work the day shift on Wednesday and Thursday and Friday and Saturday nights. Chloe worked Tuesday to Saturday at the tea room and Veronica worked six nights a week with a random night off. Occasionally, they got together and had a nice meal, the three of them, but it was rare that they overlapped to be able to do anything.

To Lo, it felt like she was settled into a family, and she felt comfortable. The only thing that unsettled her was that Veronica refused to take any money for board and lodging. Lo pleaded with her, but she said that she was pleased to see Chloe happier than she had been in a long time. Still, she collected £100 a week and stashed it in a metal box in Benjamin's room with a thank you note for when it was discovered:

You are amazing and I love you so much. A little gift for a summer I will never forget, Lo x

By then she had moved permanently into Chloe's bed, although her clothes and suitcase were kept in Benjamin's room. The pair had become incredibly close. One Wednesday when they had both been working, they collapsed into bed at just after seven to watch a movie. But before it started Chloe had a surprise.

"I got you a little something," she began, handing her a small parcel wrapped in brown paper and tied up with string. "Don't get too excited. It's nothing special, just a little gift."

"Oh, how exciting. What is it?" She gently undid the string bow and opened the paper to reveal a book – Sandettie Light Vessel Automatic, a collection of poems by Simon Armitage. "How beautiful," she said. She opened the first page and read an inscription from Chloe:

This has been the best summer. And if you ever get to live here, I'll come and join you! Love Chloe x

Her eyes became glassy and she hugged Chloe tightly, burying her head in her shoulders and neck. "I'm so grateful. For everything," she whispered.

The following day, she took her new book to the De La Warr Pavilion and devoured it. When she was alone, she had taken every opportunity to go there for coffee or lunch. If she could, she'd wear her vintage clothing and retro sunglasses to feel more glamorous. The surroundings inspired her into starting a novel set in the late 1920s.

It was a curious activity. She didn't have an end point but enjoyed playing with the characters and seeing what they did next. She didn't know their secrets. They just seemed to reveal themselves. The book could be tidied at a later date but she was in a rush to get the story down and to see what would happen.

But this day was the hottest of the summer, and she sat in the shade on the balcony of the pavilion, reading through the poems one by one and line by line, taking a break from her creativity. From the second poem onwards, "Making A Name", she was utterly enthralled.

Here is your name and a lifetime only to make it your own

She dissected the line again and again. For six hours she sat at De La Warr, going through the book but kept returning to the second poem. It had begun to play on her mind, what was next for her. Not too much at this stage, just the thought of having to think about it. Chloe had been accepted for her PHD and had said she could always join her in Oxford. Likewise, Veronica said she was more than welcome to stay on in Bexhill, but it wasn't really a solution. The poem made her drift into thoughts about the future, and hoped the answer would become apparent, like the lives of the characters in her novel.

Ever since receiving the poetry book, Lo had wanted to do something special for Chloe. She cooked nice meals, took her and her mum out to dinner, and bought tickets for a touring version of Agatha Christie's The Mousetrap at the De La Warr Pavilion, but she wanted to do something extra special.

On a Sunday morning she was up early out of bed. A sleepy Chloe asked where she was going, but she told her not to worry and to go back to sleep, which she did. Around an hour later, she was woken by a blaring car horn from below her window. Then again. Then it was held. Then it beeped again.

Chloe suddenly realised it must be Lo and raced to the window. Sure enough, there she was; at the driving wheel of a vintage convertible MG.

With her headscarf, sunglasses and bright lipstick, she looked like the sophisticated heroine from the Jazz Age that she'd always wanted to be. Chloe opened the window and shouted: "I didn't know you could drive."

"There's a lot of things you don't know about me! You've got 15 minutes. I'm going to pick up a picnic hamper. If you're not ready, I'm going without you." The car then revved loudly and pulled away as Chloe smiled and closed the window. She didn't have any real vintage clothes but cobbled together a suitable outfit to fit the mood of: high-waisted shorts, cardigan and shirt with tennis shoes. She made it to the front door in time to see the red sports car driving up the hill.

"You look fabulous!" Lo remarked and handed over a takeaway coffee. "They didn't have these in the 1930s, but I didn't think you'd survive without your morning coffee!"

"Where are we going?" she said, climbing into the car and taking the hot drink.

"Don't spill it, for God's sake. The excess on this thing is extortionate."

"I'll be careful. So where are we going?"

"You'll know soon enough," said Lo, putting her foot on the accelerator to move away, but stalling the car. They both jolted forwards awkwardly and Chloe quickly put her hand on the lid of the coffee to stop it from spilling. They both laughed at the false start before Lo tried again and pulled away with the engine growling noisily.

It had been some time since she had last driven a car. She had passed her test at 17, first time, but had only been behind a wheel maybe half a dozen times since. She wasn't particularly interested in driving, but Robin had made some remark about his belief that Lo would never learn to drive as it "wasn't in her character". Renée and Lo immediately hatched a plan and she had secret lessons and passed just six months after her 17th birthday. Robin was delighted and had no recollection of his comment, merely saying it must have been a throwaway thought. Wilf, meanwhile, who had spent so much of his youth mastering driving games, amongst others, showed no interest in putting his skills into practice in real life.

Passing the test was one thing, but Lo didn't feel entirely comfortable in the heavy MG with its clumsy steering. Her initial bravado wore off, and she took it steady through the beautiful countryside of East Sussex, which then turned into West Sussex. Chloe wasn't aware of her unease anyway. She was loving the adventure as the air blew her hair around wildly while they tried to talk above the noise of the car and rushing air until they eventually simply enjoyed the ride and the beautiful lush green countryside and occasional delightful vistas across the dazzling sea.

Just over halfway through the journey, Chloe twigged their destination and squeezed Lo's hand, which was gripping the gear stick. "Selsey Bill." Chloe smiled. "Oh fantastic." The last part of the trip took longer than expected but they eventually found themselves arriving at Oval Field Beach. They grabbed their picnic hamper and a large cloth bag that Lo had secretly packed containing towels and bathing costumes, and they carefully walked across the stones of the beach to a sandy area with the tide out.

Stretching out the blanket, they laid in the sun, and Lo pulled out two cans of gin and tonic - hers non-alcoholic - and poured them into elegant highball plastic glasses. The beach was empty as far as they could see and they got dressed into their bathing costumes without hiding themselves from any potential onlookers before settling onto the blanket.

The sky was cloudless, and the sun burned radiantly with the only noise coming from the rolling sea and a small single-seater plane flying overhead. Lo said she was hungry but Chloe said they should go for a swim first but warned that the current could be strong and to be careful.

At first, the cold water was chilling but they soon acclimatised, particularly with Chloe splashing her friend. Lo bobbed in the waves and watched Chloe effortlessly swim through the sparkling water like a jewel thief, joyfully parting a pile of shimmering diamonds. She returned to the shore and kept watching as she dried herself with a towel.

Chloe emerged from the sea and athletically dashed over to the blanked where Lo was now drying in the sun and sipping her tin of gin and tonic. Chloe squeezed the wetness from her and felt the drips of salty seawater dribble onto her lips. "It's bliss," she said, collapsing on the blanket.

The sun was hot and she towelled away the grains of sands and covered herself in factor 50 sun cream. She didn't ask, but knew that Lo wouldn't have any on, so she rubbed it into her skin, shoulders, neck and legs, finishing with a blob on her nose that she spread into her cheeks. Lo didn't flinch and merely said a thank you when she had finished.

Lying in the sun, they both effortlessly dozed off on the peaceful deserted beach. It wasn't until the sea started to get perilously close that Lo awoke and nudged her friend awake as the tide threatened to steal their shoes. They edged their belongings back onto the rocks and tucked into the simple picnic, tomatoes on the vine, crusty bread, fresh crab, pork and apple pies and mangoes and strawberries.

Clouds slowly drifted in, and as the temperature dropped, their energy returned. Eventually, they got dressed, and Chloe packed up the picnic basket and returned it to the car before taking a walk along the beach. It took just a few steps for Chloe to pull something out of a small patch of exposed sand.

"What do you think that is?" she said.

"It looks like a claw."

"It's a shark tooth. That could be about 50 million years old. We're pretty lucky to find it. Isn't it incredible?"

"It really is."

"Here, take it."

Chloe placed it her hand and then was off returning sporadically with finds. "A bivalve shell, isn't it beautiful?" "And here's the second part, wow amazing." "A scallop shell. It's perfect, oh my goodness."

Lo then spotted something in front of her that looked like a small unicorn's horn. "What about this?" she shouted. Chloe galloped back to take a look. "A turritella," she squealed. "Sulcifera, I think. That's from a sea snail from the Paleogene Period. What a find."

By now, more clouds had rolled in, and the sky was turning a burning red and pink, and the temperature was starting to drop and they circled back to the car.

"This was just a perfect day Lo. Thank you," said Chloe and they climbed back into the corner, pulling back the roof.

It was dark when they pulled into Bexhill. The MG had to be returned first thing in the morning so they left it at the car park at the bottom of the hill and walked home. They were tired but happy when they turned the key in the door.

Chloe walked in and saw a large, half-empty backpack in the hallway and immediately knew what it was.

"Benjamin's back," she exclaimed. "Oh wow, this is the best day. Come. Come and meet him."

They rushed into the empty living room and then into the kitchen, where Ronnie was unloading the dryer.

"Benjamin's back," Chloe said.

"Yes, he's back," said a startled Ronnie.

"Where is he?"

"He was here 10 minutes and then went to meet Sebastian at the George and Dragon, of course. You should go down and see him."

"I'd better take my things out of his room," said Lo.

"Oh, don't worry, Lo. There's no rush for that. He'll want to meet you," said Ronnie.

"Come on," said Chloe, grabbing her by the arm and pulling her towards the door. Lo was caught off guard and was still looking at Ronnie.

"Go on, go," she said to the pair.

The familiar swing of the George and Dragon doors flashed open, and the pub was half-empty. Chloe's head swivelled, and she caught sight of Benjamin at the pool table with three of his friends. "You go over, I'll get some drinks," said Lo.

Benjamin looked up to see his sister striding over. "Come here," he beamed, opening his arms out for a hug with the cue still in his right hand.

The bell rang, and Lo wandered over to the bar to get the drinks before the last orders. Leanne was serving: "Haven't you got somewhere better to go on your night off?" she smiled.

"My friend's brother's back from Australia."

"Yes, Benjamin. I know him. Two Horse's Necks is it?"

"I think we're gin and tonics tonight."

"Oh. How ordinary," she smiled and then turned her back to make the drinks.

Lo felt a presence and turned around. "So you must be Lo," he said.

Benjamin was tall with dark hair and a fringe skimming his green eyes. His skin had clearly been in the sun with that hard-earned colour, while his clothes were that of someone on a year out, a sky blue hoodie, khaki cargo pants and running trainers. He held out his hand, and his right wrist was covered in colourful fabric bracelets.

"And you must be Benjamin," she said, holding his hand. "I'm sorry for taking up your room."

"Oh, I don't mind one bit. I'm sorry you have to put up with my paintings."

"You did those?"

"Yes. What do you think?"

"They're very unique."

Benjamin laughed. "Unique. That's a fantastical non-commital word."

Lo began to blush but was saved by the return of Leanne.

"I'll get these," said Benjamin. "And four pints of lager, please Leanne. And you must be able to have one by now? It's last orders."

"I'll have a pint with you."

"Thank goodness."

Leanne disappeared to pour the five lagers, and Benjamin returned to Chloe.

"I didn't mean it like that."

"It's fine. I'm not sure whether I like them or not, myself. They're a couple of years old, and my latest efforts are very different."

"They have a haunting quality. What are your latest like?"

"Oh, who cares about my silly doodles? How are you finding our sleepy little town? It's not quite Manchester or Oxford."

"You know, I really like it. How do you know I'm from Manchester?"

Leanne returned with the drinks, and Benjamin paid by card, lifted his glass and said a cheers to the women who returned in kind. Chloe came over from talking to Benjamin's friends and the bell was rung again.

"So this is Lo," said Chloe.

"Yes. She was just telling me about how much she likes Bexhill."

"She works here, you know? At the George and Dragon."

"No? How marvellous. I was working on a cattle ranch in the outback and I dreamt about this place. Can you believe that?"

"Yes I can," said Chloe.

"You mustn't let me bore you about Australia. It's not the least bit exciting for you. I had a great time, but you don't need to hear about every day and night out. Stop me from being a backpacker bore, won't you?"

"We want to hear about it," said Lo.

"You're very kind. But it will easily slip into tedium. I had a unique experience. I think that should cover it for now."

"Unique as in good. Or. What do you mean by unique?" Lo said.

Benjamin looked at Lo and then back to Chloe. "Let's say unique as in special. Now, tell me what you've been up to since I last saw you."

The three of them stood at the bar, and Chloe excitedly told him about her final months at Oxford, taking exams and being accepted for her PhD. Then about working at the tearoom and how she had an amazing summer with Lo.

"That all sounds so fantastic," said Benjamin. "I'm so happy it's all going well for you."

"It really is," said Chloe.

"And how about you Lo? What are you going to do next?"

"I don't know. I've just been going with it the last few weeks. But I'm going to have come up with a plan," said Lo.

"She's writing a novel," added Chloe. "She's a terrific writer."

"You don't know that," said Lo. "You haven't read it."

"Yes, well. When you talk, you sound like a writer to me."

"I'd love to read it," said Benjamin.

"When it's finished," said Lo.

Benjamin's three friends Zak, Arlo and Sebastian joined them at the bar, and there were hasty introductions before it was time to leave. Leanne had said that normally she would have let them stay for an after-hours drink but she was going on holiday to Mallorca the following morning and was flying from Gatwick at 6am. She offered to stay for an extra hour but Benjamin insisted they leave.

He walked home with his three friends while Chloe and Lo chatted about their incredible day. Benjamin gave his friends manly bear hugs and they thudded each others' backs as they arrived at his front door and then he went inside with the girls.

"I'm a little all over the place at the moment," he said. "I'm going to go to bed and try to get back into the rhythm of things but I think it might take me some time. But I can't wait to catch up properly."

He hugged Chloe warmly and the same to Lo before disappearing upstairs. Fatigue drained the girls quickly soon after and they were in Chloe's bed shortly afterwards, drifting off to the sound of the Shipping Forecast. Chloe picturing their day at Selsey Bill, Lo hearing the sounds of the waves from when they snoozed in the sun.

Lo rose without disturbing Chloe and tiptoed down the stairs as quietly as she could. She filled the MG with petrol and took it back to the specialist where she had rented it from. She was far more cautious with her driving than she had been the previous day and was relieved to get her full deposit back even though she knew there was no damage to the car.

It was quiet that morning other than the piercing squawks of the seagulls and the odd car driving past. It was coming towards the end of the holiday season, even though it was probably the hottest part of what had been a glorious summer.

The sky was a pastel blue and pink and the air was cool, and Lo wandered along the promenade, looking out to the horizon beyond the sea. A chilling breeze whipped sand off the beach, and a grain was blown into her eye. She had a tear running down her cheek when she saw a jogger coming towards her. She blinked and saw that it was Benjamin. He took a couple of heavy steps as his run came to a conclusion beside Lo, and he placed his hands on his thighs as he got his breath back.

"What are you doing down here?" he panted, finally standing up straight.

"I had to be up early to return the car," she said. "And what about you? Jetlagged?"

"I couldn't sleep. I had maybe an hour or so, but I just lay there."

"That's tough."

"I was just staring at my paintings and thinking about what you said. Unique."

"Ha ha," she said sarcastically. "I'm going to get a coffee. Are you still running, or do you want to join me?"

"A great reason to stop running, thank you."

They headed up into the town and stopped at a chain cafe.

"I haven't got any money with me," said Benjamin. "Would you mind awfully?"

"Of course. I've been trying to do nice things for your family all summer, but mostly, they won't let me."

"Oh, thanks. A flat white."

Benjamin sat in one of the metal chairs outside the cafe. There was only one other customer, a scruffy old gentleman, sitting inside, staring out of the window. Lo returned with two large flat whites and set them down on the table, which wobbled as the pavement had a slight incline, and one leg was dangling in mid-air. Benjamin grabbed the table to stop the coffees from spilling, and they smiled at avoiding the accident.

Lo took a seat at a right angle to Benjamin, looking down the length of the street.

"I really do like it here," she said.

"I can see why you would."

"What do you mean by that?"

"Oh nothing much. It's a good place to escape to, is all. A good place to just take a second. It's at the bottom of the country, so it's where you bounce back from."

"That's not true. It's special. I think the Pavilion may be just about my favourite building in the whole world."

"Yes. It is rather terrific."

"So did you really miss Bexhill?"

"That's a difficult question for this time in the morning," he said, turning to look at Lo.

"Is it? I didn't realise."

"Well, I don't know. Sometimes, I longed to be back here. To see mum and Chloe and my friends. And I really did think about the George and Dragon and the Pavilion and all the silly, little places here. But then, other times, it felt so small. Like a tiny prison cell. Keeping me held with sentiment. Woah, sorry. I don't know where that came from."

"No, I know what you mean. I think I miss Manchester but I'm not sure either. I have a twin and a brother that I miss. And there's my dad."

"Sorry, was that a twin brother? Or a twin and a brother?"

"A twin brother and a brother. Wilf's my twin, and Robin's my older brother. I don't even know where they are right now. It's complicated."

"Complicated. Unique. You talk euphemistically. I'd love to know what you really think."

"I only say it because I'm like you. I don't really know. I don't know if I like your paintings. But they are unique. They're striking. They make me uneasy, and I don't know if it's in a good way or bad way. Same with home. I'm happy to be away right now but I don't know if I'll be happy to go back or even if I can."

"That's," he paused. "You've made me think there. That's really interesting."

"Well, how do you feel about being back?"

"Tired," he laughed.

"No, really?"

"I don't think I can really process that yet. There's a part of me that wished I'd never gone. That I'd never seen things. If I could get a plane back to Australia in an hour's time, then I'd get it. But I can't. I have to come back to the real world now. That adventure is over."

"That adventure might be over. But there's another soon to come."

"Sorry. I did say I was tired. I'm wittering on. I promised not to be a backpacker bore."

"No, not at all. It's very honest. But maybe it's just too heavy for this time in the morning."

"Yes, you're right. Let's change the subject. Give me the gossip on the George and Dragon. What about that old bastard Guest?"

"I stay away from him if I can. He's more interested in betting than running the pub."

"Yes, I'm sure he is. Well, I can tell you some stories about him. His twice-a-year trips to Thailand and the mysterious fire at his old place."

"Oh really? I'm intrigued."

Benjamin finished his coffee. "They, like most of our conversation, are for the nighttime. Even with that caffeine hit, I'm struggling to keep my eyes open. I'm going back to bed. Are you staying here?"

He got up from his chair wearily. Lo still had half a cup left and said she would stay to finish it. She was there for another 20 minutes and when she got back, Chloe was making a breakfast of different fruits.

"Hey, Lo. Everything okay with the car?" she said.

"Yes, all good," said Lo as she put a large strawberry in her mouth that she had slightly misjudged the size of.

"You missed Benjamin. He's gone back to bed."

Lo nodded.

In the afternoon, Lo went to the De La Warr Pavilion and sat in the cafe, writing her novel and dipping into Sandettie Light Vessel Automatic to read a poem. It was sticky and humid, and dark clouds gathered overhead, suggesting that a storm was coming.

Lo was sitting inside. It was still a special place, but the magic was interrupted by the general hubbub, exuberance of young kids running around and eating burgers and the wailing of babies. It disrupted her writing, and instead, she looked out of the window and gazed towards the ocean.

She was shaken out of a daydream by the sense of someone looking at her. Benjamin had arrived in the cafe with a pretty, slim girl in a thin summer dress. He came over and said hello and introduced Gillian, a friend from school. Lo was sitting at a table for two, so it wasn't big enough for them to join her. Other than saying a hello to each of them, she didn't say another word, just nodded as Benjamin spoke.

They soon left, and Gillian said a 'nice to meet you' and Lo nodded and smiled and picked up her coffee. The cafe was busy, and they took a table three down from hers with Benjamin facing Lo's direction. He looked interested in their conversation, occasionally smiling and throwing his head back in involuntary laughter. Gillian was laughing the most, though.

Lo returned to writing her book but was making slow progress. She decided to leave before the rain came and also thought it was a good opportunity to move her things out of Benjamin's room, knowing what he was up to.

She got up to leave, and Benjamin watched her, and she gave a little wave, which he returned.

For that evening, Ronnie had managed to swap shifts so she could organise a proper welcome-home dinner for Benjamin. She made his favourite food, a corned beef and onion pie, with vegetables, followed by a chocolate and raspberry roulade and bought bottles of white wine.

Lo saw the preparations when she returned and told Ronnie that she, too, had been asked to swap shifts and would be working that night. Ronnie was genuinely upset that she wouldn't be there for dinner and said was there anyway she could get out of it, but Lo said it was a last-minute change and that she'd promised.

She went upstairs and picked up her suitcase, moving them to Chloe's room. She stared at Benjamin's paintings on the wall and tried to make sense of them, giving a critical appraisal but could make little progress on her previous opinion. They were naive, she thought academically. Naive but with a raw quality. Deliberately disconcerting. They provoked emotion. But she still couldn't say whether she liked them.

With Ronnie busily preparing dinner, Lo stayed out of the way, lying on Chloe's bed and closed her eyes. She didn't sleep, just rested her eyes and thought. About the future mostly. But getting no results.

Chloe bounced into the room and said a quick 'hi' before collapsing onto the bed next to Lo.

"I'm gutted you're working tonight," she said. "Is there nothing you can do?"

"It's a family thing. It should be the three of you."

"But you've been part of this family this summer. It won't be the same without you."

"You have a lifetime behind you. You've made me feel so welcome, but let me give you tonight together."

"You're so sweet, Lo."

She lay her head on the pillow and looked towards the ceiling and took Lo's fingers into her hand.

An hour or so later they got up. Chloe went to the bathroom for a shower and Lo left while she was gone. Ronnie was still preparing the dinner and Benjamin was in the garden reading the local newspaper, the Bexhill and Battle Observer.

Ronnie again said she was sorry that she couldn't stay and told her to try to get away early if there were any opportunities and put her forearm on her shoulder, conscious not to get flour on Lo's jumper, and kissed her on the cheek. Lo looked outside and Benjamin smiled and gave a strange army salute. She smiled in a slightly baffled way.

From there, she walked down the hill and sat on the pebbles of the beach, writing her novel, until the sun went down. The storm miraculously had not arrived, but it was still horribly sticky. She walked through the town and stumbled across a typical backstreet pub, The Ship, where she drank frothy bitter.

It was half-full and buzzing with excited chat and laughter. She sat at a table, and a couple of middle-aged men occasionally made polite conversation with her, but mostly, she was left alone. She left just before last orders and returned to the house. The Newberrys were sitting outside, laughing and joking warmly. Lo went straight upstairs and got into bed and pulled the duvet around herself.

The following day was a Thursday and nobody was around when Lo woke up around 11am. Chloe had gone to work without disturbing her, and Benjamin and Ronnie were either in bed or out. She stayed in bed for around an hour and heard no noises, so went for a long bath and read her book, a collection of Muriel Spark novellas.

At lunchtime, she headed to the George and Dragon to start her afternoon shift. It was unremarkable as ever. Nick was behind the bar talking to his friend, and there were maybe 10 other people dispersed around the pub. She said a polite hello, which Nick responded to, lifted the wooden bar flap for her to walk through and then proceeded to the other side with a "I'll have a pint when you ready, thanks love."

A couple of hours into the shift the relative calmness was broken by the abrupt arrival of Harry, Dennis and Kane.

"Three pints and whatever you're having," said Harry, who then turned to his two pals. "That jumped up fucking… So what are we going to do?"

Lo pulled the three pints of lager and listened into their conversation.

"What can we do?" said Dennis. "I mean, Kane did steal that wood."

"But it's what happens," said Harry. "Everyone expects things to go missing. It's the ecosystem."

"Yeah, everyone does it," said Kane.

"There's no need for that though. Gary, the big fucking grass," said Harry.

"I'm not being funny, but Kane, mate. Take a bit, sure. But you cleared the place out. Nearly five hundred quids worth of wood," said Dennis.

"Thirteen fifty," said Lo. Harry took his card out and put it on the reader.

"Cheers," he said. "You not having one?"

"I'm good, thank you, Harry."

Harry didn't respond and turned back to his mates. "Look it wasn't clever Kane, I've got to say that. Dennis is right. Next time, just take a bit."

"Sorry Harry. But they wanted the lot and I got three for it," said Kane.

"That's as maybe. But you have to do it so they don't notice. Or notice but don't mind. A little bit here and there," said Harry.

"I was a bit skint. Rebecca's mum was mithering for money," said Kane.

"Well all right. But you don't go around telling the truth. I know Gary was feeling the heat, but fuck's sake, we could've worked something out," said Harry.

"Do you think they'll let Kane come back?" said Dennis.

Harry put his hand on Kane's shoulder. "You fucked, mate. But don't worry. We'll get you something in the meantime until you can come back a bit later. My mate Barry is always looking for good workers."

"Thanks, mate," said Kane.

"I'll give him a call in the morning. But just be a bit smarter there okay?" said Harry.

"Right, I will," said Kane.

"But we've got to send a message to Gary that we're not to be fucked with. Not so we'll get sacked. Just a shot across his bows so to speak," said Harry.

"Can't we just kick fuck out of him?" said Kane.

"No Kane," said Harry. "He's a mate."

"We could put the suspicion on him. And then save his bacon. Something like that?" said Dennis.

"I like it," said Harry.

"I like it," said Kane.

"Tell me more," said Harry.

"I don't have any more. That's a starting spot," said Dennis. He held his empty glass in the air and looked at Lo, who was still close by and had been eavesdropping their conversation. "Three more when you're ready."

"It's good though Dennis. He's been getting a lot of grief from the project manager. It's running behind schedule apparently. Anything we can do with that?" said Harry.

Kane scratched his chin like he was thinking and muttered: "It's a tough one."

"Protheroe's an old cunt," said Dennis, just as Lo returned with the pints. "Oh sorry love," he added.

"I don't mind. Thirteen fifty," she said. Dennis put his card on the reader.

"Let's take a pew," said Harry, shooting Lo a look.

"Thank you Dennis," she said.

They took a table close to the door and looked as thick as thieves as they conspired their revenge. After 20 minutes, Kane came back to the bar for another three pints. They continued chatting for another half an hour before their discussion seemed to lose momentum. Kane went to the gents. When he came back Harry went on the quiz machine. Then Dennis went to the gents. After banging the machine, Harry came back to the bar.

"Three pints, please Lo," he said. "You're looking particularly fit today." Lo hadn't expected that after his glare earlier in the afternoon and remained silent. "You thought any more about our date?"

"Nope," she said, waiting for the glasses to fill with lager.

"Don't be like that," said Harry. "I apologise. I was out of order. Let's be friends."

"How's your cunning little plan going? You should ask Larry," she said.

"What? Who's Larry?"

"Come on Harry. Get Larry to get Gary. Then you won't need to go to Barry." She laughed at her own comment.

"Funny," said Harry. "You going to have a drink?"

"I'm good," said Lo. "Thirteen fifty." He put the card on the reader and walked off, balancing the three pints to the table. His back was to the window and looking in the direction of the bar. Every now and then, they would make eye contact.

The pub was starting to fill as it got closer to tea time, and Dennis returned to the bar after another 40 minutes. Just at that moment Benjamin walked in with Max, Sebastian and another man who she would later discover was called Ed.

Benjamin waited patiently for Lo to pull the three pints, decline Dennis's offer of a drink and put the £13.50 through the card machine.

"Hey," said Benjamin, leaning on the bar.

"Hey," she said. "What can I get you?"

"Four pints please Lo. How's your day going?"

She glanced over at Harry who was staring back. "Yeah fine. Another couple of hours until my shift finishes." Benjamin looked over to where the three builders were sitting. Harry looked at him and Benjamin nodded in his direction without a response.

"We've just come in for a game of pool. I was hoping you were working," said Benjamin.

"Oh. Why's that?"

"No big reason. You were missed last night is all. I wanted to see that you were okay."

"That's nice. I was tired and just wanted to go to bed. You were all having a nice chat and I didn't want to disturb you. That's £18, please Benjamin."

"As long as you're okay," he said, taking out his iPhone to pay. "You want to come and join us when you've finished your shift? I'll message Chloe, although she drank a lot of wine last night, and you know what she's like."

"Yeah, I might do," said Lo. Benjamin's friends had already taken their drinks through to the pool room and he pointed in that direction, walking back slowly as if to suggest they were waiting for him.

The next hour and a half were busy, with the pub becoming pretty full. The building trio were virtually hidden, and only Dennis and Kane came to the bar to get their three pints. The pool room was noisy with the four lads joined by a couple more their age and a couple of girls, although not Gillian from the De La Warr Pavilion cafe.

Joe and Melody were working the evening shift and with about 20 minutes before it was time to clock off, Joe asked Lo to go around the pub picking up empties and then to call it a night.

It seemed like a fair deal so she scooped them up from the tables and put them on the bar next to the hatch. Harry's table had three empty pint glasses, and just as she was about to collect them, he picked one of them up and put it under the table.

Lo looked at him, annoyed. "Give me the glass," she said.

"Come and get it," said Harry.

Lo wasn't in the mood for games and went to the other tables for their empties. With eight or nine glasses clamped between her fingers, she returned to the bar and Harry was there waiting.

"You think you're too good for me?" he said, invading her personal space. She put the glasses on the bar. "You're not too good for me," he added. Lo tried to walk off, but he grabbed her arm.

"Don't you fucking dare," she said. The pub quietened. Nick came over. "Okay, lad. That's enough for tonight," he said.

Lo looked towards the pool room and saw that Benjamin was walking over. Harry said nothing and, after a short pause, burst through the doors to go outside, trailed by his oppoes.

"You okay, love?" asked Nick. Benjamin was now standing next to her.

"I'd kick his arse," she said. Benjamin laughed.

Nick smiled and signalled to Joe: "Get her one of those horse's arses or whatever they are."

"Thanks, Nick," she said. He winked.

"Remind me not to mess with you," smiled Benjamin. Lo smiled back. "You okay? Come and join us in here."

Lo picked up the drink from the bar, and Joe apologised for telling her to collect the glasses, but she told him not to worry. She shook hands with Arlo and Zak, nodded at Ed, and was then introduced to the four newcomers but couldn't remember their names in the whirlwind of the past few minutes.

She sat on the top of the banquette with her feet on the seat on the edge of the room. Her drink was finished in no time, and she went back to the bar to get another. Benjamin followed her.

"Let me get this," he said, ordering her Horse's Neck and nothing for himself. "Do you want to get out of here after that?"

"Thanks Benjamin. I would actually. But Chloe?"

"I think she'd be here by now if she was coming. She's blue-ticked me." He paid for the drink and rescued his remaining half-pint from the pool room and his jacket and told his friends that he was leaving. They asked him to stay but it also seemed natural for the group of friends to come and go freely.

"They seem nice," said Lo when Benjamin finally broke away.

"I've known some of them for a long time."

"Yeah?"

"Arlo and I used to live next door to each other until we were five. And Liv is his little sister, so I remember her being born."

"That's sweet. That's something really great."

"Yeah it is. What is that, by the way? Chloe was drinking it last night."

"It's brandy and ginger ale with a twist of lime. Not a true Horse's Neck cocktail, but it's good enough."

Benjamin took the glass out of her hand and took a gulp of the cocktail. "Not bad," he said.

"Not bad. You nearly finished it."

"Oops sorry. So do you want to get something to eat?"

"No, not really. Maybe another drink but somewhere else."

She drank the last of the Horse's Neck and they left the George and Dragon, Benjamin waving to the pool room in case anyone was looking over. They were walking down the hill in the direction of Vincent's Bodega.

Just as they were about to cross the road, they saw Harry stumble out of their destination, missing the bottom step and almost toppling over. They double-backed onto their side of the road and carried on walking without looking over.

"Hey," Harry shouted. "Hey, Lo." They put their heads down and walked faster. "Fucking bitch. Fuck you. Go fuck yourself."

The Amsterdam was just a few further yards down, and Benjamin ushered Lo down the pavement and into the doorway. "Get us some drinks," he said. "I'm just going to make sure he doesn't follow us in."

But Lo didn't go inside the bar. She hid in the doorway and watched Benjamin stride across the road. She couldn't make out what they were saying but saw Benjamin grab Harry around the neck of his cagoule. Kane and Dennis were now either side of Harry, but helpless as they watched him hold out his arms and palms outstretched, appearing to declare his innocence. Benjamin gave him a shove to release him, then turned and confidently walked across the road. Harry remained silent, and the three of them ambled away in the other direction.

Benjamin saw Lo in the doorway of The Amsterdam and, without words, they decided not to go inside and instead carried on walking down the street.

"Let's just go down to the beach. I want some fresh air," said Lo.

"Good idea."

Lo could tell that Benjamin was a little wired from the confrontation and they stayed silent for a few paces until they reached the wall to the beach. There he exhaled extravagantly and leaned on the wall with his hands.

"Shit, sorry," he said.

"Why?"

"I don't know. It's not my beef, and I'm sure you could handle it. You didn't need me interfering."

"Yeah, I could've done. But that doesn't make it wrong. I appreciated it."

"Yeah? You sure? You didn't need some big ape getting involved though. Sorry, that's not really me."

"It's fine, I promise." Lo rubbed his arm, and he looked relieved.

"Come on, let's go to the pavilion," he said.

It was getting darker even though it was early evening. They strode carefully over the pebbles and rocks, making very slow progress and staring down at their feet, wary of the unstable ground, with the stones shifting with every step.

"So what are you going to do next?" Lo asked.

"Oh, nothing. Not unless he's an arse again. Then I don't know."

"Not about Harry, silly. What are you going to do next?"

"What? With my life?"

"Yes. Have you any ideas? A masterplan?"

"I don't know Lo. I made some friends in Sydney and they've invited me out there. I thought about it. But I don't think it's a good idea."

"No?"

"I don't know. Maybe. I'm going to give myself a bit of time. Think about my next move."

"Get a job?"

"I want to paint, but I don't know. I don't know whether I need to think about commercial stuff."

"I hate to tell you this. But that stuff in your room is not very commercial."

Benjamin laughed. "I could do Christmas cards or something."

"What? Like the Victorian ones? Dead robins and weird Santas."

"Hey, that's not a bad idea." A large raindrop fell on Benjamin's arm. Then three on Lo and more on Benjamin. They looked at the sky, and the clouds looked demonic. "Come on, we'd better get inside."

Seconds later, the warm evening turned into a flash rainstorm. The water belted down heavily, soaking the pair and the other people on the promenade who looked like Lowry figures, bending and rushing to find safe havens.

The pair sprinted in the direction of the De La Warr Pavilion and yelped as they splashed through the puddles that had already formed. Benjamin stayed to run at the same speed as Lo who was struggling as her thin summer dress became drenched and was clinging to her body while her tennis shoes and socks were already dripping wet.

Eventually, they made it to the De La Warr Pavilion and thudded into a wall under the balcony roof to get protection. Benjamin placed his hand on Lo's cheek and gently kissed her on the lips. She responded and then they kissed enthusiastically, Lo touching the back of his head and shoulder, Benjamin placing his other hand on her hip. A raindrop trickled from his forehead, down his nose and leapt onto Lo's top lip and into their mouths.

They stopped and started to laugh. Lo brushed her soaked fringe off her forehead, and Benjamin ran his fingers through his hair. The rainstorm had abated; it was now a light shower with the sun piercing the clouds.

"You're absolutely soaked," said Benjamin, looking at Lo. She laughed easily.

"We'd better go," she said.

Benjamin put his hands on her waist again, and they kissed again. They stopped, and Lo's fingers held Benjamin's hands. "I don't know," she said.

They stood for a while, and Benjamin kissed her lightly on the cheek and said they'd better get home. The sun was now beaming, and the sticky air had dissipated. They said little as they squelched up the hill. Around a few hundred yards from their house, Benjamin took hold of Lo's hand, and they paused. "Not yet," he said.

Lo looked serious before they naturally fell towards each other and tenderly kissed. A light shower began to fall again, but they didn't notice.

"Lo," shouted Chloe. The pair turned to see her standing frozen still in the middle of the street. "Lo, what are you doing?" she exclaimed.

"Chloe," said Lo. Chloe turned and ran up the hill. "Chloe, wait," shouted Lo. But she was gone. Sprinting past the house, up the hill and around the corner.

Back at the house, their wet socks left footprints on the wood floor. They were worried about Chloe, who had run past he house and straight up the hill. Benjamin tried to allay Lo's fears by saying she was just a bit shocked – as, indeed, they were themselves.

A couple of calls from both of their phones were ignored, and Benjamin suggested to Lo that she should go for a shower to warm up and he would make some tea.

Steam quickly filled the bathroom as Lo climbed into the shower cubicle. She decided to be quick, but after soothing herself with gel, the tension began to ease, and she stayed longer, washing her hair, and then sitting on the shower floor.

She didn't rush, getting dressed, putting on a t-shirt and sweatpants with a towel wrapped around her head when she finally came downstairs.

"Any news?"

Benjamin shook his head. "I tried a couple of times. Let's leave it for a bit."

Milk was bubbling in a small pan, and he poured it into two mugs, stirring it in powdered hot chocolate before slamming the teaspoon into the sink. He handed one of the mugs to Lo and took a noisy swig of his.

He took a couple of Nice biscuits and dipped them in. Lo sat on the breakfast stool, watching Benjamin and took a few biscuits herself.

Benjamin took out his phone and typed.

"What did you say?" asked Lo. He held up the phone for her to read: *Let me know ur OK don't need say anything else but need to know ur OK.*

Lo nodded her approval.

"I'd better get cleaned up," he said. "I'll take my phone and let you know if I hear anything." Lo nodded again and watched him go upstairs with his phone and drink.

Lo took her hot chocolate outside and stood in the garden, looking up at the skies for inspiration. She took out her phone and called Chloe but it rang through to the answerphone again. "Shit," she whispered to herself.

She was sitting on the settee with her legs tucked under her chin when Benjamin came downstairs.

"She's okay," he said. "She sent me a message saying not to worry."

"What did she say?"

"She's at Liv's."

"So what did she say?"

He took out his phone and read it. "Don't worry. At Liv's. Staying tonight."

"Okay. That's good."

"I think we'd better have an early night," said Benjamin and Lo nodded.

While he went to the kitchen to wash the pan and mugs, Lo went upstairs to dry and brush her hair. The hairdryer warmed her skin. She heard the floorboards creaking softly as Benjamin went to his bedroom.

Lo took off her sweatpants with the t-shirt skimming the middle of her thighs. She walked across the landing, paused for a while before opening the door to Benjamin's door. He was sitting at his desk, and his head swung round sharply.

"What are you doing?" he said.

"I thought…"

"Jesus, Lo."

"Oh shit. No, I was just checking you were okay."

"I know what you were doing."

Lo edged backwards out of the door back to Chloe's room and hid under the duvet.

At around one in the morning, Lo heard the front door open. She hadn't slept at all and took a couple of steps on the stairway and saw it was Ronnie. She looked up at Lo and whispered: "Hi. Everything okay?"

"I'm sorry," said Lo.

"That's okay, love. Do you want anything?"

She said "Thank you," although Ronnie took it to mean "No thank you."

"Night, love," said Ronnie.

"Bye," said Lo.

A few hours later, Lo silently slipped out of the front door carrying her vintage suitcase with sunglasses covering her tired eyes.

The air was cool and the sky was pink with no one around, except a scruffy old man walking towards the promenade with his scruffy old dog.

Lo sat at the train station waiting for the first train to arrive but forgot to buy a ticket.

She took out her phone and read the recent messages between her and Chloe. In the empty box, she wrote: *So sorry.*

The grey ticks turned blue just as the train arrived. 'Chloe is online', then her name disappeared and so did the train with Lo sitting in the window, looking out to the pink reflection on the ocean.

IT HAPPENED ON AN ISLAND

Not for a second did Robin's sports editor assume that he would not be at the Cricket World Cup. He hadn't missed an England game at any format since being given the senior writer's role three years ago and had already followed them on tours to Australia, New Zealand, Pakistan, India, Bangladesh, South Africa and the West Indies.

It seemed inconceivable that he would miss the chance of another few weeks in the Caribbean even if there had been a bereavement in the family. The tickets and hotel had been booked and the first thing he did the following morning after leaving is family home was to confirm his intentions.

But he wanted to get away immediately, and he convinced his sports desk to fly him to Ireland to compose a lengthy feature on a team that could cause a surprise and maybe get to the last four. Robin didn't really believe that, and neither did his desk, but they were happy to send him to Dublin for a 2,000-word feature as long as he did a similar piece on England and another to preview the World Cup. They had already been mostly written by Robin anyway, so it was an agreement he easily reached.

A modest room was booked at an airport hotel, but he was happy to be on his own for a few days before the trip. With everything filed and a day to go, his serious thoughts moved to the World Cup. Covering it from a work perspective would be challenging but not something he was too concerned about. Deadlines were awkward, and his editor would be a pain, demanding early copy and impossible exclusives. It was a question of getting enough to pacify him and staying in with the players, coaches and press officers.

What was always a dangerous unknown was what happened away from the cricket among the press pack. Tours could occasionally be a hedonistic mix of drinking and eating while sexual liaisonsbetween colleagues or by them with strangers or paid company could occasionally cause a stir. Robin was under pressure from some to join in on nights out and would make the odd cameo appearance but mostly maintained a role as an outsider. He knew many of them thought he was uncool, but he wasn't too concerned. It was just important to have a place among the party.

He knew his closest colleague Max Halliday would be going so he messaged him to find out who would be in the group. Robin was the only cricket journalist based outside London and kept close to Max who was always in the loop. But Max had an annoying habit of sending voice notes. He knew that irritated Robin but did it anyway and he was quick with his reply.

"All right Pappy. I'm glad you've confirmed. We're all staying at the same hotels. Have you gone with the usual lot of organisers? I know your place is a bit tight, but I think everyone's feeling the pinch so it's a bit cheaper this time round. We're flying from Heathrow at about 1.30pm, getting into Kingston around 9pm local time. Are you going via London or can you fly direct from Manchester? So it's going to be a lot of the usual faces. KGB, Pinky, Whiskey Sours. Jaggi will be there and Morrissey. And there's a couple of women going. Sean Wright and someone called Mikaela Munro who I've never heard of. Great name though. Can't wait mate, should be a great trip."

Robin had a tic for when something happened he didn't like. The right side of his face would screw up, and his eye would close. He developed it accidentally from batting when a ball would cut across him. It earned him the nickname Popeye, which, after several revisions, had now evolved into Pappy amongst the cricket fraternity, a moniker he didn't actually mind. Almost everyone had to have a nickname, and it was certainly better than Max's nickname Peanuts.

He screwed up his face again after listening to the message.

KGB, Pinky and Whiskey Sours had been grouped together by Max, which was not surprising as they were essentially the same person. Kenneth Graham-Brown, Thomas Pinkerton and Mark Sowerby: privately educated, former Oxbridge students - not good enough at cricket to make it, so used the old-tie network to get cosy jobs. Sours had once confided in him that it was either writing or working for MI5 and he would have been useless at that and the Eastern Bloc somehow didn't seem as appealing as the cricket-playing nations. They were all competent but lazy writers, functioning alcoholics, apart from Pinky, and nostalgic for an era that never existed. Awaiting inevitable redundancy and retirement in the home counties, they were good fun in small doses. Witty raconteurs, apart from Pinky, between drinks three and five, then a tendency to be boorish or boring.

Jaggi Oberoi was probably the most insightful and knowledgeable writer but kept himself to himself. He also wasn't very exciting on social media and he would shy away from being a talking head on TV or radio.

That was where Ethan Morrissey excelled. 'Mozzer' had a huge following on social media and was charismatic, confident and charming as a guest. He was also a good writer, with strong opinions and had an uncanny ability of always being right. He was more of a senior writer, writing about all sports and going to major events.

Sean Wright had recently been promoted to a similar position from being a football writer. Robin had worked with her up until a few years ago, but they were no longer in touch. They hadn't seen or spoken for more than three years.

Mikaela Munro, meanwhile, was a complete unknown. Robin searched her byline and came back with a few results - mostly about local news stories and, more recently, a couple of sports interviews. They weren't very well written and she didn't seem to have any experience of covering a major event.

From there he read everyone's recent stuff and lost himself down a wormhole for the next few hours and thought how good some of the things that had been written were. Of course, that couldn't be admitted to, once he met up with the group. There was an unwritten rule to carp and criticise other's work behind their backs at all times. Positivity was very much frowned upon.

Flying from Dublin via Manchester, Amsterdam and Atlanta, Robin landed at lunchtime the following day from everyone else. Touching down in Kingston a voice note was waiting for him on his phone from Max.

"Hello Pappy, how's it going? Don't know if you've seen it, but the press conference has been brought forward to three. Don't worry if you don't make it in time. I can send you the quotes. Found this great bar last night called Horace's. Amazing in there. I think we're going back tonight if you don't make it to the presser. Let us know how you're getting on."

Walking down the steps of the plane, the fierce heat hit Robin immediately. He was dressed wrong, still wearing a cotton jacket, t-shirt and thick jeans and couldn't find his sunglasses routing through his hand luggage. By the time he collected his suitcase, which refused to roll nicely as one of the wheels had jammed, he was already sweating and sticky.

An air-conditioned taxi set off directly to Sabina Park cricket ground, and the driver spoke excitedly about the World Cup. Robin was flustered and tired and not in the mood. But the sight of the shimmering cyan sea perked him up, and he sank into the back seat and talked up West Indies' chances, which he didn't truly believe.

His upturn only lasted briefly, with the traffic piled up on the highway. It was now 2.30pm, and the last thing he wanted to do was to burst in late at the press conference, apologising, sweating and struggling with his wonky suitcase. So he asked the driver to go to The Cambridge Hotel, and he messaged Max to say thanks if he could send in the quotes.

The Cambridge was reasonably grand in appearance, but close up it was starting to fray. Some of the white walls were chipped in places, and the wood on the counter and tables were scratched and unvarnished, but it would be fine for the next six nights.

The hotel clerk, wearing a Johanna name badge, was young, beautiful, well-spoken, polite and incredibly efficient. He thanked her and felt obliged to use the intimidating porter to take his suitcase to his room down the corridor to the left. For him, both wheels turned, and he gave him two US dollars and shut the door urgently.

He ripped off his trainers, socks and jeans and went to the French window. He couldn't open it and couldn't work out why after an annoying search of the door and its various locks. The view was across to the car park, but he wanted to feel the Jamaican sun on his skin. Instead, he collapsed onto the bed and turned on the TV. Half the channels were empty. Many were cartoons or US channels showing trash. The sports stations seemed to be blocked so he put on the BBC World News, then turned it off again and drew a bath.

His phone buzzed. "Alright, Pappy. Listen I'll get the transcription over to you in a bit, but we're just getting a cab back to the hotel, so it will be a little bit longer. Nothing very interesting to be honest. Usual guff. We're here to win, won't underestimate any country, prepared for every sort of pitch, blah blah blah. You can write it now and paste it in the quotes to be honest… (*speaking with the phone in his armpit*) Mozzer, is that taxi free? That one there… (*back to talking on the phone*) I'd better go. See you at Horace's later yeah?"

Robin slid into the bath. The bathroom was small and dated but perfectly fine. His ankles looked swollen, and his belly looked white, but the water was revitalising, and he took his time to let the airplane germs wash off him.

After drying off, he sat naked at the desk and opened his laptop. The wifi was slow. Checking his email there was already one from the desk saying they'd seen the press conference and asking what was the best from the embargoed section. He ignored it, but an hour later, when the transcription hadn't arrived, he responded, saying he hadn't made it in time when it was brought forward, but he was getting the quotes.

Wearing tailored khaki shorts and a linen shirt, he took his laptop down to The Cambridge's bar terrace to get a coke and a club sandwich. Johanna, from earlier, waved to him, and he waved back.

Another 40 minutes passed until the quotes finally arrived from Max. He messaged him to say thanks and got a voice note back.

"No worries, mate. How long is that going to take you? We're just at Horace's now mate. Where are you staying? We're at the Kingston International? It's not bad. Not quite as good as last year, the pool's a bit small, but it's pretty good. Give us a shout when you're ready, and I'll get you a cold one in."

Reading through the quotes, he saw there were actually a couple of nice lines that were worth a bit more so he ended up writing a 900-word preview piece that took more than two hours to write. He got a voice note from Max and then a phone call from him, and he ignored them both. Then he got a call from Sean Wright, which he answered.

"Hey," he said.

"It's Sean, Robbie," she said.

"Hey. Yeah, I know. I have your number in my phone."

"Of course. When are you coming across? I can't wait to see you."

"Yeah, I'm gonna. I'm still working. Got a few things to take care of."

"You're in Jamaica, Robbie. Get it done, and come and have some fun."

"Yeah sure. Just got to… Where are you?"

"We're at Horace's Bar. Please come."

"I will. I'm almost done."

"Cool. See you soon."

"Yes, sure. Bye."

Robin closed his eyes for a few seconds, then opened them to look around the bar of The Cambridge, and it was still relatively empty. A married couple in their sixties, a group of sunburnt podgy middle-aged men, three preppy young men at the bar - all English and all cricket fans. He gave his copy one last read and pressed send. Then he went back to his room and waited for a reply from the assistant sports editor confirming he was happy. That took another 30 minutes.

Horace's was large and airy with a circular bamboo bar in the middle and ceiling fans ineffectively turning. It was difficult to tell where the inside began and the outside ended and bassy reggae made it disorientating until Robin finally spotted the pack gathered around two tables in the back. He decided to go to the bar and get a rum and coke first, but he was spotted by KGB.

"Pappy," he shouted. Pinky and Sours looked up and spotted him too and shouted a big "wahey" and "Pappy" and Robin smiled over and nodded. After his drink was poured, he composed himself with a swig before going over to join them.

"Hey, everyone," he said, standing awkwardly above the group. KGB, Pinky and Sours reacted like they were seeing his arrival for the first time all over again, standing up to shake his hand and loudly roaring their approval. Robin felt obliged to then shake everyone's hand starting with Jaggi, sitting uncomfortably at a slight distance from the trio with an orange juice and Max who was smiling at his unwieldiness. Ethan, sat slightly separated with the two female reporters, at the other end rose and beckoned him over.

"Great to see you, mate," he said, shaking his hand and patting him on the shoulder. "Let me introduce Mikaela Munro. She's joining us on the tour and we're all making her feel welcome."

Ethan watched her hold her hand out and say: "Miki, hi."

Robin took it and said: "Robin."

"Pappy," interrupted Ethan, and Miki giggled. She was young, awkward and far too glamorous to be part of the group. She wore strong make-up, a top that struggled to maintain her large breasts and an unsuitable tight skirt. It was already clear that Ethan was intent on sleeping with her and she was in thrall to his standing and charisma.

"And I think you know Sean," he said. Robin had tried not to look at her when he first arrived, but now he was forced to. Her hazel eyes stared back at him, and a light smile came across her face.

"Robbie, how are you?" she said enthusiastically, pulling him in for a hug.

"I'm terrific," he said, immediately feeling a lot scruffier than he had when he made his last checks in the hotel's bedroom mirror. Sean's blonde hair tousled just below her ears, shorter than the last time he saw her three years ago and the sun had brought out the freckles on her nose. "It's great to see you," he added. "How are you? It's all going well?"

"Come, sit," she said, patting a chair next to her. "I was hoping you were going to be here. I'm doing all sports now, so I couldn't miss this."

"Well, no. A month in the Caribbean. Who could?"

"It's purely sporting reasons of course," she laughed. "So how are you? I've missed you."

Robin shifted uncomfortably. "Yeah, great. I moved back up to Manchester when I left London and the desk are happy for me to work from there, so it's, yeah, really good."

"Amazing, I'm so happy for you."

"And you?"

"I'm still in Bayswater, in my old flat. But I'll hardly be there now. I'll be back for the end of Wimbledon, then obviously the Olympics, and I've got a couple of things lined up in the US after that. Busy, busy."

"And how's William?" he said eventually.

"Oh. Well. That kind of, you know, fizzled," she said.

Ethan interrupted. "Sorry. Sorry, Pappy. Sean, I was just telling Miki about that interview at the Aussie Open, but it's your story, not mine. I got to the bit about you asking him about those four double faults."

They all laughed and Sean leaned across to tell the story about speaking to a Bulgarian tennis player after his 6-1, 6-0, 6-0 defeat in the quarter-finals at the Australian Open. Robin remembered seeing it on the sports news. He had been crushed by the humiliating defeat and was barely able to speak. The punchline of the anecdote was that he had won the first game, and an Australian reporter asked him if he thought at that point he had a chance of winning, and the Bulgarian had looked almost suicidal in despair, not knowing whether it was a genuine or mocking question.

Robin spoke over the laughter and asked if anyone wanted a drink, but Ethan said a quick "no thanks" before telling a story about how he had been at an NBA play-off game in New Orleans when he'd seen it on the TV and it had even kicked a victory over the Lakers off the lead item on the news. It got a bigger laugh than Sean's story.

"So what happened to him? I've never heard of him," asked Miki.

"I think he's still playing," said Ethan. "Is he outside the top 100 in the world now?"

Robin left them to it to get another drink and signalled to Max to see if he wanted one. He got up and joined him at the bar, where he ordered another rum and coke and a pint.

"How are you doing fella?" Max said, shaking his hand again, more vigorously this time.

"Good," said Robin. "Tired, you know. But it's good to be here."

"It is mate. Better than being in Blighty. Game tomorrow and then kick back for a couple of days by the pool. Heaven."

"I see that KGB and the gang are in full flow."

"You know what they're like. They'll never change. Pinky's found a strip bar not too far away. Says it's pretty x-rated stuff, apparently."

"Jesus." They're drinks arrived, and they remained at the bar.

"Yeah. You know what they're like. You missed it before but Pinky was all over that new girl like Fat Pat's thong." That was a phrase that circulated around the group without anyone remembering its etymology.

"Christ, I can imagine," said Robin. "She needs to learn quick. What is she even doing here? I read some of her stuff. If I was being kind, I would say it had a naive quality."

"That is very generous. I can guess how she got the gig. I mean, look at her."

"She can't dress like that, man. Look at Ethan? She's got no chance. But she's got to be careful."

"Remember Tamara McGrath in Australia? Apparently, she's got the boot. That row she had the Gabba with Ethan was in some sporting gossip column. How is it she came out of that paying the price?"

"He's such a smarmy get."

"She was bloody gorgeous, though."

"I met Mozzer's wife once, you know. She's really lovely. Really sweet. Hasn't got a clue what he's like."

"Katie?"

"Yeah Katie. Two kids, too. Beautiful they are. Adore their dad more than their mum, too. Flits in and then fucks off."

"Ignorance is bliss."

"Poor thing."

"Who? Katie? Or that Mikaela?"

"Both."

Max left for the gents, and Robin considered rejoining the group but remained at the bar. From the corner of his eye, he saw Sean heading in his direction, and they smiled. She rubbed his arm warmly.

"It's great to see you," she said.

"You too," he said. "It really is. I'm pleased for you about the job, you know. You deserve it."

"Thanks, Robbie. That means a lot."

"You know I always said you were a terrific writer. I just wanted you to believe in yourself. I think you'll enjoy it more, getting away from the football beat. Some of that lot are so stuck in their ways."

"Not like the cricket pack," said Sean, nodding in the direction of the table. Robin smiled.

"You know I'm not like that lot."

"I know," she smiled back. Max rejoined them and, sipped his drink, and signalled to the barman for three more drinks. Sean was drinking gin and tonic.

"Hey, Sean. Are you glad to be here?" he said.

"Of course," she said. "So, what are your plans for the tournament? Just England?"

"Yep, just England," Max said. "I'm staying in Jamaica for the first two games, then over to Trinidad."

Sean replied: "I've got tomorrow's game, and then I'm flying to Barbados for the West Indies against Australia. Then over to Antigua for India v Pakistan, and I'll be in Trinidad for England's last two matches."

"That's similar to Ethan's I think," Max said.

"Yeah, it made sense to have a similar routine," she said.

"That's if he can get away from Miki," Robin said. Sean smiled and looked over at the pair. "Tell her to be careful, won't you?" Robin added.

"She's young and having fun, Robbie," said Sean. "She's in Jamaica for the first time. Let her enjoy herself."

"Yeah, let's have some fun," said Max, smacking Robin in the arm and carrying his pint back to the table.

"I'd better get back too. Would you like to go for dinner after the game tomorrow? I'm going early on Wednesday to Barbados?"

"I'd love to," said Robin.

Arriving at a cricket ground ahead of the game was always something special for Robin and there was that buzz of anticipation already bubbling up. The curator and the ground staff were busy on the outfield, and the security were getting ready for the teams and then the fans to arrive.

He had shared a taxi over with Max, who went straight to the press box, but Robin took a moment to stand on the boundary and take in the moment in isolation. The air was cool and the beautiful Blue Mountains looked down on the patchy green turf. Robin swept around to look at the imposing George Headley Stand and then out into the middle, picturing the great West Indian players and touring teams that had graced the sacred place.

A light breeze was drifting across the square in the direction of the short side and there was a good chance of a high-scoring game with lots of boundaries.

England were in mixed form despite having a strong squad. They had big hitters, good bowling options, both spin and pace, and batted deep, but they weren't among the favourites. If they reached the semi-finals then anything could happen but reaching the Super Eight was the first target.

Bangladesh was a tricky opener, but if they won that game then they should make it out of the first group without any issues. That was followed by the United Arab Emirates before the final two games in the

Port of Spain against Zimbabwe and New Zealand. They were all dangerous teams and England could lose to any of the four countries, or beat them all.

That's why Robin was pulsing with excitement. A healthy breakfast and tasty Jamaican coffee had invigorated him. He dressed semi-eccentrically in a pastel yellow polo shirt, Prince of Wales check Oxford bags and vintage trainers which made him feel good. As did a charming cricket chat with a knowledgeable Johanna before a brisk, bracing 10-minute walk to the Kingston International.

Max, on the other hand, was nursing a hangover. He had joined Pinky and Sours at The Silver Dollar, where they had stayed until four in the morning, by all accounts losing a fair good wedge of notes in the g-strings of the lythe dancers. KDB had been refused entry for being too drunk. Robin, in contrast, had left Horace's just after midnight and had only the three rum and cokes, although the caffeine made it difficult to sleep.

There was a dreary atmosphere on the English side of the press box where they were all grouped together when Robin finally ascended the stairs to join them. KDB belched and groaned while Pinky and Sours were tightly gripping styrofoam cups of coffee. A stringer from Florida was squashed into the corner and seemed to know Pinky but largely kept himself to himself, sucking on his vape quietly.

Below them, Jaggi was frantically typing away on his slimline Apple Mac laptop, next to Max, who was slumped in his chair, arms folded, and Robin placed his worn satchel next to him before walking over to take in a different angle of the magical stadium.

The England players were haphazardly kicking around a football while the Bangladesh side were running through fielding drills. Just inside the rope, Ethan Morrissey was wearing a headset and speaking live on the UK radio, with Mikaela just a few yards away watching. Even from a distance, it was obvious that her tight top was inappropriate as would be her cutoff jeans, if that's what they were.

Sean breezed over with a cheerful hello to everyone. Her style couldn't be more different to Mikaela's; her dapper suits and shirt and tie had become something of a trademark for covering sporting events.

She joined Robin, looking over the stadium and they made brief small talk about the game. "England won the toss and will field," came a shout from the back of the press box. Robin took his seat, and Sean sat next to him, and they made a few rough notes and talked outcomes with Max and Jaggi.

As the clock ticked down, Ethan and Mikaela arrived although there was no room for them to sit together. Mikaela sat next to Sean and said a quiet hello to everyone in that row while Ethan sat behind, clearly not happy to be alongside a sweating KGB.

"Don't worry, I'll look after you," whispered Sean and Mikaela smiled back. She turned around and Ethan was looking down compassionately.

"You've got nothing to worry about. This is the easy bit," he said but those words only seemed to make her look more agitated.

The game started slowly, with just 30 runs and no wickets in the six-over powerplay. In the front row, Jaggi typed away furiously while Max and Robin chatted about the game, as did Sean and Mikaela. Behind them, KGB and Sours groaned occasionally, Pinky rested his eyes between any shouts while Ethan and the stringer looked ostracised on each wing.

Bangladesh stepped up in the middle eight overs, taking their total to 84 for 2. With eight wickets in hand, they tried to be even more aggressive for the last six overs, but they struggled with their slogging and ended up collapsing to a disappointing 121 all out.

Between innings, Ethan and Mikaela disappeared together, and Robin and Sean went to the taco bar, although they felt bad leaving behind Max.

"They should win it from here," said Sean.

"Yeah, I think so. As long as we don't get knocked out. I can't go back to England yet," said Robin.

"Why? Are you running away from something?"

"Oh no, nothing like that. I could just do with England doing well. It's okay for you, you can prance off to Queen's Club or something. I'll be writing 'death of cricket' pieces for the next month."

"How dare you? I've never pranced anywhere in my life!"

"Sashay off maybe? Swagger off? Frolic off?"

"You can frolic off."

They took a seat behind the stand, enjoying the shade as the sun came over. They looked a curious pair, misfits that didn't belong yet also the most obvious English writers in the entire stadium.

"How's Miki? Is she doing okay?"

"You're taking a lot of interest in her. Should I be jealous?"

"I think Ethan's locked on there. Once he's got his rifle sight out, there's no escape."

"Relax Robbie. Enjoy the sunshine and the cricket."

"You're right. Where better to be? And a delightful dinner to look forward to."

"Exactly. You've been here before. Do you know anywhere nice for us?"

"I do as a matter of fact. It's a bit out of town but it's wonderful. Peaceful and has the freshest crab and seafood."

"That sounds perfect. I have to be back by midnight really. I've got to be up at seven."

"Of course, don't worry."

Applause rang around the stadium as the Bangladesh players came out onto the field. The pair quickly walked back to the press box to see the England openers striding out to the middle. And it was a good job they hurried as neither batter lasted long as they slumped to 1-2 in the first over. It got worse as they went 1-3 and then 5-4 by the end of the second.

"A bloody joke," shouted KGB, getting red in the face.

"Clueless. Absolutely clueless," added Sours.

"Nothing ever changes," interjected Pinky.

England tried to regroup and finished the powerplay on 21-4. But a potentially promising partnership was wrecked by a googly that sneaked through the gate and they were just 36-5 at the halfway stage.

"Here we go again," bristled Pinky.

"Couldn't hit a barn door from the inside," replied Sours.

"Dog shit," roared KGB.

Robin and Max were hoping for a rally, and they were pleasantly surprised. England accelerated to 75-5 from the next five overs. A run-out briefly stalled their fightback, but they needed a not-impossible 22 from the last two overs.

Hitting 12 off the 19th over, tweaked the tension up a notch further. Dot-ball, dot-ball, single left England needing nine off the last three balls. Then came a huge six, followed by a hit-and-miss that resulted in a scrambled single. Two to win or one for a super-over. The whole of the press room was baying as the fast bowler charged in. He slammed the ball into the dirt, and it smashed the bottom of the middle and off stumps, splaying them unattractively and the bowler kept on sprinting past the wicketkeeper with his arms flailing wildly as his Bangladesh team-mates tried to catch him to celebrate a famous victory.

Robin, Max and Sean subsided into their seats, Jaggi kept typing ferociously, Mikaela looked back to Ethan, and the three stooges growled and howled with their Caribbean sojourn put under threat. England had lost and were now in serious danger of missing out on the second stage of the competition already.

It was a glum mood later at the press conference and even gloomier for Robin when he got a message from the desk asking for a 1,000-word think-piece on what went wrong. He explained to Sean that he would have to push back their dinner, and they rescheduled to go to the jerk chicken cafe next to Horace's.

A good portion of his colleagues were already sitting in that very bar as Robin's head hung over his laptop back at The Cambridge bar with ice melting into his weak root beer. Johanna was finishing her shift, and they chatted briefly about the game. She said that England would need to bat smarter against the outsiders UAE as they had two similar spinners on their side. Robin nodded and then wrote the second 500 words, making exactly her point.

Among the strong, spicy smells and sweaty, sizzling sounds of Big Joe's Jerk Joint, Sean was an almost divine figure. Dressed in a lightweight white dress, she looked like a ghost hidden in the vibrant green, black and gold, the cannabis leaf prints, the noisy patois, the booming deep reggae and the local muscly men and curvy women. Yet, at the same time, she looked relaxed, leaning on the table with her elbows and giving a gentle wave to Robin when he arrived.

In contrast, Robin was utterly flustered. His forehead was already shimmering from the heat of the kitchen as he tried to find a way to Sean's table without disturbing anyone, plotting a route like a Pacman on learner level. Eventually, he stumbled into her table, wobbling her Red Stripe stubby, which was still mostly full.

"Still got that delicate touch?" laughed Sean.

Robin apologised and seconds later found himself joined by the waitress and hastily ordered jerk chicken, rice and peas to share and a Red Stripe stubby. When the drink arrived he took a big swig and finally relaxed into the stool, which wasn't easy given his rigidity. But he crossed his legs extravagantly at a 90-degree angle to the table with his shoulder resting on the wall.

"Better?" asked Sean.

"Better," smiled Robin. "You look fantastic. It's great to see you, you know?"

"You too," said Sean, putting her hand on his bare arm. "I'm glad you're doing so well, Robbie."

At that moment, he spotted Johanna sitting at a table with two girlfriends. She looked totally different out of her work outfit; maybe 10 years younger. When she looked over, he smiled and acknowledged her. Johanna responded with a smile of her own, and her friends giggled. Sean turned her head to see who he was waving to and gave a little smile at Johanna.

"Who's your friend?"

"She just works at the hotel. Johanna. She knows a fair bit about cricket."

"She's pretty."

"Sean, stop."

"No, I'm serious. You should go and talk to her."

"Sean, stop being silly."

"It's not silly, Robbie."

"As if I'm going to invite you for dinner and then go and join some other girl."

"I don't mind. And I invited you."

"Well, whatever. I'm not interested so we can just leave it."

"Okay, Robbie."

"You never change."

"I'm just having fun with you, Robbie." Robin took another swig of his beer to indicate a full stop to the conversation. "So when are you going to ask me?" she said. Silence hung in the air as Robin thought of a suitable reply. The problem was the question had been waiting to be uttered ever since she said that 'William had just fizzled out'.

Their tale began just over five years ago when Robin was working as a sub-editor and occasional cricket reporter alongside the senior correspondent William Easterhouse, who was roughly the same age. The pair became surprisingly thick, and when William was back in England, they would regularly spend nights in The Old Vine and often end up in The Two Shilling Club until the early hours.

They were a strange pair. William could be wild and was driven by adrenaline. He was a heavy drinker and cocaine user but also wonderfully charming and helped Robin get opportunities whenever he could. Robin owed a lot to his friend, who had the contacts and information to push his career forward.

William, meanwhile, found Robin as a slightly calming influence. Nights out with other friends could often go awry; fist fights, strange women, waking up in the street, everything was possible. Robin was a better alternative, plus he would always cover any indiscretions with his sixth sense of knowing when to step in with an excuse to the senior staff. They made a strong partnership.

Around 18 months later, Sean started as a football reporter and had an instant impact on the whole sporting department. Other than a meek down table sub-editor, it was an all-male environment bristling with masculinity.

Sean seemed almost immune to it with her breezy attitude that won over her colleagues, her hard work that won over her editor and her affability that led to good exclusives. On top of that, she wrote well and intelligently.

She was keen to build relationships and would often join Robin and William in the Old Vine and would encourage the night to continue at The Two Shilling Club.

In the winter, William went on the Ashes Tour to Australia. Stories were coming back that he was acting up worse than ever, drinking, drugs and prostitutes. Robin wrote several stories and columns with his friend's byline. Although the sports editor was beginning to notice, they were happy to let it slide because of William's popularity with the readers.

During that time he was away, Robin and Sean became very close friends. Their drinking adventures escalated into the odd dinner, a trip to the cinema and games of snooker.

After a late night working on the desk, they went on an impromptu night to the casino. The racing correspondent had given Robin a good tip earlier in the day, which he had shared with Sean, and they'd ended up winning a few hundred pounds. Feeling lucky, Sean had wanted to play roulette and incredibly, laying £50 on lucky number seven had paid off on the very first spin. After a couple of hours and a lot of booze, she walked out £3,000 richer, while Robin was around £40 lighter.

To celebrate, she paid for a suite at the Egerton Hotel and ordered champagne. From the balcony, they looked over the night lights of London, reflecting into the River Thames. The air was cool as they laughed and briefly danced to the sound of vintage jazz rising up from a wedding reception below.

With her arms cold, Robin draped his linen jacket over her shoulders, and she buried her head under his chin.

"You're the best," said Robin. Sean raised her head and looked into his eyes, staring for an awfully long time. He looked back, contemplating his next action, and then kissed her on the tip of her nose. "You're very drunk," he said. Sean looked at him a little longer and then finally put her head back on his chest. They stayed for a while before Sean kissed him on the cheek and climbed into bed while Robin stared across the city.

A couple of days later, Sean took a three-week break to visit her younger sister on a gap year in Australia but they messaged constantly and spoke on the phone daily.

For her last five days, she went to the fifth Test in Sydney where she met up with William. Robin never knew exactly what happened next, other than England lost in just two-and-a-half days and for the other two days, he didn't hear from either of them.

And when they returned, things were different. William and Sean behaved secretively and while it was clear to everyone on the desk what was going on, Robin was curiously naive. The new couple could never find the right moment to tell him, and it was left to a senior member of the backbench to spell it out plainly and explicitly with a dollop of schadenfreude for himself.

Sean tried to carry on as she had with Robin, messaging and calling, but the responses became shorter and less frequent, and the conversations were sparser. He stopped going to the drinking venues altogether and barely spoke with William, although their professional relationship continued. It was tough to hear about a couple of incidents involving William during a week of one-day internationals in the Netherlands. Amsterdam, with its drugs and red-light district, was a dangerous city for him to be, and he played out its worst excesses. Robin toyed with the idea of letting the indiscretions slip to Sean but couldn't go through with it. He couldn't forgive him, but also couldn't reveal his tawdry secrets somehow.

Within a couple of months, Sean had left for a more senior writing role at a rival newspaper and not long after William took a job at a magazine. Before he left, he convinced the sports editor to make Robin his successor as cricket correspondent even though they seemed set to bring in someone from outside.

Despite that, their friendship never recovered. At William's leaving party, he stayed for a single pint and said a brief thank you for his support. William hugged him and Robin responded limply before he turned and left without looking back. Climbing the stairs of The Two

Shilling Club to exit, Sean was just arriving, and their eyes met. There was something different about the way they looked at each other; the first time they really noticed each other since the casino evening. Sean looked smaller and shyer than normal, and a little embarrassed.

"Robbie," she said.

"I've got to go," he said. "I've got an early start."

"Robbie, wait." He waited. "I don't know what happened. You just never…" The end of the sentence remained unfinished. "If you need me," she added. Robin nodded and walked away. That was the last time he saw her until the previous night at Horace's.

"So what happened?" said Robin, eventually breaking the silence.

"You know Robbie, nothing very exciting. We just drifted apart. Agh, that's a cliche."

"Was there someone else?" asked Robin. He presumed that there would be.

"Me or him? No, I don't think so. We were both working hard, and we stopped… I don't need to go into it, but we sort of agreed, and that was it. About three months ago. And we've stayed friends. I think he might be seeing someone now, though. I take it you've not heard from him?"

"No. I'm not likely to."

"He adored you, you know."

Robin considered telling her all the stories and all the infidelities but decided to leave it in the past and hoped his accidental shrug didn't give any clues that there were more reasons behind his indifference.

"So, are you okay with it all?" he asked.

"Yeah, I am. I'm busy and just want to look after myself and focus on my career. There's plenty of time for all that."

They clinked stubbies, and Robin said: "As long as you're happy."

The food arrived and was delicious and moved the conversation away from their awkward discussion. Robin ordered two more stubbies and the spicy chicken was making him red and perspire. The pair were laughing and loving the street food and the evening.

Then Johanna came over, and Robin introduced her to Sean. She told them that New Zealand had beaten Zimbabwe in Guyana, and they had a brief chat about some of the players. Johanna asked them if they were going anywhere after the cafe and recommended the nightclub where she was going with her friends.

"So how about you?" said Sean after Johanna had left.

"How about me, what?" said Robin.

"Anyone?"

"I'm out of touch. Even when I was in touch, I was out of touch."

"You're better than you think." Robin bowed his head and looked at his stubby. "What about that girl?"

"Who? Johanna? I'm not going to move to Jamaica, am I?"

"You don't have to fall in love, Robbie. Enjoy yourself. You're still young, free, good looking and charming. You're touring the world and could have all sorts of adventures and all sorts of women."

"Agh. You get fed up with all that."

"Robbie!" she said, partly smiling, partly admonishing.

"You know it's not me."

"I know. You're a romantic."

It was at that point that the owner came over, and they realised that the rest of the cafe had emptied. Robin insisted on paying, and they stepped outside into the barmy night. Sean hugged him. "I'll see you in Trinidad, yeah?" she said, kissing him on the cheek and climbing into a taxi.

Robin stayed quiet and, closed the door gently and watched the scruffy vehicle drive off. When it was out of sight, he reached into his pocket and took out an antacid.

Everyone around the pool of the Kingston International was watching Mikaela Munro. A light blue bikini highlighted her deep cleavage and slim hips. Diamonds of water clung to her golden skin as she coquettishly wiggled between dips in the pool, dangling her pink-painted toes in the deep end or sucking on a long smoothie with a magazine on a lounger.

The male guests leered from behind their sunglasses. The three busboys were less conspicuous as they busied themselves with drink orders and flirting at every opportunity. When she lay on her front, letting the bikini straps cascade to her side, they found any excuse to bother her, and she giggled at their attention.

While she may have lacked confidence in her writing, she looked completely at home drawing in the admiring eyes and being the centre of attention. Robin had read her reports from the England disaster, and they were okay, although he could sense a guiding hand from Ethan. He'd read everyone's work and Ethan had written something similar, but better.

Jaggi's, of course, was the best; perceptive, intelligent and thought-provoking. There were four or five pertinent points, and Robin could take one or two of them and develop it for his preview piece. The rest were well-written and made him feel a little worse about his own effort.

But for the first time in weeks, Robin felt relaxed. The schedule was busy and this was one of the few days when he could rest. Max had invited him over to the hotel and he was happy to catch up with him properly after neglecting him over the first couple of days.

But the raging heat dried up their conversation, and they seemed content to lie on their sunbeds baking in the sun. Mikaela was a distraction, as was Robin's phone, which pinged on a semi-regular basis in the afternoon. Sean was picking his brains about the West Indies-Australia match, and then it expanded into other topics - Mikaela's bikini, good restaurants in Antigua, hotel moisturisers, etc.

Over the next few days, their conversations steadily increased with Sean calling from Barbados for some help around a story before they caught up about what had been happening. Flights had been a nightmare for her while she had felt the need to fall in with Ethan's schedule, and he was constantly doing extra bits for radio and TV stations in Asia and North America. She said she was looking forward to Trinidad and rejoining the rest of the English pack and was admiring of the tales of Mikaela's behaviour.

Robin was enjoying the tour, although it was annoying that he had to cover big matches, such as West Indies v Australia and India v Pakistan, off the TV in the hotel bar while his colleagues went to the beach or gazed at Mikaela in her startling array of bikinis.

Johanna would stop and chat when he was in the bar, and at the end of one shift, she got out of her uniform to join him to watch the conclusion of the West Indies victory over Ireland, excitedly shouting at the screen and drinking a local white rum and sparkling grapefruit juice. In a close game, the home side won with three balls to spare, and she started dancing at the conclusion when the barman turned up the calypso music to celebrate the victory. Robin watched her, smiling, but resisted when she tried to pull him up to join him. She called her friends to meet up and Robin finished his report.

The one nagging issue was England's chances of reaching the Super Eight, which had improved slightly but still looked perilous. They thrashed the United Arab Emirates, but Bangladesh had also beaten them to keep qualification in their hands.

England's victory was their final day on the island and was marred by an awkward celebration later that evening. The six English writers, plus the stringer, two people from the media team and four of the Jamaican organisers went for a stylish dinner in Irish Town.

As the hosts were picking up the tab, KGB, Pinky and Sours got stuck into the white wine and quickly sped through their charisma levels - charming, funny, irritating, obnoxious and finally embarrassing. The lowest point was when Pinkerton said that it would be better for the tournament if England qualified in the last-eight rather than Bangladesh, as there were too many teams from the subcontinent sure to qualify as it was. Graham-Brown upped the ante by calling their team 'lucky punkah-wallahs,' which had everyone shifting uncomfortably in their seats.

Robin responded by saying that the phrase was offensive and also that Bangladesh had earned both their wins in the tournament so far. KGB mumbled something about them not earning their place because they didn't have a good Test team and Robin snapped back that he was out of touch.

The table fell quiet as KGB retorted that he was a dismal county failure and a dismal writer. That left Robin smarting as he couldn't hit back as Graham-Brown had always promoted the idea that his lack of a career was due to a stress fracture in his back and that some had talked of him being a future England captain when he was at Oxford. It wasn't true, but to point that out would not have been de rigueur, even to his insult. Instead, he declared that KGB was, in contrast, a very good writer but could also be a 'loud-mouth prick' on occasions.

Pinky and Sours looked shocked, but KGB smiled, raised his glass, and told him he was right. It diffused the situation and kept their corner of the quiet from dominating the conversation.

In the taxi back to the hotel, Max and Mikaela praised Robin for what he'd say, and Jaggi was unusually strident, calling the three of them 'ignorant buffoons.' Mikaela asked everyone for one last drink back at the hotel but Robin declined as they were flying the next day, although he was pumped with pride at seemingly coming out on top in his mini-confrontation.

Seconds after touching down in Trinidad, Robin turned on his phone to discover that New Zealand had narrowly beaten Bangladesh. There were also three messages from Sean, who in the first was looking forward to coming to Trinidad, then that their flight was delayed and then that it was delayed again and asking if he had arrived yet. He sent a short reply as he descended the airplane steps but presumed she was in mid-air by then.

Max and Robin shared a cab, although they were again staying at different hotels. Max was staying at the ultra-modern De Stijl Rooms, which was all glass and shiny bold colours. A few hundred yards down the road was The Invader's Bay View - a smart, pink, colonial-style building perfectly stylish with efficient service. Robin's ocean-side room was light and airy and offered an amazing view of the sea, although there was no beach.

On his phone, Sean had left a message saying she was about to take off and was landing at about 10pm and asking if that was too late for supper. He dashed off a reply saying he would wait for her, hoping that it would arrive before she took off, but there was no instant response.

Instead, it buzzed with a phone message from Max asking what he was doing for dinner, saying that he had accidentally agreed to go out with KGB, Pinky, Sours and some 'local dude called Angus', who was working the game and was going to 'show them the best spots'.

That felt like code for strip joints or possibly even brothels, and he replied that he didn't think it was a good idea after their little spat. He received another long audio message telling him that no one had even mentioned and it had probably been all-forgotten and not to worry about it, adding that Angus apparently knew loads of great places. But Robin said he would leave it for now and do it another night. Max didn't reply.

Sean messaged when she arrived, and by then, Robin was already sitting in the Cool Cafe and Bar with a white rum and grapefruit juice and a rumbling tummy. The air was chilly, and through the dark, barely lit by the fairy lights and flame torches, entwined couples could just be seen, wrapped around each other in warm cardigans under heaters with the noisy groups of friends inside.

Other than the light from his phone, Robin was almost hidden in the corner in his dark jacket and trousers. He was going through his colleagues' work and was shocked to discover Mikaela's exclusive interview with the England captain, who declared: 'We can still win it'. Annoying as it was, he had to admire her 'get' and messaged her to say well done but didn't receive a reply.

Sean arrived and looked around for Robin but couldn't see him. He waved and finally stood up to join her, and she smiled in relief, and they hugged sideways with one arm and he kissed her on the cheek.

"Thank god you're here," she said.

"Thank god you're here, I was going to start eating the bamboo fence."

"It's nice here," she said, rubbing her bare arms.

"Do you want to go inside?"

"Christ, yes."

There was a warm ambience inside the Cool Cafe and Bar with young groups of sophisticated Trinidadians. Loud reggaeton drummed out repetitively and some people were dancing and swaying along. Robin had felt like he would have been conspicuous in the trendy spot on his own, but sitting alongside Sean he felt comfortable and welcome, although he was in a hurry to order the chicken and seafood platter.

"How's it been? Are you enjoying the trip?" Robin shouted over the sound of the music.

"It's been tiring. Good. But tiring."

"It will be spending that much time with Mozzer."

"He's okay. I know he's not your type, but he's funny."

"I like him."

"I couldn't have got through Barbados and Antigua without him. I don't think I'll see much of him now he's in the same place as Mikaela."

"Oh yeah? Are they getting on well?"

"I wouldn't say well. I think she pesters him a lot, but at the moment, he's happy enough."

"He will be, but his wife and kids might not agree when they get back to England."

"Now, now, we're not going to get another sermon from Pappy the Preacherman, are we? Just let them get on with it. What does it matter to you?"

"She's a nice girl."

"Oh, I know her appeal. Ethan showed me some of the selfies she sent. Nearly turned me."

"Yeah?"

"Almost pornographic. In fact, there probably were some that I didn't see. Calm down, Robbie. I haven't got copies."

"Oh shucks."

"But I can recreate them," she said, striking a few poses, parting her mouth and putting her tongue in the corner of her lips, then thrusting her head back and half-closing her eyes and finally putting her arms under her breasts and pouting.

"I haven't got the tits!" she said, and Robin laughed awkwardly.

"I dread to think what she got back in return," he said. At that point, he took a bite of a large king prawn; Sean began to laugh, and soon they were in hysterics.

They laughed a lot for the rest of the night until the Cool Cafe and Bar closed just after one. Next door's Cool Club was still going, and most of the revellers made the 22-yard pilgrimage, but Sean was getting sleepy.

"I think I need to go to bed," she said.

"That sounds like a good idea," he said.

They made their way outside, and Sean clung lazily to his arm as they waited for a taxi to pass. A shiny black Mercedes pulled up and they got inside and relaxed into the leather seats with Sean leaning her head on Robin's shoulder. First stop was the Invader's Bay View and Robin put his hand on the back of her head and gently lifted it off him when they arrived.

"Don't fall asleep before you get back," he said.

She smiled serenely as he closed the door. The car drove the last few hundred yards and, on his tiptoes, he could just about see Sean as she got out. He wasn't sure, but she might have been looking back. She disappeared inside just as his muscles twitched to wave.

While everyone was lying by the pool at the De Stijl Rooms, Sean went the other way to join Robin at the Invader's Bay View. Both were feeling the rigours of the tour and chilled lazily, drinking rum and grapefruit juice and eating fruit and then Escovitch fish, followed by more fruit.

Max had left a message but Robin knew it would be an invitation and left it until mid-afternoon before listening to it, but by then a second had arrived. He was wrong on this occasion, though. In the first, he talked about feeling dreadful and that the previous night had got pretty wild and that he wasn't entirely sure what happened, but he had a vivid image of Sours getting a blowjob from a rotund prostitute and getting back at about six in the morning. In the second, he was starting to come around, but he broke halfway through, and vomiting could be heard in the background before he came back and said scratch that I'm going back to bed.

He played the message to Sean, who shrieked, laughed and gave a mock face of incredulity. She was stretched out in the sun, enjoying the doing nothing part. After Robin sent a lengthy reply, Sean lay on her front and asked Robin to rub sun cream on her.

Around late afternoon, as the heat died down, they talked and joked and played silly quizzes until Sean asked what they were doing for dinner. She said she had brought some clothes with her, and they decided to eat at the hotel. Robin suggested she go up to his room to get changed, and an hour later, when he politely knocked on his own door, she scrambled out of the bath in just a towel, apologising and saying she had lost track of time.

Sincerely, he told her not to worry and went out to his balcony while she got ready and he checked on the stories that had come out of the World Cup. Only Jaggi from their group had written anything, a feature on the Queen's Park Oval pitch and why batting first might be a good idea. His room smelt deliciously of Sean's coconut and mango moisturiser and Robin took in deep breaths as he got undressed before his shower.

Dinner was delightful on the hotel terrace, and they talked about all sorts of subjects, eventually landing back on William and whether it was done. Sean said they had a great time but it was closed; no way back. Her phone rang, and she whispered that it was Ethan.

"That sounds good. I'll see if Robbie wants to come," she said, putting her phone to her shoulder. "Ethan's hired a car and driving up to the north of the island tomorrow where there's this amazing beach. He's taking Miki. Do you want to come to?"

"I can't. I'm going to the New Zealand-UAE game tomorrow. I've got a short report to do, and I want to check out the pitch and conditions."

"Are you sure? Can't you get someone from the office to do the report and say you're busy on something else?"

He pondered for a while before finally saying he couldn't really.

Sean relayed the message to Ethan and then hung up. She said she was getting tired, and Robin walked the few hundred yards back to her hotel with her. At the entrance, she kissed him on the cheek, and he told her to have fun at the beach.

New Zealand batted first and won easily against the United Arab Emirates. Robin also bumped into a former Australia captain and that made a nice exclusive to go with his preview piece for England's game against the UAE the day after.

His phone was mostly silent all day, although he got a voice note from Max early in the evening. He'd gone on the day trip to the beach, and he said they wouldn't be back until later as they were staying in the area for dinner.

The following day, Robin joined the four of them at the De Stijl Rooms, where they hung around the pool before watching Bangladesh's game against Zimbabwe. England's hopes of staying in the competition were looking ominous, needing to win their last two games, including against a strong New Zealand team, while their run rate was also poor in comparison to their two rivals should they all finish on three wins.

It got worse when Bangladesh started in style in their last match, hitting 221-3 to set Zimbabwe an almost impossible target. Robin was getting antsy with the group as they watched in the hotel bar, along with a crowd of sunburnt England fans, and was slightly patronising to Mikaela when she asked a simple question, and Ethan shot him an annoyed look.

At the end of the innings, he decided to take a stroll to get a coffee and calm down. Sean joined him and successfully got his mind off the cricket and more chilled. And by the time they arrived at the Cool Cafe and Bar, his mood had improved.

The cafe had only one small TV, and it was showing a repeat of a classic World Cup match. He took out his phone to confirm the reason why: "It's raining!" he said. They stayed for an hour, chatting and watching his phone until the message came through that the match was abandoned and ended in a draw without a ball of the Zimbabwe innings being bowled. It was a tough break for Bangladesh but winning their final two matches would now guarantee England qualification.

Max left a voice note to tell him the news in case he didn't know, and Sean said they should invite them over to join them, which he wrote in reply.

Inside 10 minutes, Ethan, Mikaela and Max arrived, and the mood was joyous. They drank a lot of white rum and grapefruit, with everyone seemingly easy in each other's company, although Sean caught Robin's unease at the public petting by two of their party.

Drunk, they all easily continued onto the Cool Club, where they danced and partied with the local Trinidadians who made them feel welcome. The atmosphere was charged in the small, dark room with sweaty bodies grinding to the thumping primal bass. Flashing colours swirled in the darkness, and bare flesh, arms, and legs shimmered in the disco ball. Ethan and Mikaela were getting particularly carried away with the uninhibited freedom on the dancefloor, moving closely and sensually like they were the only two people in the room.

Sean watched them and smiled. Her movements were gentler and less obvious, but she was enjoying herself. A local boy in a white vest, with thin muscly arms, came close to dance with her, and she matched his rhythm, bending her knees and throwing an arm around his neck. But she brushed him off when he tried to get a little closer, turning to dance in another direction and shoving him away when he tried to follow.

Two girls from the group also moved close to Max and Robin. Max was not a good dancer, although he was trying to enjoy the moment, but his partner quickly disappeared.

Robin was better, and when the girl backed into him, he responded by resting his chin on her shoulder and hands on her waist as she wrapped her arms around his head. Among the smell of perspiration and cigarette smoke, she smelled delicate and fresh, possibly of sandalwood and peach, and he closed his eyes to inhale the aroma. At that moment, he lost the rhythm of their movement, and the back of his hand accidentally brushed the underside of her large breasts. He immediately said sorry, and she moved away, more annoyed with the way he stopped to apologise than the incident itself.

Sean was laughing, and Robin soon started laughing too. As the song changed, she took the girl's place and danced close with him, backing into him. Robin took up the same pose and was careful not to follow suit, although he was distracted when she exposed her long neck to the side as she enjoyed the sway of the song. Robin was too embarrassed by his physicality and stepped back to maintain a gap between them until she turned, and they danced facing each other.

By then, Max was somehow back with his local partner while Ethan and Mikaela were nowhere to be seen. But Robin's eye contact with Sean was broken by a kerfuffle to the side. They couldn't hear what was being said, but Max had clearly done something to upset the local girl, and her friends were piling in to seemingly protect her, attacking Max.

Robin moved quickly to try to calm the situation and within seconds, had bundled him out of the club with Sean following behind. Fortunately there was an old Vauxhall taxi waiting outside, with the driver in place, and they moved off with the group still shouting after them angrily.

In the short distance to the hotel, Max protested his innocence, saying something along the lines that he thought she was up for it. At the De Stijl Rooms, Max climbed out and thanked Robin for stepping in to save the situation. He asked Sean if she was coming, and she smiled at Robin before following him out.

They moved off and, in the few hundred yards to the Invader's Bay View, the driver said: "A good night, brother?"

"Yeah. Well, I think so," Robin said.

Robin's head was throbbing when the bedroom telephone rang. It was reception, telling him that there were two local gentlemen here to see him. He bolted upright and said that there must have been a mistake and they were asking for the wrong person. But the receptionist insisted that they wanted to speak to Mr Miller.

After getting back in the early hours, Robin had thrown up all over his bathroom before passing out on his bed. It was only as he walked down to the lobby, in shorts, t-shirt and sliders, that he remembered that fact and also that he hadn't cleaned his teeth.

Before he could grab a glass of water, the receptionist introduced the two men, and Robin said hello. They perceptibly winced and motioned towards two sofas, and moments later, a waiter brought over coffee, which the Englishman guzzled rather rudely.

They introduced themselves as Gaz and Wheels from the Cool Club. They said they would like to speak to his friend from the previous night, but they were having trouble tracking him down.

"Wait. How did you find me?" Robin asked. It briefly crossed his ego that they might have recognised his byline picture.

"We know the taxi driver," Gaz said. "He told us he drove to the Invader's Bay View, and the ride was charged to a Mr R Miller. He remembered you because you didn't leave a tip."

"Shit," Robin muttered.

"So is he staying here too?" Gaz asked.

"Who? Max?" he said, followed by another "shit".

"Yeah, Max," said Wheels. "Where's Max?"

"I don't know. He came back here, and then he took off. I don't know where he's staying. We're just here for the cricket, you know."

"England?" said Gaz.

"Yeah," said Robin.

"England are shit," said Wheels and they both laughed.

"Well, yeah but. Look, I'm sorry I can't help you."

"Will you see him at the game?" said Gaz.

"Maybe, I'm not sure."

"He was out of order, last night. We need to straighten things out," said Gaz.

"I don't know what happened. I was just trying to calm it all down."

"My sister was very upset," said Wheels.

"I'm sorry to hear that."

The pair looked at him closely. "Okay. If he's staying here, you're gonna be in a shit-ton of trouble too. You get me?" said Gaz.

"Yes. I get you," said Robin.

They got up to leave, and Wheels said: "And clean your teeth you dirty cyat!"

Robin did a confused sort of hat-tip in their direction and watched them depart. Then he raced up to his room to call Max who didn't answer. He rang again but no answer or the third time. So he jumped into the shower and cleaned his teeth then tried the phone again.

"Oh man, what is it?" said Max, wearily.

"Those two guys from the club. They're after you," exclaimed Robin.

"What two guys?"

"You remember. The end of the night. Something happened with that girl and then we had to make a quick exit."

"Yeah but. I thought she was. You know, she was dancing and. It was a misunderstanding. Nothing serious."

"Well they just came to my hotel, and they seemed pretty serious to me."

"What the fuck?"

"Yeah. They threatened me. Well kind of. But they're after you."

"Shit, what the fuck?"

"I don't think they wanted to discuss your 800-word think-piece on West Indies' top order."

Max was clearly rushing around the room and panicking, muttering: "Think, think."

"Look, just don't come over here, okay?" said Robin. "They don't know where you're staying. All they know is you're here for the cricket and that your name is Max."

"Shit, how do they know my name?"

"I don't know. They must've heard someone say it in the club."

"Right, right."

"Look. Get your shit together. Jump in the shower, you'll feel better. Just don't come here."

"Okay. Thanks Pappy. You're a real pal."

Robin then phoned Sean and relayed what had happened and also said it was probably a good idea that she didn't come to the Invader's Bay View to which he agreed.

After telling her to be careful and hanging up, he switched his phone off in a panic, the perceived threat washing over him. He went to the restaurant for a buffet lunch but hardly ate anything before returning to his room, where he spent the first hour on the balcony until it came into his head that a gunman could take him out from his first floor perch. Ridiculous as the idea was, he moved inside and lay on the bed.

The phone was strangely quiet, and he remembered that he had switched it off. Putting it on, he found a flurry of messages from Sean and a voice note from Max.

He read Sean's messages first:

"Max's in a bit of a mess. He wants to go back to England. Will you talk to him?"

"I'm going to go with him to the airport."

"Is everything okay?"

"Let me know you're okay, you've not answered."

Robin dashed off a reply saying that he was fine and that his phone had died before listening to Max's message.

"Hi mate. Listen, I think I'm going to get out of here. I've spoken to my desk, and I'm going to get over to St Lucia early for the Super Eight games. I was going over anyway after the groups whether England go or not and they don't mind me going a bit early. I've got a couple of contacts there, so might get a head start on a couple of features anyway. I'm sorry about all the fuss. Honestly, I thought it was on, like fat Pat's thong, and the next thing it's all kicking off. You're a real pal and I appreciate everything. Be careful. I don't suppose I'll see you in St Lucia, but you never know. Stranger things have happened. New Zealand might rest a few. And keep an eye on Mozzer. And if you could send me the quotes from the presser that would be great. Cheers pal."

Two things came into his head. Firstly, it seemed a good solution and secondly, he'd forgotten all about the press conference. He got a taxi, seeing no sign of Gaz and Wheels, and arrived just in time.

The pack stayed to write up their pieces, and Robin was the last to finish.

"I hear it all got a bit exciting last night," said Ethan.

"You know what Max is like," said Robin.

"I thought you were all lovers not fighters," said Ethan, and Mikaela giggled.

"What are your plans tonight? Miki's found a nice seafood restaurant. Not far from here," Sean said.

"I'm still feeling a bit rough. I think I might have an early one," Robin said.

He watched the three of them disappear and heard his phone vibrate with a message from Max. "Thanks for the quotes, pal. Jesus, it's absolutely beautiful here. The hotel's right on the beach and you can even get wifi on it too. Sitting in the bar with half a coconut, listening to Barry Manilow and I feel like the luckiest guy in the world. We do okay don't we? It's a simple life. If I don't see you here, I'll see you in Edgbaston okay? St Lucia's like Birmingham anyway, without the wow factor. Come on England!"

Robin smiled and returned to his hotel, going straight to his room to watch a dead rubber between Kenya and Scotland.

England's victory over Zimbabwe passed off without major incident. Robin spent the day by the pool, eschewing an invitation to go to the De Stijl Rooms. Around tea time, he went to the ground and this time headed straight to the media centre and didn't leave until the game was over.

He scoured the stands looking for the presence of Gaz and Wheels and the darkness of the night and strange and unfamiliar sounds of the fans, the mesmeric calypso beat, and a vociferous angry MC put him on edge. He saw what he thought were two suspicious characters midway through the first innings on the open side to the right. He watched them for the next four overs, and they disappeared, which made him nervous. It wasn't until they reappeared towards the start of the second innings with a third man and three women - two in England shirts - that he relaxed.

Sean was sitting to his right and could sense his anxiety and tried to ease his nerves, firstly by being relaxed and then by openly telling him to calm down and that there was nothing to be concerned about. Ethan was more flippant with his reassurances, but his nonchalant air was strangely more comforting.

The game itself was pretty straightforward, with four wickets in the powerplay, meaning that England were always ahead of the game. Copy was filed shortly after the last ball, and just before midnight, the pack headed to a local bar for drinks, although Robin declined.

All the nervousness and stress had left him shattered and he slept through until late morning. There were three messages on his phone from Sean when he woke up:

"Hope you're feeling better about it all. Don't stress Robbie x"

"I wish you were here tonight. This bar is amazing, you wd love it xx"

"Wanna go for brek or lunch? X"

He quickly replied that lunch sounded good but Sean apologised and said she had now arranged to have lunch at the hotel with Ethan and Mikaela before going to the press conference, but he was more than welcome to join.

The three of them were sitting around the pool in their swimming costumes, and not only did Robin feel overdressed, he felt over overdressed, deciding to wear long - if thin - trousers - and a smart shirt with a press conference in the afternoon. Ethan seized on it. "Did you think you were still in Manchester, Pappy? Those gangsters will never spot you in that gear. You look like a local."

The girls laughed, and Mikaela gave him a playful slap in rebuke. But then they stretched out in the hot sun, their bodies turning golder, while Robin sat at a table a short distance away with a glass of bitter blood orange, waiting for a club sandwich.

Behind his sunglasses, Robin watched them and felt apart but idly assessed them. Ethan wasn't muscly but his body was taught and fresh compared to Robin's skinny fragility. Mikaela was like a glamour model, buxom and seductive, but also a touch cheap.

Sean was wearing swim shorts and a matching crop top, fleshy but subtler. Her freckles were more visible and her trademark buck-tooth smile was never far away with her joy and lust for life. Her delicate fingers smoothly rested in mid air. While her restless right leg shifted between bent and straight with her ankles and toes taking on ballet points.

A heavy slap on the shoulder disrupted his gaze. "Pappy, how are you doing my friend?" said KGB.

"Hey, KGB. How are you?" said Robin.

"She's a bloody goddess isn't she?" said KGB.

"Yes she is."

"That Ethan's a lucky dog. Good on him. If I were 20 years younger." A busboy came over before he could finish his sentence and Graham-Brown ordered a double gin and tonic and bacon burger.

After a little small talk, they moved on to tomorrow's game and while they were in discussion, the other three disappeared to get ready for the press conference. It started out as a friendly chat but soon got overly heated. Robin had asked what line-up England should go with for tomorrow's match, suggesting four-seamers to bowl cutters into the pitch. After politely saying that was ludicrous, KGB argued they should have three spinners with a back-up fourth option as New Zealand struggled to slog-sweep. Robin said that there was zero evidence of that, and the conversation got more and more aggressive until Sours and Pinky arrived and sided with their drinking pal.

The other three returned, and they went off to a straightforward press conference. Having not seen Gaz and Wheels since their visit to the Invader's Bay View, Robin was starting to feel more relaxed and joined the others for dinner at a charming restaurant out of town.

Sean and Ethan were guests on a cricket podcast so joined later and Robin sat between Jaggi and Mikaela and accidentally got drunk very quickly. It was in stark contrast to the majority of the party, who were feeling jaded after the previous night's excesses, other than the usual heavy-drinking trio and with the thought of joining them in the Cool Club and a 10am game start, the night ended abruptly with Robin feeling short-changed. For the majority, they would be covering the rest of the tournament whatever, but Robin's desk had told him he would be returning home to cover it if England were knocked out so it could have been his penultimate night in the Caribbean.

He was particularly peeved that Sean was ending the night early and she got a little cross with him, saying he should have come out the night before and that she was shattered and couldn't go wild every night.

Back at his hotel room, Robin sent a message to her: "Soz, was just in the mood. Been a bit stressed last couple of days. See you tomorrow x". He watched his phone, but it didn't immediately blink. He went down to the hotel bar and had a rum and coke, while watching the highlights from a game from 2005.

Eventually, his phone lit up with a message from Sean. "I'm fine x" she replied. Robin ordered a double rum and coke and settled into his wicker chair.

There were nerves in the Queen's Park Oval media centre before the game had even started. It was a cool and misty morning, and England, after losing the toss, were put into bat. After a promising start, they finished on a 162-6 as boundaries became harder to come by.

By the time New Zealand came out to bat it was the hottest day of the World Cup, and the pitch was dry and dusty. After reaching 101-2 off the first 10 overs, the match was swinging heavily in favour of the Black Caps. And choosing four fast bowlers, as Robin had suggested, was looking like a mistake.

Robin was fraught, biting his nails, running his fingers through his hair and ignoring KGB's jibes about going with spinners that were being echoed by Pinky. In the 11th over, the one spinner bowled a wicket maiden, and he was torn between being happy that it improved England's chances and that it proved their point.

By the 15th over, he was all bowled out, and New Zealand had moved onto 124-4 but were struggling for boundaries. A mixture of off cutters, leg cutters, slower ball bouncers and yorkers were proving hard to hit.

Robin was sweating in the heat, but as the game ticked down to an agonising climax, he was suddenly struck by a sense of serenity. He rocked back in his seat and took in the Queen's Park Oval, from the sun over to the Northern Range backdrop, the partying and noise in the stands and the smells of curried goat that wafted in and the succulent fresh fruit being eaten by colleagues.

On the pitch, the Kiwi batsmen wiped their brows as they took on water. The England captain with dirty trousers, held his cap as he and the bowler manoeuvered the fielders around the outfield. Jaggi was boiling with enthusiasm, even KGB, Sours and Pinky were fevered. To his right, Sean was biting her knuckle and he looked at her lips and watched her breathing. She turned and smiled at him and asked how he was doing. He nodded confidently and thought how lucky he was to have this life.

New Zealand were happy to take singles from the next two overs and moved onto 136-4. They targeted the 18th over and hit a boundary and a massive six as they moved to within 14 runs. But the critical 19th over started with a superb catch at fine leg. After two dot balls, the batters tried to scramble a single but the non-striker was run out. Two singles took them to 150-6 needing 13 off the last to win.

Robin's tranquillity had long since passed. The possibility of a win was on. He mopped his brow as the pack argued over fielding positions. Eventually, the over started and, after a single, the ball was launched into the stand and the crowd went crazy. Six to win off four runs, they hit an easy single but the fourth ball passed through to the wicketkeeper, just at eye-level height.

A brave ball and the media centre seemed to gasp as one. Even better was the next one, a slower ball yorker that smashed the wicket and the England fans roared. So too did the press pack who were now on their feet or wandering around to stave off the tension. A six to win or a four for a tie off the last ball.

The New Zealand batter ambled out to the middle slowly and it took almost five minutes until the ball was finally delivered. Aiming for a yorker, the ball pitched too short and in the slot for the batter to smash a massive straight drive. The entire ground watched it loop into the sky as the fielder desperately ran round the boundary. He thrust out his left hand, and the ball bobbled off his fingers. His right hand tried to take it but it bounced up again, before he grabbed it at the third attempt and sank to the turf in relief as his team-mates sprinted over.

Cheers erupted around the media centre, and Robin punched the air before hugging Sean. After holding on for too long, she wrestled free and hugged Mikaela and then Ethan while Robin high-fived Jaggi and then Sours and Pinky.

Euphoria ran through his report and he gave a satisfied slam of his laptop after getting the all-clear from the desk that they were happy with the copy.

"I'm going to take you for the best meal of your life," he said to Sean, who was still finishing her copy.

"What's that?" she said.

"Let's go for dinner. Somewhere amazing. Get stinking drunk and do something stupid."

"Oh Robbie. I'd love to. But I've got an early evening flight."

"What do you mean?"

"I thought England were going out so we're off to Barbados for a few days. It's Australia v India in a couple of days."

"You're going tonight?"

"Yes. In like two hours."

"Have you got time for a quick drink?"

"I don't think so. We've got to swing by the hotel to pick up the bags and then we're off to the airport. What's your plans?"

"Well I was booked on the flight to St Lucia tomorrow lunchtime already so I'm just sticking to the plan. I'm gutted. No you, not even Max. The best game I've ever covered."

"Sorry, Robbie. Why don't you ask Miki? She's staying."

Ethan wandered over. "Great game, Pappy," he said.

"Amazing. Absolutely amazing," Robin said.

"How are you doing, Sean? There's a taxi outside for us," Ethan said.

"I'm done," she said, quickly typing a sentence, re-reading her intro before pressing send and closing the lid of her computer. She stood up gathering her things and said: "What a game." She put an arm around and gave a brief kiss on Robin's cheek. "Meet me in St Lucia," she said.

"Zing, zing, zing went my heartstrings," sang Robin.

"Huh?" said Sean, smiling and frowning at the same time.

"Meet Me In St Louis. You know, Judy Garland? Great film," said Robin.

"We'd better go," interrupted Ethan and the pair bundled their way out, shouting goodbyes to the rest of the room.

Robin looked out onto the pitch as the ground staff worked away with the roller trundling along in the late afternoon sun. The stands were now empty and the magic of the day had already floated off into the sky.

Knowing that Ethan was going away, Mikaela had arranged a beauty treatment and an early night, KGB, Pinky and Sours had found an Irish pub full of England fans and Jaggi had disappeared unnoticed.

Robin got back to the hotel, ordered a pint of lager and listened to a voice note from Max.

"Yes Pappy. What a win. What a fucking win. I thought he'd dropped it. My God that was amazing. Mate, get yourself over here tomorrow. It's bloody paradise. I'm so happy you're coming. Who is it? Pakistan, West Indies and Australia, that's bloody tough that. But if you want to be the best, you've got to be the best. But at least we made it out of the group. I've got to be honest, I'm a bit blotto. Met a couple of people out here, and we're having a great time. Don't know where we're going to end up tonight."

He texted back: "Have a good one," finished his pint and went up to his room.

St Lucia was paradise, just as Max had said. This time, Robin was staying at the same place as his colleagues, at The Challengers Club Hotel. It was a relief to get away from Trinidad and the threat of Gaz and Wheels. Particularly as they were both outside the Invader's Bay View Hotel when he got his airport taxi before stopping to pick up Jaggi and Mikaela. He slunk down in the back seat, even with the tinted windows. When his colleagues came down, the local pair got interested and spotted Robin just as the cab pulled away, shouting and swearing after them.

It wasn't until they took off in the small twin-engined jet and looked down on the little island that he could finally relax. Barely an hour later, they were touching down and making the short bus ride to the north of St Lucia.

A couple of new reporters as well as Max, were already waiting there to join in the tour, having flown in from London. Tristan Constable was a former player and part-time journalist who hung out with the radio teams and generally didn't mix with the written press.

The other was Daryl Queensland, another former player but from Australia, who worked as a freelancer for publications across the world. While the Aussie press were staying at the nearby Royal Villas and Daryl knew the majority of them, she wanted to stay with the British reporters as she was covering the tournament from an England angle.

Unlike the superior Tristan, who looked down on anyone that hadn't played the game, Daryl was warm and friendly with everyone and had a phenomenal understanding of cricket that she was more than happy to share. Her and Mikaela instantly became very close, with Daryl generously taking her under her wing. She loved her new nickname of 'Queenie' bequeathed by KGB while Tristan smarted at being called 'Coppers' because of his name and red hair. The latter of those traits kept him off the beach while the rest of the gang hung out there during the day, working and relaxing between press conferences and matches.

The Super-Eight started with Pakistan beating Australia. Robin and Sean exchanged messages about the tournament but they were less frequent than they had been. It was hectic where she and Ethan were with New Zealand winning against South Africa, on the final ball and then Afghanistan beating India, which was a huge story.

India's possible exit meant she would delay her journey to St Lucia as she would cover their next game against New Zealand, and her frustrations seemed clear in her brief messages to Robin.

In St Lucia, drinking and entertainment were mainly contained to the Challengers Club Hotel, partly because it was beautiful and peaceful and partly because of the unfortunate events at the Cool Club and Robin's insistence of avoiding a repeat. Max and Robin still enjoyed themselves, mostly on the beach with white rums and grapefruit.

Relaxing on the loungers, they made friends with the two young beach waitresses Rhian and May, who were giggly and flirty. They laughed at everything Max and Robin said even though it was clear that sometimes they didn't understand the lame jokes they were forced to listen to. Their reward was handsome tips, particularly from Max, who would whine and lust after May before and after she brought the drinks. Their uniforms, baggy grey and white striped shirts with tight unflattering navy skirts, were plain and neutral, but still it would be enough to get him overly-excited, worse after a couple of rums. His comments to May became more and more overt, but they were, at least, not as bad as what she was subjected to by Sours after a heavy afternoon of whisky.

Rhian didn't take any messing about from him and he then put Sowerby in his place on her behalf, and they carried on serving them like nothing had happened. With May dragged into conversations with Max, Rhian was occasionally left to stand and talk with Robin, and she was perfectly charming. He asked her about cricket, 'not interested', St Lucia 'wonderful, but I want to see the world', what she did for fun 'not much, studying, for a law degree' and a whole of other things that she didn't seem interested in. Still, she was perfectly polite and asked questions about London despite him repeatedly saying he didn't live there.

On the morning of England's first game, they spent a few hours on the beach, Robin drinking apple juice and Max on rum and chasing May. He didn't notice the dark clouds move in overhead as the worst fears about the weather forecast came true. Max stayed at the beach while Robin went to his room, and just as he opened the door, he heard the rain slowly then quickly begin to pelt down on the balcony windows.

He stared through the glass and watched the last of the beach dwellers, including Max, sprint for cover as the rain smashed down. It was torrential and lasted hours, flooding the patio, and the normally benign sea crashed in white waves, curling and spraying magnificently. Robin watched it all and felt helpless as the call came through that the game with the West Indies was called off.

Despondency would be washed away by a long bath he decided, and messaged Sean from his supine position, but she didn't instantly respond, presumably at the India press conference ahead of their game the following day, and they exchanged only a couple of brief messages with Sean saying she still didn't know what her plans were.

Frustratingly, the storm disappeared by around 6pm and was replaced by marvellous sunshine. Max and Robin headed off for dinner with Mikaela and Daryl. The women wanted to talk cricket and how they thought a point against the West Indies might be a good result. Max wanted to talk to May.

That afternoon in the bar, he'd asked her out for dinner, and she'd said 'maybe' rather than a straight 'no', and he was tediously talking about how beautiful and effervescent she was. The women laughed at his out-of-character description, while Robin slightly rudely commented that there was nothing more boring than listening to someone pine for an unrequited love. Max snapped back that he didn't know that it was unrequited, and who was he to talk to anywhere. Robin shifted apologetically in his seat and let him continue to talk about May while he ordered a second bottle of white wine for the table and half-listened.

The tournament continued to throw up surprises and the drama was making it a must-watch around the world. India were beaten again, narrowly by New Zealand but still remarkably had a chance of progressing after South Africa beat Afghanistan in the other game in Group A.

England's chances, however, were on a knife edge. West Indies won comfortably against Australia meaning defeat to Pakistan would make it almost impossible for them to progress.

Robin was nervous on the morning of the match and spent the afternoon exploring the cliffs by himself and then heading down to the delightful Donkey Beach, listening to an audiobook. He took in the island's beauty, the delicate flowers that grew on the cliff edge and the occasional orange orioles that flitted by like an amber warning. On the beach, the salty air tingled his tongue freshly and the sea aroma filled his lungs. It cheered and rejuvenated him, away from the heavy drinking and heavy work of the past weeks.

Sean wasn't coming over for the game. She and Ethan had flown to Barbados for India's final game and would come to St Lucia if there was anything riding on England's last match.

He had tried to convince her about the beauty of the island and what it had to offer, but Sean was too conscientious to ignore what her desk wanted to do. Laser blue seas, hideaway coves, elegant untold restaurants, he poured himself into messages, spending more time trying to persuade her to come over than he did on his copy. But she apologised and said it was impossible and her later messages even hinted that she was slightly annoyed about it all.

Two jet skis whizzed past noisily, drowning out L P Hartley's The Go-Between on his headphones. It was Mikaela and Daryl, and they whooped and cheered as they skidded around the ocean. Mikaela waved and shouted at Robin when she spotted him, and he politely acknowledged them before they sped off to where they had come from.

Mikaela seemed distinctly unbothered that Ethan was not returning either. The pair of them had been like a honeymoon couple in Trinidad, constantly disappearing and reappearing, unashamed that everyone knew what they had been up to. But her carefree attitude remained constant throughout and arguably, her work was better than ever. Daryl was selfless with her advice and they made a good team as Mikaela soaked up her knowledge of the game and was repaid by her ebullience.

The interruption had distracted Robin and he put down the headphones and decided to wade into the sea, not too deep, just enough to cover his ankles and then shins. The North Atlantic Ocean was cold, but he tried to stick it out for as long as he could. He returned to where he had left his bag and sat in the sunshine, thinking about home and his family. Then about, Sean and he played with the sand, watching it run through his fingers. He picked up a delicate shell to take home with him as a reminder, but part of it was broken. He tried to find a better one, but there were no others that he liked.

Back at the hotel, Max was still on the lounger and was in high spirits. "We're going for lunch tomorrow," he said.

"Sure. Where do you want to go?" said Robin.

"No, stupid. Me and May."

"Oh. I see."

"She's the most incredibly sexy woman I think I've ever seen. I knew I'd wear her down eventually. Peanuts always gets results."

"I'm going for a shower," said Robin, wandering off. He thought it was strange that Max had referred to himself as Peanuts. He had a premonition of the future, that he was the heir to KGB, Pinky and Sours; a drunken old hack, red-faced louche, nomadic cricket bore, never thinking a new thought, never writing a new word. He slapped himself in the face, angry at his meanness and under the tumbling water of the steaming shower, tried to reset his brain and focus on the cricket.

It would be painful - even more painful than his slap to the face in the shower. England were atrocious in a resounding defeat. Batting first, they faced the ignominy of scraping 90-8 off 20 overs, not even being bowled out for such a low score. Pakistan took just over 12 overs to win, losing only a single wicket. Such a big defeat meant England were essentially out. As a flick over the rope sealed the result, a message pinged through from Sean: "I'm not coming to St Lucia, soz x".

On the day before England's final game, the entire pack went for dinner. West Indies had beaten Pakistan on the previous night meaning the match against Australia would mean nothing to either nation. It was a huge anti-climax; a flat ending after the incredible way they had qualified. Robin would be flying back to England the morning after the game as would Mikaela, KGB, Pinky, Sours and Coppers, with the rest going to Antigua for the semi-finals and final.

Sean would have flown over on the morning of the game, but now there was no point. She was in Bridgetown for the excitement that was unravelling in the other group. New Zealand had beaten Afghanistan emphatically on the previous night meaning India only had to win against South Africa to make the last four.

At the Challengers Club Hotel, they gathered in the bar and watched the start of the India game before heading out for dinner. Sean and

Ethan were both featured in the pre-match build-up on the TV and both looking relaxed and handsome. Sean in a cream muslin jacket, white silk shirt and black tie, looked incredibly stylish and spoke eloquently about South Africa's chances. Ethan wore a sky blue jacket and dirty yellow relaxed collar shirt that looked incredibly cool and was something no one else could pull off. He too spoke confidently, about India, and the pair laughed and chatted easily with the host.

They were the best of the English press pack. He looked around the table: the ugly physicality and opinions of Graham-Brown, Pinkerton and Sowerby, the shyness of Jaggi, the superiority of Tristan, the lack of knowledge of Miki, the Australianness of Daryl, even the self-aware discomfort of Max and Robin on TV and radio, he had to confess the pair were easily the best to represent them.

Mikaela smiled enigmatically at the TV. "You missing Mozzer?" asked Robin.

"Not really. He's a bit full of himself. But he does look great in that shirt," said Mikaela.

"We're in St Lucia, mate. There's only you moping about," interjected KDB. Robin gave him an angry look and Mikaela was clearly uncomfortable and started a chat with Daryl. "Oh come on, lighten up," added KDB, but Robin got up to go to the bar.

He was sad about England's exit but wanted to have an enjoyable final evening, final day and final cricket match and resented the remark. He watched the group from the bar and wondered where he fitted in. KDB's gang were rowdily guffawing, Jaggi and Tristan were waving their arms around animatedly, Max, Mikaela and Daryl were sharing a joke. At times, he saw himself as a bridge able to join two differing views. A kind of Istanbul - a meeting point of two different continents, belonging to both and neither. Tonight, he was more like Perth, remote and isolated, yet a part of things.

Dinner was at The Estate House, where they joined the Australian pack, with many of them heading home as well. The food was fabulous;

an unrelenting relay of plates of fresh fish, seafood, steak, light curries, noodles, salads, fruits and cured meats, which they picked through all evening.

Either side of Robin were two Australian reporters, Nathan Cooper and Shane White, names that he recognised and respected. They talked mostly about cricket, a little about where to visit on the next Ashes tour and touched on other subjects, but his mind was on the India game and also about Sean and Ethan. He was jealous to not be with them. On the TV, the wild atmosphere had been building before the game with India's passionate and vibrant fans taking over the Kensington Oval.

He checked the score regularly on his phone and messaged Sean, but she was probably working hard. South Africa had batted first and made a decent but not insurmountable 164 for five. As much as the food and evening was incredible, when Daryl suggested going back to the hotel, he leapt on the proposal and rounded up the English pack. Pinky and Sours in particular, wanted to stay, but their minibus soon arrived, and they were corralled into it.

India were 78-3 off 10 overs when they got back to the hotel, with the pack regrouping in The Challengers Club bar to watch the conclusion. It was set to be an exciting finish and Robin couldn't decide who he wanted to win. India added something special to the tournament, but it also seemed a little unfair that they could still go through having lost twice while England were already out after a washout and single defeat.

KGB on the other hand, was very clear that he wanted South Africa to go through. He had friends, family and colleagues from there and an affection for the country and there was always a feeling that he and his two friends hankered for a colonial past where the white man knew best and was in charge.

With a brain anesthetised by an overdose of white wine and now topped up by an injection of single malt whisky, his lips became looser. In the 13th over, the black fast bowler sprayed the ball over and went for 20 runs. "Pathetic," launched KGB. "You can't let someone like that bowl."

"Someone like what?" replied Robin, angry and full of booze himself.

"Bloody brainless," said KGB, glaring back. The bowler came back on for the 15th, and the black captain came under fire. "I'm sorry, but they need a skipper who knows what he's doing." It wasn't overtly racist, but Robin knew what he was getting out.

The first delivery was smashed to the boundary. "Fucking clueless," rasped KGB. The second beat the bat. "Poor shot, that was a bad ball," he said this time. The third slammed into the India batter's front pad, but the umpire turned down the lbw appeals. After a quick chat, the captain signalled for a review. "What are you doing?" shouted KGB. "That's never out. Can't someone take charge of these two."

Finally, the screen showed the review, clipping leg stump. The batter was out. Robin roared. "Good job, you're not in charge KGB," he said. There was no reply.

After two play-and-misses the last ball was a brilliant slower ball yorker that banged into the middle stump. KGB squealed with delight. "You've got a fucking nerve," muttered Robin.

"What was that?" said KGB.

"You were having a go at him in the last over, and now he's got two wickets."

"Oh hello. Pappy's come to life. I know you're sulking, but don't take it out on me."

"I'm just sick of hearing your shit."

"You can't blame me for what's going on." Robin looked puzzled while KGB shared a joke with Pinky and Sours.

"You haven't got a clue what's going on," said Robin.

"No my friend. You're the one that hasn't got a clue what's going on," said KGB.

"I don't get it," said Robin.

"You might know a bit about cricket, but my god, you know so little about everything else."

He saw Mikaela's and Max's heads swing around quickly to Robin with shocked expressions on their faces. But he still looked quizzical.

"What do you mean?" he said.

"Do I have to spell it out, honestly? Sean and Robin. Paradise, and you lost. You had your chance. Just like your shitty playing days, you missed your opportunity."

Robin stormed off angrily and was followed by Max. "There was no need for that."

"He's a cruel bastard," said Max.

"All I wanted when I was growing up was to be a cricketer. That's below the belt, the fat twat."

Max nodded but looked quizzical as he tapped him on the neck compassionately. They went onto the terrace, which was chilly and deserted, but the giant TV was still showing the cricket. It wasn't that thrilling a finish. India won with 15 balls to spare.

"You want another drink?" asked Robin.

"Aw mate. I'm meeting May in 10 minutes."

As Max wandered off, Robin checked his phone but he had no messages and went up to bed. He passed the press pack on the way to the lift and KGB was holding court with the others, laughing along.

England was cold and wet. The Springboks were touring and the first two days at Edgbaston were abandoned without a ball being bowled.

Robin sat alone in the corner writing short think-pieces on each day and occasionally reading his Graham Greene book.

Max was a couple of seats away, and they conversed occasionally as the hours ticked down. He was lusting after a young woman who helped to serve the lunch and tea but he still had time to lengthily describe his last evening with May, returning to the subject regularly and seemingly without any self-awareness. Also forgetting the long voice note he'd sent to him.

KGB, Sours and Pinky nodded when they bumped into Robin, but they kept apart. Jaggi somehow busied himself on his computer, presumably, some fantastic piece on no cricket would be coming, while the rest of the England media were made up of semi-acquaintances and footballer reporters on secondment for the summer.

Mikaela was at the golf, Coppers was on the radio, and Daryl had returned to Australia. Sean and Ethan were at Wimbledon, which was somehow escaping the wet weather and the country was engulfed in tennis-mania with a 16-year-old from Sunderland reaching the quarter-finals.

The morning of the third day was delayed, and Robin stayed in bed in his hotel before wandering down to the ground in mid-afternoon, just as her game commenced. Edgbaston was almost empty and they bowled 15 overs before the day was abandoned. By the time he got back to the hotel, the young Sunderland star was knocked out but emerged a defeated hero.

Days four and five were pointless as the game petered out to a tired draw before they debunked to Lord's for the second Test.

Robin's metropolitan hotel was dreadful. From the outside it looked like a traditional London villa and was located within walking distance of the ground in Marylebone. But it was badly beaten up. Flea-bitten carpets, off-white white walls, bath without a shower, a locked window without a key, TV without a choice of channels.

He was stale and fatigued when he arrived at the ground, and as he walked through the nursery towards the Media Centre, he felt a tug on his arm.

"Hello stranger." It was Sean, and she pecked him gently on the cheek. She was radiant and fresh, freckles dancing around her face from a season in the sunshine.

"Hey," he took the kiss clumsily. "I didn't know you were going to be here."

"Yeah. Just this Test I think. I'm heading out to California next week so I don't know if I'm going to be back. I might take a couple of weeks before the US Open."

"I saw you were covering the tennis. Did you enjoy it?" Robin had read every word she had written, and the rhythm and vocabulary was very different from her cricket pieces and popped with a different energy.

"It was good. It was only my second time there, but it's a special place."

"Ethan was there too. I'm sure he could show you the ropes."

"Listen. I've got to go and do some reports for Australian radio. They're paying me a fortune. I'm going to be in the radio box, but we could meet after the game. Go for dinner, maybe?"

"That would be nice."

"I got to go," she said, touching his arm and rushing over to a young red-haired man with a headset who was waiting for her.

Lord's has a special aura that never fails to excite and Robin's mood was uplifted at the hum ahead of the first ball, looking down at the lush green turf and across at the historic pavilion. He talked enthusiastically with Max over coffee and even made a comment of support at KGB's indifference at the batting selection. They were both wrong. England bludgeoned their way to a brilliant 404-4 by the close of play.

After filing his copy, he realised there was a message waiting for him from Sean. She hadn't written since he replied to his message on his final day in St Lucia. "Happy landings x" she'd written. Shattered on touchdown, he had opened it and considered writing that he was back in England but decided against it. There had been no correspondence since.

"I'm just behind the media centre. Let me know when you're ready x."

"Coming now," he dashed off before dashing down the steps to quickly join her.

London was at its best with the early evening warmth and a hazy golden glow of light. They walked slowly through Regent's Park, past the lovers still lying on the grass through their lazy day and the couples softly shuffling through the sunshine.

They talked about everything and nothing. Tennis, cricket, California, writing, friends, enemies, family, love, leisure and how to say scone. At The Riverside, they continued for hours sitting outside, even when the chill became too much. They'd forgotten to eat, other than four packets of crisps and got gently drunk on gins and tonic.

Shortly after they called last orders, it was time to go. Standing to leave, Robin pulled Sean into her chest and, wrapped an arm around her and rubbed her goosepimpled muscles.

"You're freezing," he said.

"I've missed you," she said. He continued to cuddle until her phone pinged, and she broke free to read it. "I'd better go."

"Okay. It was great to see you again," Robin said.

"You too," said Sean, and she walked off, turning around to blow him a kiss.

It was to be a remarkable Test. England declared on 555-6 just before lunch on the following day. After taking a wicket in those 10 minutes, South Africa were bundled out for just 86 in the afternoon session and made to follow on. They were even worse after tea and were all out for 70 after an extended session.

Robin revelled in the victory, and it was a hectic postmatch with interviews and extra pieces required after such an extraordinary victory. After finishing his work, he saw another waiting message from Sean. "I came to see you, but you looked really busy. I'm going to head to the States early now. Great to see you. x".

"Great to see you too, have a fab time x" he replied.

"I'm sorry about everything x" she added.

"You don't need to be" he replied.

After a win at Trent Bridge and defeat at Southampton, he returned to London for the final Test at the Oval and messaged Sean in case she was back in the city. She sent back a picture of herself on a beach, with the caption: "California, baby x" He sent back a picture of himself in front of a window, with drips falling down the glass and a woman struggling with an inside-out umbrella in the background with the caption: "London, baby x"

She sent back a crying with laughter emoji. The final Test was a rain-affected draw with action on each day but never more than 40 overs. Somehow, it was Robin's favourite match of the summer.

I LOVE YOU, BUT I'VE REALLY GOT SO MANY THINGS TO DO

Dr Barelli-Minch had been a big help to Nigel in the past months. They talked over his past indiscretions and what they meant, picking out each of the people involved and how it had affected them. Maybe Renée knew and was at peace with it? Maybe she passed away in happy ignorance? Maybe it would have been selfish to have confessed everything to her?

The last one was tricky as the therapist didn't know about his revelation to his children. When Nigel told her, typically, she took his admission in her stride and freestyled a positive response, saying that it was obviously something he had wanted to do, and that made it important.

She was a master of soothing his guilt and helping him to want to rebuild a constructive final few years of his life rather than let them go to waste. He was busying himself, painting - landscapes rather than nudes now and would regularly get out to the Lake District, Pennines, the Moors and even had a few days in the Highlands of Scotland. He also started volunteering - as a litter picker, at a food bank, and as an assistant cricket pitch curator at Robin's old club, and took up walking football to stay fit.

Home was still a strange place, frozen in time. The warmth was gone, and images from the past could be chilling. Renée with the baby twins, a beautiful radiant picture but out of frame, the secret shadow of Melanie in her lovenest apartment. Renée and Nigel in the searing heat of Nice, moments after he had held back in a cool cafe to text a love note to Carrie.

Memories were everywhere. From the obvious reminders like her clothes in the closet and her books in the bookcase to the spices in the spice rack that he would never use and the bath bombs that would never explode, or whatever it was they did.

Any silence was torture. Creaks from above sounded like Renée's shuffling footsteps but then he felt it was just the house punishing him after also being present at his confession. He felt like he'd let the home down too - a cosy shell cracked by his dishonesty. A kitchen cupboard slammed violently in a draught, had him instinctively racing to see she was okay but, of course, there was no one there. It felt like the house was angry, too, and he audibly apologised.

He made it his mission to cheer them both up. Blue Note jazz played regularly throughout the house and audiobooks throughout the night. Fresh flowers every week added a sweet smell, and all those tiny blemishes - chipped paintwork, squeaky windows and stained grouting - were all upgraded.

Slowly, the ache began to ease, but sticking plasters would never be enough. Renée's absence left a gigantic hole and he was trying his best to fill the space. But there were so many other gaps in his life that he wanted to bring back together.

He hadn't heard from Robin, Lo or Wilf since they left and didn't want to push them into contact. However, Dr Barelli-Minch encouraged him to 'reach out' as she put it. Eventually, Nigel nervously sent out a WhatsApp message to each of them individually. They were all different, but the crux of the sentiment was the same: I'm sorry, I'd love to see or speak to you, but I understand if you don't want to. Please let me know you're okay.

The messages went out mid-afternoon, and Nigel took a long walk through the uneven, scruffy streets with his phone in his hand the whole way round. But there were no replies, not even blue ticks. He sat in the Shakespeare, which had now become a regular haunt, with a pint of Heatons 47 and the mobile resting on the table.

After a bath, he listened to some Blue Note jazz and flicked through a library book of a collection of modern landscape painters. He thought he saw the screen of his phone light up and expected to be disappointed. He wasn't, it was Lo. "I'm good, hope you're okay x". At that moment, Dexter Gordon's Cheese Cake kicked in through the speakers, and it felt magical. For something so seemingly ordinary, it was one of the most special moments of his life.

He replied instantly with a simple red heart and then decided to leave it there. For the next 48 hours, Nigel felt amazing, but there was no response from Robin or Wilf. After careful consideration, he sent another message to Lo. "I'm not going to bombard you with messages. But I've not heard from Robin or Wilfred. Do you know if they're okay too? X"

It took another couple of days before a reply came through. "They're fine x". Simple as that. Nigel was relieved. He didn't know if he would ever see them again, but it was some sort of start.

Tidying the house, he found one of Renée's lockets in the sideboard. Inside was a picture of a young Robin with the twins on the other side. Nigel could swear it hadn't been there before and considered it was possibly a reward from the house for giving it some relief too. He knew it was crazy but he was happy to go with it and whispered: "Thank you. I'm not losing my mind. I just want to say thank you for whatever made this happen."

After a week and another summit with Dr Barrelli-Minch, he tried another message to Lo. "Are you in Manchester? It would be great to meet up. I know I've let you down. But you and the boys mean everything to me x".

This time, it took 72 hours before the response came through. Lo wrote: "I'm not in Manchester. What's done is done. Not just now but when I'm ready. I love you, but I've really got so many things to do x". Nigel's heart missed a beat, and he turned up Chet Baker a little louder.

Crossword solving was getting better, and one joyous morning, Nigel completed the cryptic puzzle flawlessly and relatively quickly. He celebrated by taking a drive out to Macclesfield and painting the hills above Cheshire. He went for an experimental style, plastering on bright colours thickly, hinting at the landscape rather than an accurate recreation. Completing it, he took a step back. Was it any good, he wondered. Probably not, but he liked it, and that was enough.

At home, he left his brushes and paints in the car and headed straight to The Shakespeare. Mayumi was working, a delightful film student who served behind the bar, and they chatted regularly. She was a shining diamond in the dump and admitted it was not a place that she would ever have been seen dead in. His arrival always seemed to be a relief to her, too, someone different from the bawdy regulars and the glaring stares.

Nigel stood at the bar for a few minutes, and they conversed gently. Mayumi was having a few problems with her girlfriend. He listened and offered no advice. She loved her, he knew, and they would work it out. His feeling was informed by accidentally seeing them walking through Manchester city centre, holding hands and giggling together.

As Mayumi served another customer, Nigel took his Heatons 47 to his familiar corner, and on the TV screen he never usually watched was a Test match between England and South Africa. He thought of Robin and assumed he would be there. He took out the locket, looked at the pictures and smiled. Robin would be okay, he thought. And so would Lo. Wilf was more of a concern but Dr Barelli-Minch had suggested perhaps it was his time to flourish. He really hoped so.

Rain lashed down on his way home. Nigel was still in the light jacket, polo t-shirt and slacks he'd worn for his day painting, and by the time he turned the key in the door, they were all sticking to him. He dripped onto the welcome mat in the darkness and flicked off his squelching shoes.

Looking up, he saw a warm shaft of light streaking down the hall and watched it grow bigger before being disturbed by a gentle shadow. "Hey. You're soaked," said Lo.

"It's absolutely chucking it down," beamed Nigel.

"I'm going to stay for a few days," she said.

"Stay as long as you want."

"I'm still mad at you."

"I know."

Lo wandered over and gave him a small hug, but it ended quickly with his dampness. "Jesus. Go and get changed." She walked off back into the living room.

The shower was hot and Nigel's tears mixed with the steam. Drips ran down the tiles as if the bathroom was sharing in the emotion. Lo's Medea of Mayfair products were already balanced on the edge of the bath, along with a lady's razor. She'd already taken a dip, messed up the towels, and the dull soap now seemed to be a more vibrant white.

Composed again, Nigel boiled milk in the kitchen. "You want a hot chocolate?"

"Yeah. I will. Thanks," shouted Lo. He stirred the drinks and carried them into the living room, burning his index finger and rushing for his daughter to take her drink. He settled in the armchair with Lo stretched out on the sofa.

"What are you watching?" Nigel asked.

"Not sure," she said. "Something about vampires."

"You okay?" he said.

"Yeah, I'm fine."

"What have you been up to?"

Lo didn't take her eyes off the television and at no point altered the intonation of her voice. "This and that. I've been to see friends for the summer."

"But you're okay?"

"Yeah, I'm good."

They both slurped their hot chocolate and watched the teenage drama. Nigel eventually broke the silence. "I am sorry," he said.

"I know," she said matter-of-factly. The lack of emotion was a kind of forgiveness. She laughed at the bizarre love triangle unravelling on the screen. Nigel sneaked glances at her when he could and smiled, and looked at the photograph of Renée looking down - her smile seemed bigger, higher at the sides and cheeks more pointed.

"Are you hungry?" he said.

"No, I'm fine."

"Do you need anything? You know where everything is, but if you need anything."

"I know."

"Where's your washing? I'll put it on tonight."

"It's all right. I'll do it in the morning."

"Okay."

Nigel washed the mugs and stood momentarily in the back garden, looking up at the sky that had now cleared after the shower. A fox was at the bottom of the garden and emerged into the moonlight, staring back angrily. He looked at it, marvelling at its elegant red tail, soft fur and piercing amber eyes. It wasn't going to be intimidated, and it was Nigel who backed away inside.

He tidied up the rest of the kitchen, wiping down the sides and putting the crumpets next to the kettle so that Lo could see them if she wanted any. Outside, the fox had disappeared into the night, and Nigel returned to the living room. "I'm going to bed," he said.

"Okay," said Lo.

Stopping briefly at the door, he said: "It's great to see you." There wasn't a response, but he didn't leave any time for one, closing the door and climbing the stairs quietly.

Wilf's return was a bigger shock. The weeks had passed away quietly with Nigel's life largely undisturbed by the return of Lo. A pattern of painting, therapy, volunteering, walking football and a couple of nights at the Shakespeare continued.

Conversations with Lo were slow - uneasy at first but became more comfortable the more she settled. She was subdued at first after what had happened in Bexhill, back under her childhood roof and the reminders of her mother and the lack of trust for her father.

Gradually, that wore away, although his infidelities were never discussed, almost like the confession had never been made. Sometimes, she looked at him with pride, he was living a positive life. Sometimes she felt a frustration at the disappointment that he'd delivered. Over a period, it became like an annoying itch, a permanent irritation like a tickle under a tattoo that couldn't be reached.

It was just something to live with, and she opened up over time. She talked about her summer; her job, her time with Chloe, but not Benjamin. She spent a lot of time writing and hanging around in her pyjamas.

Nigel was happy to have Lo back but was also concerned for her. She was drifting a little without an engine or rudder. He thought about what Renée would say to her. It was difficult to approach but he had to say something to get her out of her slumber. His natural thought was to say something like: "Your mother would want you to get out there and go for life rather than hanging around here." But he'd lost the privilege to speak on behalf of Renée to their children like that, and anyway, it felt like a cop-out; it needed to come from him. It was difficult but he finally brought it up over a lunch.

"Lo," he stuttered. "It's great to have you back. It really is."

"Thanks," she said.

"Wait. It's great to have you back and I know you've had a difficult few months. But I'm a little bit concerned about you."

"You don't need to worry about me."

"What are you going to do Lo? I know it's been hard, but you can't hang around here in your pyjamas forever. Have you got a plan? Any ideas on what to do next?"

"I'm writing. I'm writing a book. I've given myself another couple of months to finish it and to see what happens."

"That's great, Lo."

"Well, we'll see how it goes. I've got a friend from Oxford who's had a look at some early pages. She really liked it."

"Chloe?"

"No. She was a scientist."

"Oh I see. Why don't you invite her up? She was very kind to you."

"We fell out. She won't answer my messages." Before Nigel could speak, Lo shut him down. "We're not talking about it."

After a short pause, he said: "It's just. You don't go out. I've not seen you with any of your friends."

"You don't need to worry. I've got my books and my writing and Vampire Diaries. Honestly, I'm all right."

"The Shakespeare is looking for someone behind the bar. Now you've got experience. I could get you a job."

"The Shakespeare? That dump. Is that where you go drinking? I remember going in there when I was 16. It's a right hovel."

"Yeah, it is. But what do you think?"

"I'm not working at The Shakespeare. I'll get a job if you want some board."

"It's not that. I just want you to be doing something. Something to get up for."

"I've got something to get up for. My writing and my books and Vampire Diaries."

"Okay, something to get dressed for."

"Okay, okay I'll get a job."

Nigel collected the plates and gave her a kiss on her cheek as he walked past. "And by the way, Vampire Diaries is crap."

"Hey!" she smiled.

Just 48 hours later, she did her first shift at Ragged Wood, a trendy cafe bar in West Didsbury. It couldn't have been more different to the George and Dragon in Bexhill. Daytime it was full of single workers with their Apple Mac laptops, ordering coffee and salads and using the wifi. In the evening, it got lively with younger locals squeezing in for continental lagers and listening to the incredible playlist compiled by owner Marcus.

Lo liked it there. In the daytime, she could work on her book, sometimes being there for an hour without needing to look up to serve anybody. At night, she made friends with her new colleagues and Marcus, who bought a good bottle of South African brandy and a case of homemade Somerset ginger beer made with chillies, which was not for customers, and they would drink together in highball glasses with organic Seville lemons over ice.

Nigel walked past one evening and saw her looking relaxed and enjoying herself. She was soon working five and sometimes six shifts a week and would get there early or stay late, even spending a couple of hours there on days off as her novel progressed rapidly.

Returning home after a game of walking football, he heard Lo talking and laughing in the living room. He clicked the front door quietly, gently lay down his bag, slid his shoes off and tiptoed upstairs in his socks as silently as possible so as not to disturb them.

It was a couple of hours later that Lo saw the shoes and bag and realised he was home. "Dad," she shouted from the bottom of the stairs. He didn't initially respond. "Dad. Are you up there? Come down."

He emerged on the landing and halfway down the stairs, Wilf stepped out of the living room doorway. "All right," Wilf said insipidly. Nigel had not asked anything of Lo about her brothers other than assurances that they were okay. His return was a total surprise.

Nigel hugged him tightly and whispered: "I'm sorry."

"All right," said Wilf again.

"You want a cup of tea?" interrupted Lo.

"I'd love one, love," said Nigel.

"I'm all right," said Wilf.

Nigel laughed and put his arm on his shoulder. "Are you staying?" he said.

"If that's all right?" said Wilf.

"It's all right," smiled Nigel.

Christmas sneaked up. After a low-key autumn tour to New Zealand with the cricket die-hards of the press pack, Robin was back in Manchester and would occasionally call in for dinner, but lived at his flat a few miles away.

He was decidedly frosty towards his father, and their differences were never really settled. Even a clear-the-air drink at The Shakespeare didn't truly resolve the matter. Robin was angry and could never fully forgive him, but the kindred harmony between the siblings kept him hanging around.

There was a lot Robin wanted to say to his dad, but mostly he sulked. His mother wasn't faultless, but her blemishes were small and cute compared to his monstrous carbuncular dishonesty. He wanted to call him names, wanted to drive his face into the shame he'd crapped over all of the family and his memories. But he concluded it was pointless and would only increase the hostility with the atmosphere restful with the others.

He came close, once, in the garden. It was a nothing event that provoked a violent eruption of anger. Nigel shifted a plant pot around the back of the garage, and Robin told him to leave it. It was in the way his father insisted. Robin repeated again to leave it, remembering the Mother's Day he'd hauled it into its spot.

"Just leave it," he screamed spectacularly, picking up his glass of coke and almost hurling it at his head.

"Throw it," said Nigel, seeing him pause. "Throw the glass at me if you want to." He did want to, but he put the glass down on the table and left. The plant pot, at least, was to move back to its previous position, although Nigel still didn't know why it was so important.

The twins had moved on, though. Lo was content working on her book, now going through a heavy rewrite in its second draft. Wilf was freelancing computer work from home and getting handsomely paid. As the weather turned, Nigel slowed down and spent more time at home, yet saw less of the kids which, contradictorily, made him pleased that they were getting on with their lives.

Christmas Day would be awkward - the first without Renée. But they all made themselves busy to avoid any mawkishness. Ragged Wood invited a group of local homeless for lunch and Lo insisted on working for free. Marcus gave her a bottle of her favourite South African brandy, and they enjoyed three or four Horse's Necks later in the afternoon, getting gently squiffy. Lo left at the right time with the potential that something might happen that she didn't really want to.

Robin had stayed at his flat, and Wilf stayed in bed until lunchtime and then played video games - downstairs rather than upstairs in a sort of acknowledgement of the day. Nigel went for a long walk, calling in at the Shakespeare for a short drink and watched the thugs and drunks in there, celebrating with their paper hats, and somehow enjoyed being part of it.

He got talking with Ronnie, a heavily tattooed labourer who was in Manchester to see his brother and to pick up his three kids early on Boxing Day morning and take them back to Birmingham. Ronnie kindly offered to get rid of the fox that was now forever in Nigel's garden.

"I've got two pit bulls that will rip that fucking thing apart," he said. "Show no mercy. They're a pest, foxes. Vermin. Princess and Leia will love it. It will be good exercise. And you'll enjoy watching that fucking thing having its neck pulled open."

"I really wouldn't," he said, declining the offer.

Around 4pm, he returned home to make dinner while Wilf was reading one of his books. It wasn't anything overly exciting, a large roast chicken, roast potatoes and parsnips, carrots and peas. He forgot the gravy and stuffing, but Robin had some and brought them over.

The family opened small gifts, nothing too exciting but a thoughtful array of books, perfumes and clothes, and Lo put on ubiquitous Christmas songs that the others had heard regularly for the past few weeks. She hadn't; the music at Ragged Wood was far cooler than to give into the festive fare, but now she was enjoying it in an unironic way.

Dinner was okay, the meat was dry, and the potatoes weren't crispy enough, but the gravy covered over the issues. After eating, Nigel decided to make a very short speech.

"I don't want to make a big thing," he started. "Just to say, you'll never know what it means to me that you are able to join me today. I won't ever forgive myself for what happened and what I did. I'm just so proud that you're all better people than me."

With that, he picked up a couple of plates and hurried out of the room to stop the emotions overwhelming him. Robin rolled his eyes in the dining room, and the twins smiled back.

They thought they heard a knock at the door above the familiar sound of Mistletoe And Wine. They heard the door open and wondered who it was. Nigel didn't have too many visitors now that the excitement of Renée's passing had died down and the well-wishing vultures had moved on to another cadaver. They tried listening but couldn't make out who it was. Robin turned down the music but other than it being a woman's voice, none of them could make out anything that would indicate who it belonged to.

The dining room door opened, and the father stepped in. "There's someone here to see you," he said. The three of them watched as the woman appeared by his side and smiled nervously.

"I'm sorry. I shouldn't have…" she took a deep breath of composure. "I was in love with you, and I didn't realise."

By the middle of January, the offspring had left Manchester. It happened sharply but semi-serendipitously. Robin was back on tour with the England squad; Sri Lanka followed by Bangladesh this time. Lo's book had evolved into a gothic vampire allegory that had attracted interest from major publishers, and she was in and out of London offices as a deal and decision became closer. Wilf was offered a role in California for a smaller gaming company for a lower salary but would be given almost free reign over creativity and direction and he moved instantly once it was confirmed.

Back home the weather was awful. A snow storm and freezing temperatures lasted for weeks. Nigel was alone but the house was glowing with warmth, and he hibernated surrounded by the comfort of his familiar things. He listened to jazz regularly and, drank tea and ate ginger nuts.

From the back bedroom window, he painted a snowscape of the white rooftops over West Didsbury and his garden below. At one point, the fox appeared its majestic red fur in the snow like a ruby-stoned ring on a pale finger. It reversed away slowly, briefly looking up at Nigel, but they never saw each other again. He hinted at the animal in his painting, but it was more of a celebration of the surroundings.

Later, as the snow melted, Nigel re-emerged to take in the new world. He wandered around the park as the earliest snowdrops began to break through, and the pushchairs were taken out by proud and fatigued mothers for the first time in weeks. New flats were being built on the other side of West Didsbury and a new small cafe bar had opened.

Dr Barrelli-Minch was moving to Australia, and before she left, he wrote a charming thank-you letter and gave her a generous voucher for a case of wine. She recommended her successor, a slender man from the Home Counties, but he politely declined, truthfully saying that he now felt no desire to go to therapy.

"I'm cured," he joked to the pair of them following his last session.

"If you ever need to talk to someone, don't be afraid to reach out again," said Dr Barrelli-Minch soberly.

Nigel felt the same about The Shakespeare, he no longer felt attracted to it. During his time at home, Wilf had stopped drinking Heatons 47 and had moved onto a refreshing Filipino lager called Dian Masalanta which he had developed a taste for. Of course, there was a bar in West Didsbury that served it, and he would occasionally call in at The Jampot for a bottle.

More than anything, he felt a new tranquillity. A painful period had subsided significantly, although the scars had made him move a little slower and more warily. Phone calls were occasional with his children, but they all seemed to be blossoming, and he asked for no more. Occasionally he would hear details that would cheer him.

Lo's life was hectic and it suited her. She moved into an extravagant shared warehouse loft in Shoreditch with a graffiti artist and a young TV producer. Her novel was creating a buzz even before it was published, and she'd signed to the notorious hard-edged publicity agent Martha Parker.

Smart and straight-talking, she was semi-famous as a representative of many stars and dedicated her career to getting incredible deals for her clients. She wanted Lo on her role call, and that in itself was an incredible achievement for an unpublished author. A leading company offered a three-book deal, but Martha negotiated a five-book deal with a more favourable advance and the opportunity to renegotiate better terms after the second came out.

Lo admired her drive. She was in her fifties but looked fabulous and dominated whatever environment she found herself in. Her frenzied worklife between London, New York and Los Angeles was all-encompassing, and Lo wondered what she did for pleasure. She had no husband or children or seemed to do anything other than dinners and red-carpet events.

After a couple of Horse's Necks at a glamorous party, Lo once bravely asked what she did for fun and got the enigmatic response: "You don't need to worry about honey. I enjoy myself when no one's watching."

In Sri Lanka, Robin was enjoying cricket and touring again. The characters were all the same, but he had found the centre of his own Venn diagram, a sweet spot between colleagues and friends and doing what he wanted.

Walking on the soft sand of the beach in Galle after the first Test in the warm sun was a special moment, peaceful and beautiful. An early finish in the game saw him take an uncharacteristic wellness retreat in the hills near Dambulla. Following the third test, he stayed on for a week, volunteering at an elephant orphanage. Sri Lanka had echoes of St Lucia, heavenly and intoxicating, and he immersed himself in its splendour in a more considered way.

In California, Wilf was more relaxed than he had ever been in his short life. The small company was flourishing, and he worked when he wanted, hard and ferociously, and relaxed on other days when he wanted a break. It was quiet in his little villa, looking over the vineyards of Mendocino County and he could lie in his lounger and feel the gentle breeze on his face or take the 15-minute skateboard ride downhill to the beach.

Jenny liked California, too. Though she seemed to have an east coast attitude, the move to the other side of the States had smoothed down her edge a little. She was still sharp and fiery. But her little bohemian coffee house was an idiosyncratic success.

She claimed her vulnerable side had been unlocked by Wilf, like an extra character in a video game. That's what she told him. But Wilf was just thankful that she'd taken the leap to visit him in England on Christmas and thankful to Ciprian for helping her find him from his £500-a-night rehab centre.

They would sit under the stars, talking for hours, Jenny with her less harsh Lebanese marijuana, Wilf now drinking a light Mexican lager called Monterrey 70. They talked about their pasts and found comfort in their two-way connection away from the madding crowd in their California retreat.

Wilf had changed too and thoughtfully sent a good luck card to Lo on the night of her book launch. It meant a lot to her, as did the one sent from Bangladesh by Robin, particularly as she received no response to the invitations sent to Benjamin or Chloe. It also meant a lot to see her dad there too, even though he spent far too much time talking to her literary agent.